SACRIFICED
The Last Oracle

Emily Wibberley

Sacrificed (The Last Oracle, Book 1)
2nd Edition
Copyright © 2014 by Emily Wibberley

Published by Wibbs Ink

www.emilywibberley.com

Edited by Ellen Clair Lamb & Melody Guy

Cover Art by Adrijus Guscia

ISBN-13: 978-1505896787
ISBN-10: 1505896789

CHAPTER ONE

The back road was empty. Which was good. She had about twenty paces to get up her nerve. Twenty paces before she was in front of the most powerful person in all of Sheehan. In all the world, for everything Clio knew. And if she didn't have her rage, then she would be left with nothing between herself and those Seeing eyes.

Darkness hid the fevered flush that was spreading across her cheeks like spider webs carrying flaming silks toward a trapped prey. Shadows fell over the tremor that shook her left leg—just a slight twitching, but enough to belie the sureness in her step. Perhaps put there by anger. Perhaps fear.

Her shoulder was still wet with her sister's tears, searing the painful memory of her sister's sobs into her flesh. Clio had to do something.

Or at least try.

As she trudged through the too long grass, the sound of a nearby brook battling with the resounding pounding of her heartbeat, Clio did her best to convince herself that she could do this. She could confront the Oracle. Clio had never believed in the Oracle's power,

1

anyway. Flashy smoke and cheap tricks. That's all the woman had. Nothing to be scared of.

Right?

The moonlight was caught on the edges of the temple, giving off an eerie shimmer that seemed to shake with Clio's every step. The place looked deserted. Felt deserted too. Not a single creature made its dwelling here, none but the Oracle and her Vessels. The Oracle's place of worship crouched near to the ground, yet standing in its shadow always made Clio feel smaller than even the most imposing peaks of the city's pyramid.

Clio shouldn't be there. She knew that. But she also knew that if she turned back, it would be to more tears. More desperate attempts by Clio to fill the empty air with empty promises. Flat words vowing everything would be okay. That the sun would set tomorrow and Ali would still be Ali. It always came out all wrong, because Clio knew that come daybreak Ali would be the Oracle's. And Clio would never get her sister back.

No. That wouldn't happen. She would do whatever it took to convince the Oracle that she didn't need this girl too. Not this one.

But standing there, looking down into the gaping mouth of the temple, the thought of drying her sister's tears almost sounded more appealing than facing *her*.

"You shouldn't be here. It's late." The voice came from behind Clio, startling her.

Taking a deep breath, she turned to face the Oracle. The moonlight seemed to reach toward the woman, illuminating her white-blonde hair and casting fingers of shadow across her face, revealing just enough for Clio to find the harsh lines of the Oracle's grimace.

"I came to ask…" Clio's eyes fell to her feet. This had been a mistake.

"Yes?" The Oracle's tone was impatient.

"Don't take her. You—" she willed strength into her voice as she spoke. Calling upon the rage that had been burning through her blood only moments ago. "You already have two Vessels. You don't need another. Ali, she's too young—"

"She's sixteen, the required age." The Oracle cut her off. "The same age as my other Vessels when they entered my service. I will not take the time to explain centuries of custom to a fourteen-year-old girl."

"Fifteen." Clio's voice dropped.

"Excuse me?"

"I'm fifteen," and for the first time Clio met the Oracle's gaze.

"It hardly matters." But something flashed in the woman's eyes. Guilt. Fear? "You are too young, and I owe you no explanations. Ali will join my service and learn the ways of the Oracle. The Deities set her aside for this duty ever since the day she first drew breath."

"*You* set her aside. But you don't need her. Please spare her. She doesn't want this." Clio's voice was growing thinner with each word.

"You may be surprised."

"Don't tell me how *my* sister is feeling!" Tears were welling in her eyes.

A figure moved in the darkness just beyond the road. The Oracle's eyes flicked in that direction. She must have seen something that Clio's eyes could not make out because the Oracle nodded once and then turned to head into the temple.

"Wait!" Clio cried. "Please. Please stop." Clio fell to her knees, desperately clasping the Oracle's silk robes in her hands.

"I do not have time for this, Clio."

The sound of her own name shocked Clio enough to make her release the robes. She fell to all fours as her tears peppered the ground below her.

"Please don't take her from me. You've already taken...Ali's all I have left." She spoke with deadly stillness.

A foreign look passed across the Oracle's face. Like a lost memory, fighting to be recalled.

"Mother, please." Her words tumbled out of her mouth before she could stop them. But it didn't matter. The Oracle was already lost in the darkness of her temple.

She allowed herself only a moment. One moment to staunch the flow of tears. One moment to check the shaking in her chest. Her hands curled uselessly into the dirt as she fought her emotions for control of her body.

"Get up, Clio," she muttered under her breath. Ali didn't have time for this.

With a final look at the formidable temple, she turned and ran.

They would leave. Go to the Great Sea. The Oracle wouldn't

spend the time to search for her two youngest and most superfluous daughters. She had two others to take up the Oracle legacy. Clio laughed as she ran. How had she never thought of it before? Nothing was keeping them here.

By the time she got back home, she felt lighter than she had in years.

She pushed through the furs that sealed off their home, nearly colliding with chairs as she sprinted to the back room that served as her and Ali's bedroom. "Ali!" Clio called, excitement bubbling through her voice.

Ali was exactly where Clio had left her—sitting on her mat, staring up through the circular opening of their domed roof at the night's sky. Their quarters were lit only by the moon, which hung like a beacon promising what could never be.

"Ali." Clio dropped to her knees in front of her sister, taking her hands in hers. "Let's go. We're leaving."

"What?" Ali pulled her gaze down to Clio. "Leave?"

"Leave, run away. Let's go! We don't have time to waste. We could be in the city by morning." Clio jumped up and started to gather their things from the chests around their room.

"Clio, stop."

Clio turned back, surprised to see that Ali hadn't moved.

"I know you're scared, but we can do this." Clio returned to the tangle of dresses she held in her hand.

"I'm not." Ali's voice was barely more than a whisper.

"You're not what?" Clio looked at her sister. Really looked at her for the first time since barging into their room and noticed what she had failed to see before.

Ali's eyes were dry. Clio could barely make out the now faint remnant of red that had rimmed Ali's eyes. Beyond that, nothing, absolutely, nothing in her face suggested the slightest disquiet.

"I'm not running away. I—I can't believe I'm saying this, but I want to be a Vessel."

"*What?*" Clio's mouth fell open. "You were bawling in my arms just moments ago."

"I know. I know." Her sister actually smiled. "While you were gone, something clicked."

"What happened? Did Mira or Vire come in here?" Clio looked around for one of their older sisters—sisters who had already abandoned them in service of the Oracle—but the room was empty.

"No, nothing like that. I just…I want to fulfill my destiny."

"Deities, listen to yourself." Clio could barely look at her. The range of emotions she had felt this evening was finally taking its toll. Her knees buckled and she was forced backwards onto the chest. She was shaking when Ali's fingers tentatively searched out hers.

"I don't want to hide from my fate anymore," Ali said, her voice raw with conviction.

The glow in Ali's eyes made Clio pause. She'd seen it before. Never before on these soft features. But she knew what it meant all the same. Devotion, faith, rapture.

It meant it was over, and Clio had lost another.

But how? How could anything have changed my sweet Ali? With her older sisters, Mira and Vire, it had been expected. They grew up believing in the Oracle and what she did. Of course they would embrace the offer to be inducted into their mother's cult. But Ali and Clio had been different. They had always relied on what they could actually see, and never, never in all their years had they seen any hint of the Oracle's power.

Clio sharply pulled her hand out of her sister's. "You sound like them already. All this talk of duty and destiny, and fate. Ali, you know it's a lie." Along with Clio, Ali, her two older sisters, and their mother, there was fate. The sixth voice in Clio's house. Just as real, just as articulate, fate was always the one dictating this or demanding that. Fate was the father they never had. He set the rules, enforced them, and watched over the family. Everything came back to fate, and Clio couldn't be more tired of it. It wasn't fate that made their mother turn her daughters into Vessels; it was their mother, the Oracle. Pure and simple. She was the one who was going to take Ali away. Remake her into a tool. Change her.

And Clio would be more alone than ever before. She crossed to the other side of the room in a futile effort to put as much space between herself and the living reminder of her "destiny."

From behind her, Ali spoke without the slightest trace of emotion. "I promise it won't change me. I will always be your sister. Nothing, not even she, can take that away from me. And then in just another year, you will be a Vessel too. We will be back to doing everything together. You'll see. Tomorrow at dinner, I will still be me, just with some extra duties."

"Don't you pretend that's how it will be." Clio couldn't say it, couldn't put into words what had been gradually unfolding before her eyes for years. Clio and Ali never spoke about what happened to their older sisters. As if articulating the reality could give the whole thing weight, substance, and leaving it unsaid kept it unreal.

But it was real, even if words had never made it so. Clio and Ali faced the truth every time they looked into the vacant eyes of their sisters. Mira and Vire were never the same after they were ordained, and now it was Ali's turn.

Next year, it would be Clio's turn, and she would have to face whatever it was that irreparably changed her sisters.

"I can't just sit by and watch as you—" Tears choked the words in her throat.

"Shhh, Clio. It's going to be all right." Ali sat back down on her mat, motioning Clio to join her.

"Why are you all right with this? How can you just accept it?"

Ali took Clio's hand in hers and squeezed.

"It's not up to me to either accept it or reject it. It's fate, destiny laid out for me long before I was even born." Ali's voice was eerily calm.

"But how do you know that it's fate?"

Ali smiled. "I just know, Clio. I want this. Doesn't that prove everything? Despite it all, all the fear over all the years, now, when the moment has come, I want it. You will too."

In a voice so quiet it was almost a whisper, "But aren't you scared? She does...something to her Vessels...something to our sisters, and then they aren't our sisters anymore."

"She is our mother. She would never hurt us. And if I have to change a little in order to serve, then that's the sacrifice I am called upon to make." Such conviction heated Ali's voice, giving her words an almost tangible texture in the empty air.

"She's always been the Oracle first, and our mother second. And when you go to her tomorrow, it will be as a Vessel, not a daughter. She knows the difference. You should too." Her mother's cold look as she tore her robes from Clio's fist flashed across her mind.

"Being a Vessel is an honor. Her blood—*sacred* blood—runs in our veins. And I feel it, pulsing through my body, making me stronger. These last couple days leading up to my ordainment, I have felt myself getting stronger, quicker. I can see farther and hear the sand that stirs under my feet. I didn't want to tell you because it scared me. These changes, they go against everything we thought was true. But my body is preparing itself, and my mind must do the same."

Clio couldn't look at her sister. The things she was saying, they didn't make any sense. Someone must have talked to her. Somehow convinced her that this was worth her freedom and her life. Convinced her that it was somehow real. Clio didn't want to think about it. It didn't matter. Nothing did, except for Ali. Clio didn't have much time left with her.

"I was scared before. But it was because I was weak. I was looking at this all wrong." Ali spoke quietly. "You will see when it's your time."

Clio nodded her head. She didn't want to argue anymore.

Ali was already lost.

"That's better," Ali chirped. "Come on, we have all day tomorrow. What do you want to do? We could climb the ridge, try to get a glimpse of Sheehan's pyramid? I think we are going to have a clear day." She looked up into their hole to the sky as she spoke.

"Sure, Ali. That would be nice." Clio tried to sound excited.

"Great, at dawn then," and she squeezed Clio's hand before lying down.

Stillness and silence sat between them, and the unmovable barrier of destiny. Clio's mind was blank. Too exhausted to try to work out where she had failed. If she hadn't left Ali, maybe she wouldn't be acting like this. Maybe Clio could have gotten her to run away. Maybe they would have been on the road already, the whole world and all its time before them.

"You want this? Truly?" Clio just could not understand.

"It's not a question of want anymore, Clio. It is who I am."

Yes, well, Clio thought. *It's not who I am.*

When Clio awoke, she was surprised to find the sun high in the sky. Something was wrong. Ali should have woken her at dawn. Panic shot through Clio's veins as she turned over.

Ali was gone.

Clio jumped up. Her eyes darted around the room. All of Ali's things were gone, removed as if they had never been there in the first place. Her room was left uncomfortably bare—only Clio's wooden chest and her feathered mat remained. The sun seemed to shine in dismal and muted tones.

The Oracle. She had come for Ali in the night. It didn't make any sense. The ceremony wasn't supposed to be until sunset.

A heavy emptiness settled in Clio's chest. It had always been there, nesting, digging a little deeper each year, growing bigger as Clio felt herself growing smaller. As each of her sisters had been drawn into the Oracle's cult, Clio found herself left with less and less. She wasn't one of them—she refused to become one of them—and so they had little to do with her. What was a kid sister compared to a calling from the Oracle? One by one her sisters moved on until Clio felt as if she was looked through rather than looked at. And now, without Ali, there was no one left who could see Clio. See her as the girl she was rather than daughter of the Oracle.

This was how it was going to be from now on. Well, at least until Clio's own ordainment. Until then, she was going to be alone—the last of four sisters to enter into the Oracle's service as a Vessel. She would see her family only at meals. Most of her time would be confined to this house, alone while everyone else did whatever it was they did in the temple.

She had to try to find her sister, had to talk to her one last time. Strange prickling currents ran up and down Clio's spine, making her feel like something was most definitely wrong. No matter what, Ali would have wanted to say goodbye. She couldn't have changed that much already. Maybe she wasn't gone. Maybe she just got up and wanted time to herself before the big day. Maybe she woke up and was scared again. Too scared to climb the ridge as they had discussed.

Something nudged Clio's thoughts away from that conclusion, guiding her to a place of uncertainty. She couldn't explain the feeling, and honestly, she didn't want to. Premonitions rang a bit too close to the Oracle's supposed gifts for Clio's taste. But she couldn't deny that somehow she just felt that something was wrong.

After pulling her thick black hair into a knot in the back of her head, she ducked under the heavy curtain that separated her quarters from the family hearth. Clio hated the inconvenient length of her hair, but her mother wouldn't allow her to cut it. It was supposed to be sacred. Her mother said that the locks of the Oracle marked her for who she was, that her mother's sterling white hair meant she had been touched by the Deities. Clio thought it was much more likely the touch of some kind of white bark found in the jungle. It might have been one of the Oracle's more poetic lies, but to Clio it was just inconvenient. She was forbidden to shear her own hair out of the slightest possibility that the Deities could "touch" her too, and mark her with their gift. So her ebony black hair hung in heavy locks down her back, each strand a shackle holding her to an unwanted fate.

This common room was shaped much like her own. It held the memories of smiles and warmth so distant from now that they felt more like dreams than truth. A long time ago Mira had sat here, pretending to be a princess and biting delicately on a leg of lamb that left gristle and grease all across her mouth while her sisters sat on laughing. Now the room was as bare as her sisters were distant. Only a fire pit occupied the space, sitting under the opening in the ceiling.

Fingers of smoke curled up from the flames and billowed out of it.

The room was hazy with smoke, the air colored a gentle gray. Someone pulled aside the black pelt that shuttered their home from the outside world. For a moment, sunlight parted and danced with the smoke in the air, a menagerie of color, blinding her. Then the pelt fell back into place, and Clio could make out the outline of a woman in the flickering firelight.

Clio smelled something foul. A mixture of blood and soot and something else sickly sweet overwhelmed her senses. The woman limped forward, and when her face caught the light, Clio realized it was her older sister, Vire.

And something was horribly wrong with her.

CHAPTER TWO

The sight of Vire sent a chill through Clio's body. Vire shouldn't have been here. Her sisters entered the house only after dusk, and then only for their meal. But it wasn't just the shock of seeing her sister in an unexpected place that caused Clio to cringe away from her. It was that she was covered in blood.

She could hardly make out the leather gear, but she knew Vire was wearing it. It was special gear reserved for the missions, or "callings" as her mother referred to them. Callings were the duty of the Vessels, but never had any of her sisters returned from a calling with even the slightest scratch. The leather straps that wove around her sister's body, hugging her vital organs while leaving her limbs free for motion, were caked in black soot—and dark brown blood.

Clio's heart nearly stopped as she stared at her sister standing in a puddle of blood that stretched all the way to the entrance. *What had she done?* Vire just stood there, looking off into the distance as if her mind were somewhere else entirely. Every so often, she would flinch as a flame from their hearth licked out toward her.

Clio didn't speak much to Vire anymore, and Vire spoke even less to Clio. Once she was ordained, she made it abundantly clear that the concerns of anyone but the Deities were a waste of breath. But despite the years of distance and coldness between her and Vire, Clio approached her sister to see if she was injured. Thick droplets of congealing blood dripped off her sister's hands, down her thighs, off her hair, landing with heavy splats on the floor below. Clio's mind was moving fast, like the heavy beating of waves against the shore.

What happened last night? Who did this to her? Why would anyone want to hurt one of the Oracle's Vessels?

"Vire, what happened? Are you hurt?" She didn't really expect an answer. Clio couldn't shake the feeling that this had something to do with why Ali had been taken away prematurely. She took a deep breath and tried again.

"Vire, talk to me! Where were you last night?"

Vire's eyes remained fixed on a distant, unseen point. It was as if she didn't see or hear Clio. Vire was like a specter, a wraith, risen from the beyond, present but separate from the world around her.

Slowly, Vire turned and looked at Clio. Empty eyes and a hollow voice spoke. "My wounds need attention."

"I can see that."

Mira, the eldest sister, came in through the front, gliding in that eerily silent way of hers. Mira was undoubtedly the warrior among her family. Hard lines wrapped around her biceps and her calves. Her hair was knotted down behind her neck, and her eyes held the promise of strength. "Is it done?"

Vire gave a barely perceptible nod of her head.

"Good. Clio, see to her wounds."

What was going on? Clearly the sight of Vire like this was not a shock to Mira. This was expected, planned.

Ordered.

But what had she done?

Clio had always imagined callings to be mundane errands that the Oracle tried to dress up in some meaningless ritualistic trappings. Like all the ceremonies she did in her temple. But maybe the Oracle asked Vire to do something else for her today.

Clio didn't want to think it. She couldn't consider the possibility that her mother had asked Vire to endanger her own life in service to one of her lies.

"First," Clio said to her eldest sister, "where is Ali?" That strange tug was pulling harder and harder in Clio's mind. Something awful had happened. *Had Ali had been a part of it?*

Mira looked at Clio, really looked at her for the first time in longer than Clio could remember. "Ali is a Vessel now. She is serving the Oracle."

"What did you do to her?" Clio yelled, desperate for a real answer.

"Yours is not to question. You are to do as you're told. See to Vire."

Before Clio could protest, Mira swept out of the room, moving with an unnaturally graceful and powerful stride.

Clio got up to follow her, ready to hold Mira back until she got some answers, but Vire stood in the way. Clio could see faint tremors shaking her sister.

Vire was scared about something. Clio couldn't leave her like this.

She led Vire deeper into their home, where a trough held their bathing water, and gently began to rub all the sticky gore off her skin. A series of shallow slices covered her forearms, and deeper ones ran down her thighs, but it was abundantly clear that most of this blood was not her own. "Deities, Vire, what happened?"

Clio jumped as Vire's hand flashed out, grabbing Clio's wrist. "Things are changing, Clio. Watch yourself." As suddenly as she had spoken, she fell silent again, retreating back into the stoicism that held her in a distant place.

"Great," Clio muttered under her breath. "One more sentence and we might have gotten something useful." But Vire might as well have been gone already.

Clio finished cleaning and bandaging Vire. By the end, her own hands were trembling. Clio had half a mind to run out, leave whatever was coming behind her, escape and live her own life.

But Clio knew that she couldn't leave Ali behind. She had to see her, to make sure she was all right.

Clio couldn't fight back her tears anymore. She knew it was futile, but she raced through the clay corridors of their home anyway, desperately looking in each room for Ali, hoping that Mira had been lying and Ali was still here. She had to find her, had to make sure she wasn't a part of whatever had happened. But the house was as empty as it was always going to be.

Something awful *had* happened.

And it had been *expected*.

A sinking feeling in her chest told her that she was too late to change anything, but she pushed it aside.

She had to get Ali out of whatever mess had brought Vire back bloody and bruised.

CHAPTER THREE

She ran through corridors until, after what felt like an eternity, she burst outside, savoring the sting of the cold morning air as it freed her skin from the suffocating heat inside. Being outdoors cleared her head, it always had. When she was outside, looking at that skyline that seemed to reach on forever, it was hard to feel trapped, even though she'd been born into an inescapable fate.

Even though every passing day brought Clio closer and closer to the Oracle's altar. When she turned sixteen there would be no turning back. She would be ordained as one of the Oracle's own, and Clio would become a prisoner to the temple and its empty rituals. Each day would be an echo of the one before—filled with blessings and the broken pleas of people desperate enough to call upon the Oracle for signs of the end of their sufferings. Clio would have to listen to her mother as she pronounced prosperity for some and yet more hardship for others. And then watch as those poor fools stood from the altar and departed, thinking that the Oracle had somehow seen their future. They would spend the rest of their lives waiting for her words to come true. When her mother died, Clio had no doubt that her eldest sister would take up the mantel. The Oracle was clever. She had always claimed that when she was returned to the Deities, her powers would pass to her oldest living heir. The whole city of Sheehan believed it. But Clio knew it was all a clever trick to keep power within the family. Mira would take up the title of the Oracle, and Clio would be trapped serving yet another cold and distant woman.

But Clio wouldn't lose herself. She would never become like her mother, like Mira and Vire who went from innocent children to unfeeling stone. Clio would always be Clio.

But Ali's words from last night fought with this promise. *"I was scared before. But it was because I was weak. I was looking at this all wrong. You will see when it's your time."* In the course of one evening, Ali had completely changed. And Ali had seemed to think that whatever had changed her would also change Clio.

Clio's head started to feel light. It was all she could do to drop herself down on a large stone as she tried to slow her panicked heartbeats.

Without Ali, Clio had no one to remind her of who she was. Over the years she had lost everyone she cared about one by one. Without them, Clio worried that she, too, would retreat into the same silence as her sisters.

As her vision cleared, Clio realized she was looking out on the skyline of Sheehan, the distant city that gave the Oracle her power. Sheehan stood mockingly in the offing, just within Clio's sight. She could see everything she wanted but she could never be a part of it. The temple was kept just outside the city's perimeter. But Clio loved Sheehan all the same. A city nearly in ruins, with the fragile beauty that was only found in a final tenacious hold on life. By all reasoning, Sheehan should have crumbled to dust by now. Its wars with Morek's empire had been devastating. And yet somehow the king had negotiated a few more years for his kingdom. It was what Clio loved about her city—it fought to remain itself while everywhere else the will of the Empire was law. Sheehan was subservient to Morek, but at least Sheehan was able to keep the rule of its own king. As long as he lived, the laws of Sheehan would govern. Which was an especially good thing for Clio, because under Morek's laws the Oracle and her entire line would be executed.

More than that, Clio couldn't stand to see the gentle and warm culture of her city replaced by the distant directives of a foreign Emperor. Her city was small. It was weak, and it couldn't last long. But it was a beautiful panoply of simple people who knew how to live off their own land. Never had Sheehan conquered anyone else. All it needed was its own soil and its own people.

Clio could make out the distant fields now. They were mostly dried up, abandoned when farmers were forced to take up spears against Morek. In the heart of it all was the spattering of homes that made up the city's center. And somewhere behind the chaotic spread of moldering clay huts and winding roads was the palace where the king lived with his son.

Derik. Her one friend in the world, now that Ali had changed. It had been five years since she last saw the crown prince of Sheehan. Five years in which he had probably forgotten her. Forgotten the nights that they spent lounging like jungle cats together on the tallest tree in the city. It was the only place that they had ever felt alone. He had always been trying to escape the pressures of the king and the palace, and she, of course, had been desperate for a break from the eyes of the Oracle. Up in that tree, high above the confines of duty, they had shared so many secrets. So much of her heart would always be among those crackling branches and swirling breezes.

It didn't matter that he was the prince and she was the daughter of the Oracle. They were just kids whenever they were together. The last time Clio had seen him had been the night Mira was ordained. It was then that Clio realized her sister would not only be taken from her, but made into someone she didn't even recognize. There was never any mention of a father in their house, and Clio had learned young never to ask about him. It was Mira who had taught Clio how to read and write, a rare skill for even a noble child, who had taught her music and even did her best with history. Only a child herself when Clio was born, Mira had taken on the responsibilities that should have been their mother's.

But on the day Mira was ordained, everything changed. Mira came back from the ceremony with a new responsibility and made it very clear that she no longer had time to raise her kid sister. She had been called away to serve a greater power. That night, Clio ran all the way to Derik's palace and climbed through his window, crying about what she had lost and how one day she would have to serve the

Deities too, that they would take everything away from her as they had Mira. If Mira could so easily forget Clio, Clio feared she would forget Derik, and then there would be nothing for her but the life of a compassionless Vessel.

He told her that she was too strong for that. He had promised to remind her of this if she ever forgot. But when Clio returned home that night, the Oracle told her that she was too old to be playing with boys, that the Oracle's children could never marry and have children. Clio shouldn't be wasting the prince's time. At that age, Clio hadn't understood what the Oracle meant.

Clio hadn't seen Derik since that night. But she liked to imagine that he still climbed that tree and thought about the friend he used to have. He would want her to be strong now. If she gave up on Ali, it would be the first step in retreating into that poisonous acceptance of fate.

Clio hurried across the courtyard that stretched between her house and the temple. As always, when Clio set her eyes on the single-story stone structure that was her mother's temple, her heart sank. She hated its oppressive silence, its immovable weight, and the way that even in the daylight it seemed to hide in a pit of shadows. As much as she didn't want to step foot inside, she knew that Ali could be in there.

She opened the heavy doors and descended the steps that led down to the altar.

The temple was an inverted pyramid of sorts. Stone steps descended from three walls to the altar. Water ran down the steps of the far wall, feeding a deep pool in the center of the room. Clio supposed the room was beautiful, but all it made her feel was how much she didn't belong here. She couldn't help but think about how cold the stone and water were, how they never saw the sun—like her mother and sisters. Clio could never belong here, underground like this. But she was stuck here all the same.

She descended into the pit of the temple, taking the steps two at a time, but she already felt that Ali wasn't here. Another premonition that Clio wanted to ignore.

The temple wasn't empty, however. She stopped when she saw a man standing on the edge of the pool. He wore long sweeping robes of deepest red.

Mannix.

Clio shivered. Something about Mannix had always unnerved her. He had come to Sheehan not five years ago, and already he had somehow gotten himself a position as the king's prized adviser. She knew he had played an instrumental role in brokering a peace with Morek.

A thin-lipped grin spread across his pale face as his eyes fell on Clio. His head and face were completely hairless. In the place of eyebrows, Mannix wore a multitude of ruby piercings. He turned to her, his red eyes lighting up as she approached.

She barely spared him a glance. She was racking her brain for ideas of where Ali could be. "You shouldn't be here."

"Is that so? Tell me, why is it that men cannot come in here unattended?" His gaze fell on her like flames.

"Not my temple, not my rules."

"Ah, but it may be your temple one day." He walked around the pool to get a better look at her.

"Not likely. Youngest of four, remember?"

"I do. And yet you really are…flowering." His grin ripped itself higher into those hollow cheekbones, giving light to those red, empty eyes.

"It's probably comments like that why men aren't allowed in here." Ali could be anywhere, doing anything by now, and Clio was stuck dealing with Mannix in an empty temple.

She could still feel his eyes moving over her body. He wasn't like the other men who came to see the Oracle. Their stares seemed to strip Clio of her clothes. Mannix looked like he was stripping the very skin off her bones. Rage flickered up in her chest, but the best way out of this was to move him along as quickly as possible. She had to find Ali.

"Can I help you with something, or are you just here to bother me?"

He ignored her and bent down at the pool's edge, skimming his fingers along its surface.

"I wouldn't do that if I were you," she warned.

"The sacrificial waters, yes? I wondered if the lore was true. They say it carries the power of the Oracle. That she cannot be the servant to the Deities without it. Have you ever gone in?"

"I don't know about all that, but yes, once. I fell. Came out covered in blisters. Truly, you are ugly enough already." The water was another of her mother's flashy tricks, poisoned in a way to seem as if it held power from the Deities.

"Interesting. So only the Oracle herself can touch it?" he wondered to himself, his fingers curling around his chin. "But Clio, that mouth of yours will get you into trouble one day. Learn to guard yourself in the presence of powerful men."

"Is that what you are now? You serve the king—the servant of men. I serve the Oracle—the servant of the Deities. Whatever power you have stops at the doors of this temple."

They glared into each other's eyes until—

"Clio, escort Mannix out of the temple and help him with the offerings." Her mother's voice broke their eye contact.

Unnoticed by Clio, her mother had entered the room. She stood at the top of the steps, a vision in her white robe and headdress made of pure white pearls almost indistinguishable from the striking white of her hair. While all of her daughters had hair the color of darkest night, hers was whiter than sunlight reflected on a snowy field. She stood at the vestibule to her private chamber that attached to the temple. Clio didn't know what was in there, and she never would. It was for the Oracle's eyes only.

Mannix lowered himself into an obsequious bow. Clio couldn't help but snicker. The Oracle looked down on her. "Clio, I won't ask you twice."

"But it was only one new moon ago that we sent the last batch of offerings." As part of the peace agreement, Sheehan had to send temple maidens to Morek. According to Sheehan law, the girls had to be blessed in the temple before they could perform their duties.

But they hadn't been due for another transport of offerings for several more moons.

"The Emperor requires more," Mannix said.

"And what did he do with the last twenty girls we just gave him?"

"Clio, it's not your place to question what the Emperor does or doesn't do with our offerings." Her mother's voice was firm, resolute.

"Where is Ali?" Clio's voice was just as hard.

Mannix raised an eyebrow at her.

"She is doing her duty, as you should be doing yours." With that, the Oracle retreated back into the vestry. There was no arguing with the Oracle, try as Clio might.

Mannix looked up at her. "After you." He swept his arm out, motioning her to lead the way to the door.

Outside, the girls were tied up and waiting at the entrance to the temple. The hot sun beat down on them, and their skin screamed out in angry blistered protest. They couldn't have been much older than Clio, but the rags that clung to their peeling skin told stories of a suffering Clio couldn't imagine. Most of them were slaves sold by their masters to the king, but some were just destitute girls who thought that becoming a temple maiden would bring them a better life. Clio hoped they were right, but as a temple maiden herself, she knew that it wasn't much different.

Clio and Mannix untied each girl from the wooden beam that

she carried on her shoulders before she could be led down to the temple. As Clio worked, she tried to put as much distance as possible between herself and Mannix, but his eyes followed her.

"So," he said, "as you are nearing adulthood, you must be looking to your future. Are you prepared for the reality that you will remain in this temple with your sisters for the rest of your life?" He drew out his words, stretching them to unnatural lengths that twisted around Clio. He went on, only looking at her out of the corner of his eyes. "I can't imagine *your* three sisters are fine company for such a *lively* girl as yourself." His eyes held a spark, as if he could see exactly how she had been feeling and was using that to hurt her.

"And what would you know about fine company? When you came here you were alone, no family, nothing." She bit her tongue. Stupid. She shouldn't waste her time goading him.

He looked right at her and smiled. "Oh, I'll be the first to admit that my family was the worst of company. The absolute worst. It's precisely the reason I came to Sheehan. There came a point when I realized I had no reason to remain loyal to people who had done nothing but hurt me, and so I ran away."

Clio couldn't stand the way his words got inside her. They touched her own secret desire to run away and have a normal life. Instead, she braced herself. "Well, I'm sure it worked out better for them in the end without you." She finished with the bindings and led the girls through the temple doors. Part of Clio knew that she shouldn't speak so to a royal adviser, but Mannix was the least of her concerns.

He rounded on her, pulling her up painfully close to him. "You're lucky that sacred blood runs in your veins. Without it—" but he swallowed whatever he was about to say.

He released her just as the Oracle came up to meet them.

"They will be brought out to you when we are done." The Oracle spoke to Mannix, who nodded his assent.

Clio turned to go, anxious to continue her search for Ali.

"Clio?" Her mother's voice was commanding in its question. "You are to assist me today."

"What?" She caught Mannix's eyes on her as she balked at her mother. She had never been privy to any of the Oracle's ceremonies before. Clio couldn't help but think the only reason she was now was to keep her from Ali.

"That was not a question, Clio."

Mannix swept aside, inviting her to enter the temple. With a last glance over her shoulder, as if Ali would suddenly appear behind her, Clio shuffled inside.

She descended the steps and took her place at her mother's side for the blessings. The Emperor didn't know that the king was having the offerings blessed before their departure. If he did, then surely he would have all the offerings killed before they stepped foot in his temples. He had long ago had his own Oracle killed and replaced her with a priest.

Clio knew about the execution of the Oracle of Morek. She had been an old woman who, the stories said, had conspired to have the

Emperor's son murdered. The reason behind her action had always remained a mystery, but Clio's mother speculated that the Oracle of Morek foresaw that the boy would grow into a ruthless killer. The Oracle's family disappeared too, leaving no doubt in anyone's mind that the Emperor would not tolerate anyone related to the Oracle. Regardless of how it all occurred, Oracles were not welcome in Morek, and even Clio could never set foot in the city for fear of being recognized and then executed.

If the peace failed, or if the Emperor found out that the Oracle was being used to bless his own temple maidens, he would sack Sheehan, and no amount of brokering could save the Oracle or her family from his wrath. But the king would not send any of his subjects out into the world without the proper blessings, and so they all toed a dangerous line.

Clio's mother stood behind the stone altar in the center of the room. The sacrificial waters gleamed palely around her. With a glance, the Oracle indicated that Clio was to kneel at her side. Each girl filed eagerly down the steps, taking their place one at a time before the altar.

The first girl approached and knelt before the Oracle.

Clio's mother spoke. "The water before you comes with divine sacrifice. Come before it with a sacrifice to the Deities and they will bless you. Come unworthy, and they will take from you so you may learn the feeling of true sacrifice and devotion." The Oracle cupped her hands in the water. Clio's skin stung with the memory of blisters.

Another one of her mother's Oracle tricks, no doubt, that she could touch the water without pain. The Oracle probably had some ointment, something that made it so she could look as if the Deities truly blessed her above others. Clio felt sick. Somehow her mother was willing to hurt these girls with poison just so she could appear powerful.

The Oracle continued, holding her cupped hands above the head of the kneeling girl. "With this water, you are anointed as a servant of the Deities. Your body will do their will. Your life given as the most sacred offering."

As the Oracle spoke, the girl's eyes shone, glowing with the fervent belief that this was the start of a better life. But when the Oracle released her hands, and water cascaded down the girl's forehead, a shrill scream rang throughout the temple.

Angry red welts trailed droplets of water down the poor girl's forehead.

The Oracle was unmoved, clearly used to the sight before her. "You will be marked so that you may remember the feeling of sacrifice long after you have forgotten the pain."

Her mother handed Clio an urn from her altar, and Clio realized that she was to do the actual marking.

Everything in her recoiled from the task. Inside the urn was very finely powdered lead. Clio knew it would seep into the girl's wounds, leaving an ugly black mar across her face.

"No." She mouthed the word at her mother as she put the urn back on the altar, and was rewarded with a slight crack in the Oracle's appearance. The Oracle's mouth, just at the corners, bent downward in frustration.

The whole room was looking at them. Clio saw one girl whose hair was completely sheared off, leaving only a wispy brown fluff covering her head, smirk at the halt in the proceedings.

Her mother hissed at Clio out of the corner of her mouth. "If you don't do this, you won't be seeing Ali in the near future."

"Where is she?" Clio asked, all the blood rushing to her face in anger. She didn't care who heard her.

Her mother only handed her the urn.

Clio had no choice, which wasn't anything new. She could, and she always would, rebel as much as possible against each part of her mother's lies, but in the end, the Oracle always won.

"Girl, you want your blessing, do you not?" the Oracle asked the prostrated girl.

The girl nodded. "Please. I need to be worthy for my new life. The mark of the Deities will keep me pure."

New life. It was all a lie. These girls weren't being sent to some sacred and meaningful life. They were just going to be slaves in a strange place. Girls at the mercy of yet more powerful men.

But the girl wanted this, and Clio had no choice if she wanted to find Ali.

Biting the inside of her lip until the warm, sweet taste of blood flooded her mouth, she doled out each of her mother's blessings. Girl after girl was burned by the water, while the Oracle remained unblemished.

When she looked into the eyes of each girl before her, Clio

willed her eyes to say what her mouth could not—*get out, this is no honor, it is a prison.*

Finally, it was the girl without hair's turn. She was obviously sick. As she approached the altar, she did her best to swallow the wet coughs that filled the sacred space of the temple. She knelt just like all the other girls, waiting patiently for the blessing. Unlike the rest, she looked upon the Oracle as the scalding water was poured over her head. Only, the water wasn't scalding. Not to her. It ran off her sallow skin like nothing more than the rain.

Silence filled the temple. Clio glanced anxiously at her mother, expecting her to be upset that another was invulnerable to whatever burned all the others.

But instead, the Oracle smiled with more kindness in her eyes than Clio had ever seen. "The Deities thank you for your sacrifices," the Oracle said. She crossed to her altar and pulled out a small bowl. Dipping her fingers into its contents, the Oracle then anointed the girl's forehead.

The hairless girl's expression never changed. She wasn't like the others—her eyes held no love or fear or idolatry.

As the girl walked away, Clio saw her subtly wipe the oil from her forehead.

Countless times throughout the ceremony, Clio glanced at the door, hoping to get a glimpse of Ali, hoping that she was all right. With each passing girl, Clio's legs jittered with restless energy. The blessings dragged on for what felt like an eternity. As the sunlight that spilled in from the entryway dimmed and faded, Clio couldn't stop a stream of horrible visions of Ali from filling her head. She tried to halt them, tried to hold onto the smiling Ali she had always known, but deep down she knew that Ali would already be different.

Something had happened, and it was only wishful thinking to hope that Ali had been kept apart from it.

After the ceremony ended, Clio hurried back to the house and waited anxiously by the hearth where they all took their meals. Ali had to come. She still had to eat.

Finally, Vire led Ali in.

The shock of her sister's changed appearance forced all of the breath out of Clio's chest and launched her to her feet.

There she was, already wearing the leather gear. The soft skin of Ali's stomach above the protection of the gear showed a black bruise the size of a warrior's club. However, it wasn't the bruise that had Clio up, it was the puffiness around her sister's eyes—evidence that she had been crying for hours. And behind those raw pink lids was something much worse—eyes cold and fixed to an unmoving point in the distance.

After less than one day, Ali wore the same expression as Vire and Mira.

CHAPTER FOUR

Before Clio could reach Ali, Vire imprisoned Clio in the steel vise of her grip. Clio couldn't get to her sister, so she settled for yelling.

"What did this?"

No response.

"Ali, please! Tell me what did this to you. It's me. It's Clio. Please, Ali!" Her voice cracked on the last word, and she dissolved into sobs that wracked her body.

Ali said nothing. She was gone for good. The morning after Mira had been ordained, Clio and Ali had stolen into Mira's room very early in the morning. They hadn't fully understood all the changes in their sister yet, and they had thought that everything could go back to normal. But when they woke Mira, she barely even looked at her two younger sisters. When they asked her to take them into the market in the city, she remained silent. Clio could still remember the way Mira's body shook and her eyes darted back and forth across the room. There was no way to know what the Oracle put her Vessels through on that first night. Whatever it was, it scared them into silence.

The Oracle stepped into the room. Clio's eyes found hers in accusation, burning with all the rage Clio had for her mother. Her tears of despair turned to ones of fury.

"How *could* you? Give me an answer! Something that could explain this"—she gestured to Ali's face—"and this"—to the bruise. "She's hurt and scared, scared like Mira and Vire were on their first nights. Tell me what you put them through!"

Pearl beads threaded into her mother's gossamer hair, and black ash rubbed around her pale and wrinkled eyes signaled that the Oracle had been doing some kind of séance. She was cool, as always. "One day, Clio, you will have an explanation. On your sixteenth birthday, you will begin to fulfill the destiny that the Deities have chosen for you. You will help us to carry out what the Visions call us to do, as your sister Ali did today."

Disgust for her mother, for all her lies, tore through Clio. She was trapped—in this house, with these statues for family; in a tradition that was so confining she could never break free.

That wasn't the worst part, though. Clio had always felt that everything would be bearable if she didn't know what she did. If she hadn't lived through the same transition three times over with her sisters. If only she had lived in ignorance, she might have been able to enjoy the first 16 years of her life. But the sight of her sisters served as a constant reminder of what was to come. Clio couldn't stop herself from counting down every moment until that dreaded day.

"*Visions*. Listen to her!" Clio turned to her mute sisters. "You believe that the Deities talk to this mortal through *visions*? Have you ever seen any evidence? Anything at all? I've watched my whole life, every moment I could, I watched for any sign that there was something behind it all. But I've seen nothing but a woman desperate to convince the people around her of her power. What did she have you do?" Clio couldn't say it yet. Couldn't bear to put words to the blood that had been dripping off Vire, blood that was not her own. Blood that was too much to be anything but a crime. She didn't know whom, but someone had been hurt. Killed maybe. And her mother had been behind it.

Her sisters stood silent, watching the Oracle as if waiting for her command.

"That's enough, Clio," her mother said.

Anyone might have interpreted the slight fall of the Oracle's eyes as sadness or regret. But Clio knew her better than that.

The Oracle was angry. For the first time in Clio's life, her mother actually looked upset.

"You think I have offered my daughters up to this bloody business of my own accord? That I would use them for what? To silence people who may doubt me? That's what you are thinking? You saw Vire come back covered in blood and you can see Ali before you bruised, and you actually think that I sent them out there on one of my own errands. What was it you said? To convince people around me of my own power?

"You are more foolish than I had imagined."

Clio's mouth gaped silently. She had never heard her mother speak so many words in her entire life. Her mother had never once looked at her with anything but the Oracle's lofty stare. But now, Clio saw something new in her mother's expression. She saw disappointment.

"Then what did you make them do?" Clio couldn't back down. She had to understand. For once, her mother was speaking to Clio as a mother might her daughter. She had to find out whom the Oracle had hurt today. A horrible sinking feeling that made the very air feel heavy on her chest told Clio that today hadn't been the first time, either.

"The Deities show me what must be done to protect Sheehan. Sometimes that involves acting on their behalf to silence any threats." Her mother's voice was smooth and matter-of-fact.

"You have people killed," Clio whispered, her eyes wide with the final truth of it all. The reason why none of her sisters were ever the same. How could they be? After doing what the Oracle asked, after killing, how could they go back to being the loving and carefree girls of before?

"I obey only what the Visions ask of me," The Oracle answered, unconcerned.

"The *Visions* don't tell Ali or Vire or Mira to do anything! You are the one with the supposed connection to the Deities. You should do it."

"It is the job of a Vessel, Clio. The Oracle can only See."

"How convenient." Clio nearly retched on her words. "Who did you have them kill?" She almost didn't want to know. She didn't even want to be in the same room as these people anymore. She didn't care if the Visions were real or not, she didn't want to be witness to whatever crimes they were committing. Most of all, she didn't want to become a part of it.

"Our king was in danger. Surely you can't fault us for stopping that danger. There is a reason you are not in my service yet, Clio. You are too young. And clearly, you are too naïve. I know you don't revere me as a girl should revere the Oracle, that you don't respect me as a child should respect her elder, and that you don't love me as a daughter should love her mother, but listen to me now. You are not involved in this for a reason. You are powerless to your emotions; they consume you. As long as that is the case, I cannot trust you with the secrets of the Deities, but I will make this final caution. Learn to rein in your temper, your love, learn to separate these feelings from duty. Accept that Ali is a Vessel. Accept it because it is her duty and yours as well. We all must make sacrifices, Clio. That is what the calling of the Oracle is all about. As long as you allow yourself to feel everything with such devastating magnitude, you will be unable to perform your duty."

And with that her mother was gone and the Oracle had returned.

It was all too much. Mannix's words came back to her: *I saw no reason to remain loyal to people who had done nothing but hurt me, and so I ran away.* While Clio hated the thought of following in Mannix's footsteps, of letting his words worm into her, she couldn't stop the warmth that began to spread through her at the thought.

"Your time will come, and then you will understand," said the Oracle. She turned her back on Clio and started to walk out of the room.

"No, Mother, I could never understand this."

It was too late for Ali, but she was not going to submit to this. Clio twisted out of Vire's grip and bolted to the doors. She didn't turn back to see whether anyone was following her until her home was out of sight.

She was simultaneously relieved and disappointed that the road was empty behind her. While her aim was to escape, she couldn't help but want her family to come get her, maybe even comfort her the way her sisters had before they were changed. Tell her that she was wrong.

But they didn't come, and she wasn't wrong.

She'd been running for hours before Clio realized that she had absolutely nowhere to go. The only person she had even spoken to in years, other than her family, was Mannix. And he was the last person she wanted to see.

Five years ago a much younger Clio had run down this road under the moonlight, her head filled with thoughts of escape, her feet pounding toward the distant lights of the palace. It had been instinct then to run to Derik. And just as before, Clio found herself turning down the royal road before realizing what this meant.

She hadn't seen him in five years, but he was the only person in the world she trusted. He was the only one who could understand it all, and she needed that. She needed him, the boy who had sat with her in their treetop canopy and held her hand silently when Clio's world had been turned on its head. He'd promised to be there for her whenever she needed him. She could only hope that was still true after all the years of silence between them.

CHAPTER FIVE

Clio's feet kicked up dust that clouded her eyes as she darted through the cramped streets and alleyways of Sheehan. Sheehan had once been huge and sprawling, but most of the young men had died in the wars with Morek, leaving behind the women and the weak, who clumped together around the palace for what little protection it could offer.

The close quarters meant that disease spread like wildfire. Clio covered her mouth as she passed lepers whose limbs had started to fester and fall off.

Clay huts crumbled around her. Only the palace and the Oracle's temple were wealthy enough to be made out of stone. The city was dying, but Clio felt alive, more alive than anything.

As Clio skirted a tight corner, the palace suddenly emerged out of the crumbling huts and diseased alleys. Its façade was markedly more decrepit than the last time she had seen it. The jewels that had once lined the door were gone, stripped off the stone. Clearly, the king was using every possible resource to fund the city's defense.

Clio hid in the shadows at the gates, waiting for the guards to walk their rounds, but they wouldn't leave. Instead, more and more streamed from the palace doors.

She couldn't get anywhere near the palace with all of these eyes about. Something was definitely going on tonight.

Clio backed away. She had been a fool to think she could just march into the palace. She had been even more foolish to think that Derik would want her there. For all she knew, he had completely forgotten about her by now. The fact that her life hadn't changed didn't mean that his hadn't either.

She couldn't bring herself to go back into the decaying city to spend the night among the lepers and the streetwalkers. Night was bright around her, alive with chirping and buzzing. No, she didn't want to be inside.

It was on nights like these that Clio and Derik used to climb to the top of their tree and watch the fires being lit in each hearth, whispering to each other so as not to disturb the chatter of the birds around them. It was to that very tree that Clio found herself heading. She didn't know why—maybe out of habit, maybe because she didn't have anywhere else to go.

The tree stood just outside the palace gates. It wasn't as tall as Clio had remembered. Of course, she had been smaller then. It felt the same, though. She laid a hand on its thick trunk and looked up. Branches stretched out above her like cracks in the night sky.

As she made to lift herself on to the lowest branch, a

commotion above surprised her. Some animal must have been moving around. Clio took a couple of steps back, then let out a clipped shriek when whatever it was fell heavily to the ground beside her.

"Clio?" The mass straightened up into a tall man with dark hair that curled in tightly wound spirals across his forehead. "Is that you?"

"I'm sorry," she muttered, "I didn't mean to disturb—wait." She stopped. "How do you know my..." Her eyes widened as she realized who was standing before her. Those same gray eyes from years ago sparkled in the moonlight. "Derik?"

She hadn't prepared herself for the simple truth that Derik would be a man by now. A man who looked as if he might one day be a fierce and powerful ruler. They were the same age, but Clio couldn't help but think that five years wrought so much change in him and so little in her. All she could get out was a shaky, "Oh my."

He cracked a grin. "You come to my tree in the middle of the night after disappearing from my life, and *you* are the one who is shocked?" His voice was so much deeper than she remembered, so much more powerful and commanding.

"I just didn't expect to—what are you doing here?"

"I spend a lot of nights out here, ever since you left. The real question is what are *you* doing here?" He smiled as if she was the greatest sight he had ever laid eyes on.

"I—well, I came to find you, actually."

"Five years of total silence and *now* you want to find me?" There was hurt in his eyes.

"Derik, surely you don't think that was my doing?"

"I didn't know what to think. I came to see you so many times in those first days, but Mira kept telling me you didn't want to see me. What else was I supposed to think?"

"Of course she did," Clio said under her breath. Her jaw tightened in anger at the thought of her sister helping her mother to keep Derik away. "She was lying. The Oracle wouldn't let me see you anymore. I wanted to. Believe me, there were so many times that...I just needed you, but I couldn't get away. And now—"

She didn't get to say anything else because suddenly she found herself wrapped in his arms, with her head nestled against his chest. They had hugged when they were younger, but this was different. To begin with, he was now a good head taller than she was. He was also rock solid. A man's muscles lay beneath his tunic.

Before she knew it, she was crying. She hadn't been hugged like that in a long time.

"Clio, what is it? What's wrong? I'm guessing you didn't come here just because you missed me."

Between sobs, she managed to say, "Oh, Derik, I couldn't stay there anymore. Ali is gone. And today..." How could she tell her only friend that her family was nothing but a bunch of murderers? "Derik, she has them killing people for her."

To her surprise, he nodded. "I suspected as much. For ages now, more and more sightings of your mother and your sisters have coincided with suspicious deaths. Clio, I'm so sorry." He clasped the back of her head in his hand and held her to him.

It was amazing. All those years, and still she could tell him anything. It felt right. They stood in silence until Clio's eyes finally dried.

"Hey, it's all right. You can stay here as long as you need. I haven't forgotten my promise, you know." At this, she looked up into his gray eyes and really smiled. "Deities, Clio, you've grown up. When did all this happen?" As he looked her body up and down, she blushed.

"Oh, probably about the time this happened." She punched his hard chest lightly and laughed. Clio couldn't help but feel self-conscious about her appearance. After her run, she was covered in sweat and mud and the Deities knew what else.

"Your hair," he said as he twisted a lock between his fingers. "It's so long now."

"Yes, well, that's because the Oracle won't let me cut it," she said. "I hate it."

"Hmm, well. She isn't here now, right?" He went back to where he'd dropped the blade in his fall. "You don't like it? Let's cut it."

A huge grin spread across her face. A change. It was exactly what she needed. She just wanted to distance herself from her family in everyway possible. She nodded. "Yes, please do."

He gathered her hair in his hand and gently sawed at it near her shoulders. As the hair fell around her feet, her head felt lighter. It wasn't just the hair she was shedding, but all the fear and anxiety she had been keeping for years. Never in her life had she felt like this, as if she could do anything. She could have a family one day, and be whatever she wanted. She could fall in love, and she never had to go into that cold, heartless temple again. She was free. And it was glorious. It didn't matter that she had no idea where she would go next. That was part of the freedom. No future was set for her.

"I think they did something especially bad last night. Vire, she was covered in blood, and she spoke to me—"

Derik cut her off. "Wait, Vire? Vire actually spoke to you?"

Clio laughed, remembering all the times that they, as children, had tried to get two words out of Vire.

"I'm sorry," Derik said. "Go on. What did she say?"

"She told me that things were changing."

Derik seemed to mull this over. "Things *are* changing," he said. "Lately, my father has been emphasizing my training. He says I will have to lead an army soon."

"Against Morek?"

Derik shrugged. "I've never wanted to do that, to command men in battle, but I guess I don't have much of a say in it."

"I know what that's like," Clio murmured.

"Well, whatever it is, we will face it together now." Derik brightened.

"I've missed you, Derik," she said quietly.

He spun her around until she was facing him. "I've missed you, too. We have years to make up for. You've always been my best friend, Clio. Without you it's been…tough. Mannix, he's all but taken over. My father is barely even in the city anymore, he spends all his time trying to negotiate alliances with the north."

"Is that why there were so many guards outside the palace?"

"It's because my father was supposed to return from Morek this morning." Derik looked out to the horizon, as if trying to catch a glimpse of him.

The Oracle had thought that the king was in danger. Clio couldn't tell Derik. She had no reason to believe the Oracle truly knew something of importance. If she did, though, hadn't she sent out her Vessels to protect him?

"Come on." She grabbed his hand, pulling him back toward the tree. "Let's climb to the top, like we used to do. Maybe we can spot him."

They raced each other, laughing as they pulled and kicked their way to the top. When Clio poked her head through the tree's dense canopy of leaves, she couldn't help but gasp. The retiring sun's red glare was just barely visible, like a fog that clung to the edges of the world.

It was beautiful, but they saw no hint of an approaching king.

"We should go inside." Derik's voice came from beside her.

She grabbed his hand in hers, squeezing it tight. "Not yet, please." As long as she was out here, on this tree that seemed to stand apart from time, the rest of the world felt too far below to touch her.

They sat together as they used to when they were children, on the top branch, Derik's back against the trunk. Clio nestled in his lap. She nodded off to the sound of his gentle breathing, oblivious of everything on the ground that was about to change forever.

CHAPTER SIX

Clio smiled in her sleep.

She was outside, and nothing had ever felt so good. The sun was beating down on her face. She smiled, savoring the warmth, but a distant and wavering cry pulled on the edges of Clio's memory, beckoning her back into the dark. She tried to get back to the feeling of the sun on her skin, of its blissful emptiness, but those thin voices held a part of her. Their shrill echoes sounded throughout Clio's mind, unwavering and remorseless. Clio felt in her bones that she had to get away. She ran, as if that could bring silence, and collided with something hard. Or rather someone. Looking up, she felt the warmth flow through her again. The voices were completely forgotten as she stared into Derik's eyes. He took her hand, and they raced toward the sound of trickling water in the distance. He jumped in and beckoned her to follow. After a moment's hesitation she did so, plunging herself into the icy stream.

The cold water was a shock after the warm air. Her mind froze, shooting pain through her limbs. This wasn't right. The pain was growing and growing, it felt as if her head would burst at any moment. Instead of bursting, however, everything just went black.

She opened her eyes and was surprised to find herself in her mother's quarters at their home. It was night, and her mother and sisters were all sleeping in the dark. Something obscured the moonlight coming in from the window—a black outline. Clio strained her eyes to figure out what it was when it dropped down into the room and straightened out into the shape of a robed man. Several more soon followed. They were completely silent. As they crossed into the faint moonlight, Clio caught a flash of red...Mannix's red.

Clio tried to call out to her sleeping family, but her voice made no sound. She tried to step toward them but found herself held back.

She stood helpless as the men motioned to each other and took their positions over each sleeping figure. The man nearest her mother threw a rope around her neck and dragged her outside. Clio could hear her gagged struggling and the unmistakable sound of a blade being drawn followed by a wet thud.

Clio tried to follow her mother. She had to see if she was okay, she couldn't be dead, but some unheard signal must have passed among the men, because in complete unison the men pulled out their blades and sliced the throats of her sleeping sisters.

All but one. Ali was pulled up, groggily kicking out as she realized what was happening. One of the robed figures brought her to another man. Clio recognized him as one of the guards who had streamed out of the palace earlier that night. He bore the plumage of one of the king's men.

"This is the youngest?" he asked.

The robed figure only nodded.

"She is to be brought directly to Morek. Do not stop for anything."

Clio was screaming, but no sound came out. The pain in her head was back, worse than it was before, growing and growing to a breaking point.

Clio woke with a jolt. Something was wrong with her eyes; the branches and the stars around her looked like a reflection in a pond. Everything rippled and swayed, as if the wind were moving water. She tried to stay as still as she could, to make the rippling stop, and found herself looking up into gray eyes.

Derik.

He was saying something to her, but he sounded as if he were underwater, his voice warbling out in thick, heavy vibrations.

If she could just quiet the pounding that seemed to come from everywhere, she could focus enough to break through the water that separated her from the world. Taking a deep breath, she stilled the lapping waves. Slowly, the blood reached her eyes and ears, bringing everything into focus again.

Derik had been shaking her, repeating over and over, "Clio, what it is? Clio, come back!"

She opened her mouth to respond—terrified that, as in her dream, she would be voiceless—but a thin, low moan came from her throat. Her head was still pounding. Each beat was like a club to the inside of her skull.

Clumsily, she got to her knees and crawled to the end of their branch just in time to be sick. Her body seemed to be rejecting her very insides. Finally she rose, gasping for air, and Derik held a canteen of water at her lips. She sipped and felt the water cool every part of her body on its descent. It cleared her head, too, except for that dull pounding in the background.

Derik looked at her with concern creasing his forehead and

pulling his jaw taut. "Clio, your hair. It's…it's white."

She pulled a fistful in front of her eyes and was shocked to see pure white hair where black had been. It was just like her mother's.

Like an Oracle's.

She was going to be sick again. She crouched over the edge, but nothing was left in her stomach.

"What's going on?" Derik's voice shook. "What's happening to you?"

Her dream must not have been a dream at all. It was a Vision. It was real. The Visions her mother had always spoken of, the Sight. It was all real. Clio couldn't deny it any longer. The white hair falling in front of her eyes, the resounding pounding in her head—it was all proof that the Deities were doing something to her.

The only way she could have a Vision would be if all of her family were dead, but wasn't that what she'd just seen? They had been butchered in their sleep, and she had inherited the Sight. Power passed down through her bloodline, her mother had never lied about any of it. The Oracle hadn't been trying to trick the hopeless into worshipping her and her family, after all. The Deities had indeed spoken to Clio's mother.

And now they spoke to Clio, bringing a horrible message that someone had killed her family.

But who would do something like that? The Oracle was a sacred and beloved fixture in Sheehan. Clio knew about the execution of the Oracle in Morek, but her own family had always been an ally to the king of Sheehan.

"Derik, I saw my family murdered," she managed to say when her stomach stopped trying to force up what was no longer there. But Ali…Clio didn't understand. Could Ali still be alive if Clio had the Sight? Ali should have inherited the Sight before Clio, unless she had died too and Clio just hadn't seen it. Clio pushed that thought away, unable to accept it.

"What do you mean you *saw* them? You were dreaming." Derik was backing away, as if he was afraid.

"Then how do you explain this?" She grabbed her hair. "I Saw it, Derik. In my Vision, they were killed in their sleep. Or are going to be killed. I don't know." She was suddenly hopeful. "It might not be too late. Maybe I can stop it."

"Are you insane? You can't go somewhere that you know is going to be full of murderers! Think! You wouldn't have been able to See anything unless they were already dead. If everything your mother told you was true, then she was the Oracle up until the moment she died. I'm sorry, Clio, but I can't let you go. It's too dangerous. It could be a trap." He moved toward her and put his hands on her shoulders.

"No they can't be dead, I saw…" Clio's hand came up to mouth as she realized what she was saying. She had Seen it. "I have to go. I have to see them." Her whole body was shaking. Derik's words finally sunk in. "Trap? What do you mean 'a trap'?" The pounding made it hard for her to understand what he was saying.

"If they took out your entire family, it can only mean that they planned to get rid of the possibility of there ever being another

Oracle in Sheehan. They must not have been expecting you to be out of the house. Maybe they didn't even know how many daughters there would be—your mother has done a good job hiding you all away. But you can bet that if you walk into that house with your hair like that, they will finish the job."

"But Ali, they might not have killed her! She was taken—"

He straightened up and motioned for her to be quiet. She tried to pick up what he was hearing, but the pounding in her head still made everything duller.

Finally, she heard it. Footsteps, getting louder.

"Prince Derik, are you up there?" A voice slithered up to them. *Mannix.*

Derik swore as he prepared to climb down.

The red robes from her Vision flashed before Clio's eyes.

"Careful," Clio urged under her breath, "he has something to do with this all. It was his men who…"

He nodded his understanding, then dropped lithely from branch to branch, landing with a dull thud right in front of Mannix. Clio flattened herself down on the branch, hidden in brambles and darkness, and hoped that Mannix wouldn't think to look up for her.

"Derik." There was that slippery voice again. Clio could almost hear his grin. "I came to wake you and tell you the news, but found your chamber empty. Were you talking to someone out here?" The whites of Mannix's eyes flashed up as he searched the branches.

Derik strode away from the tree, trying to pull Mannix's gaze from Clio's hiding place.

"No," Derik answered.

"I thought I heard voices." Mannix looked up again.

"I don't owe you any explanations. Do I need to remind you that I am the prince and you are but an adviser? It is highly inappropriate for you to question me in this manner." Derik's voice was strong and commanding.

"Of course, my prince." Clio heard his robes rustle in what must have been a bow. "It's just that my position and yours have been slightly, how should I say, altered this night."

"What do you mean?" Derik asked.

"Dreadful betrayal. We should have followed Morek's lead and sacrificed the witches before something like this happened."

Clio's heart stopped for a moment. He was referring to the Oracle and her Vessels.

"What are you talking about?" Derik asked.

"It is my sad and unfortunate duty to tell you that the woman who has called herself the Oracle is responsible for the death of your father." Mannix's voice dripped with false grief.

The king dead? And her mother responsible? Maybe it was her pounding head or maybe it was the news, but the branch seemed to be sliding out beneath her.

But her mother said that the Vessels had fought someone to protect the king.

Clio saw Derik lose his footing in the darkness, the wind knocked from his breast at the news. He recovered almost immediately, not showing weakness. Straightening, he faced Mannix, all authority again.

"As my first duty as king regent," Mannix added, "I ordered the witches executed in private. No need to stir up the public."

Clio rolled onto her back and stared up at the stars. They were dead. And Mannix had killed them. Any hope of saving them died with Mannix's words. Clio felt her heart shudder, fighting to let out the sobs buried within. Clio locked her jaws together and willed herself to take slow breaths through her nose.

"King regent? I am nearly 16, old enough to rule on my own. There is no need for a regent," Derik said.

"Well, I'm afraid your father felt differently. His latest will names me as regent until you are ready. Come to think of it, he really should have specified an age. How am I to know when you are truly ready?" The implication was clear: Mannix would never give up the throne.

Derik must have been too shocked to say anything.

"My deepest apologies, Derik. Your father was a good man, but he should not have trusted those women. I had advised against it."

"Why kill the daughters? They shouldn't pay for what their mother did."

"Sadly, they are just as guilty. You see, the old woman was not strong enough to do the job herself, and so she had her daughters do it for her."

"What proof could you possibly have?" Derik's words were an accusation.

"My prince, several villagers spotted the younger ones walking from the temple to the house covered in blood. Your father's body was retrieved just behind the temple."

Clio's blood froze. She couldn't get the image of Vire standing in the hallway, dripping with blood, out of her mind. Could Vire have possibly...? But the thought was too horrible. There she was in Clio's mind, skin slick with blood, hollowed eyes, cold and distant. And there was Mira, asking her if it were done. *It.* The Oracle said they had protected the king, and Vire thought she had accomplished whatever her calling was. If Vire had failed in saving the king, wouldn't she have said so?

Deities, it was so messed up. The revulsion boiled away at Clio's insides. She didn't know whom to trust. Her sisters? Her mother? They were murderers. They had all but admitted it.

Yet something wasn't right about Mannix. Every drop of her blood called her not to trust his words. Clearly Mannix had the most to gain from the king's death, while her mother and her sisters had everything to lose.

Derik was talking again. "Surely the youngest daughter, Clio, should have been saved. She hadn't even started her training."

"Ah, I had forgotten that you had a special relationship with the youngest girl." But Mannix sounded as if he hadn't forgotten that at all. "She is one of them, but because she had not yet entered the Oracle's service, I thought it prudent to gift her to Morek. They have a certain method of dispatching Oracles."

Why send one away and kill the rest? It didn't make any sense.

Mannix went on. "I know how hard this must be for you. Try to rest tonight. I will take care of the affairs of the city." With that, he left.

Clio slowly came down from her hiding spot. Her brain was churning, trying to understand everything that just passed. Why did Mannix think she was on her way to Morek? Had his guards lied to him? Most importantly, however, had her family killed the king? But if they hadn't, why had they been butchered? It was too much to make sense of.

"Did you know anything about this?" Derik rounded on her, doubt flashing in his eyes.

"About your father? No, of course not! It doesn't make sense. My mother told me that she had foreseen something befalling the king, but she had sent Vire and maybe Ali out to stop whoever was going to hurt him. Vire said she had done it. Derik, I'm so sorry."

She laid a hand gently on his arm, and his face crumpled in grief.

"I can't." He pulled away from her. "Why does he think you are on your way to Morek?" he asked, wiping his eyes under the cover of darkness.

"In my...Vision," her tongue tripped on the word, "I saw Ali being taken to Morek. They said it was because she was the youngest."

Derik's eyes widened. "They thought she was you."

"I have to go. I have to stop them from killing her."

"To Morek? They made their policy toward Oracles very clear when they sacrificed the last one. You are just going to get yourself killed. The Deities spared you for a reason." Heat rose in his voice, panic setting in.

"I can't do nothing while they kill her! Plus, it's not safe for me here anymore. If Mannix finds me—"

"He won't. I can hide you." He grabbed her just above the elbows, holding her steady.

"No, you can't. You have a city to rule now."

Pain lanced through her head again, settling just behind her eyes, bursting into light.

Mannix walked through a crowded street, his red robe billowing behind him like a bloody wave. He sliced between people, stopping when he reached a door guarded by one of his own crimson men.

"She's in there?" Mannix asked, anticipation rough in his voice.

The guard only nodded.

Mannix brushed past him carelessly. Clio felt a pull, telling her to go with him. Somehow she knew that her real body was moving with her, unlike before when she had been trapped in Derik's arms.

He entered a small, stuffy room. Two more crimson men lined the wall, as well as the one guard from the palace. But it was the center that drew Clio's eyes. Ali sat bound and motionless, her head hanging limply forward. Her hair was so matted with dirt and mud that it looked brown.

Mannix knelt beside her. Almost tenderly, he brushed away the hair that covered her face.

He hissed and drew back when Ali's face was revealed. "I said the youngest girl, you fools!" Rage flared in his face, twisting his mouth into a thin grimace.

The palace guard spoke. "This was the youngest, sir. The other three were much older."

Mannix stopped. "Three? No, there should have been five! Four to kill and one, the youngest, to bring to me."

"There were only four in the house, sir. We searched everywhere."

Ali stirred on the ground below him. "Clio..." she murmured.

"Where is she?" He spat at her, taking her face in his hands.

Slowly, Ali opened her eyes. Both Mannix and Clio flinched at what they saw—Ali's eyes were pure white. "I may be blind, but Clio can See you. You think we knew nothing of your plan?"

"You didn't foresee the king's true death." Mannix smirked.

"The king is dead?" Ali's blank eyes widened in shock. "But we killed your assassin."

"My decoy." He waved away her word. "So it's true. The Oracle cannot foresee her own death. I imagine the Deities knew humankind well enough not to drive the Oracle mad with such knowledge. But it leaves a very gaping hole in their Sight, don't you think? The king died alongside the Oracle. She couldn't see his death without foreseeing her own."

Mannix crouched down in front of Ali and cupped her chin in his hands. "Your mother, what did she do to you?"

"We did know some of your plans, though." Ali smiled, but Clio could see the fear in the faint tremble of her lip. "The Deities come to the Oracle through her sight. When she took my eyes, the gift passed over me. She made it so Clio would be the Oracle. You won't have her."

Mannix smiled. "Is that so?" He turned to his guards. "Take her to the pyramid. They will know what to do with her."

Clio came back sputtering. Her eyes burned, but already the pain was less than before.

"Mannix is lying, Derik. He killed the king. He killed him at the same time as my mother. That's why his body was found at temple. Mannix brought the king there."

"How do you—" Derik began.

Clio cut him off. "Mannix is going to send Ali to the pyramid in Morek. She will be executed for everyone to see. I *have* to go." Her tone made it clear there was no time for questions.

Reluctantly, Derik nodded. "I *will* come for you, all right? I promise. As soon as I can. I didn't just get you back to lose you again." His eyes blazed. Clio couldn't help but trust him.

"Here." He took the small pack he had on him and handed it to her. "Morek is a little more than a day's journey. Just follow the sunrise and you can't miss it."

She turned to go, but his hand caught hers, pulling her back. His gaze was uncertain.

"Clio...I..." Their faces were getting closer. Something flashed in his eyes. Doubt? Hesitation? "Be safe, and keep an eye out for the Untouched. No matter how dark it gets, do not light a fire, you hear me? They will find you if you do."

She nodded numbly.

He brushed his lips along her forehead and held her hand for a long moment.

All too soon, she was on her own, running again. But this time, Clio's world and all its laws had been rewritten. Her mother truly had been the Oracle. She had been given messages from the Deities. Everything Clio had ever fought against, everything she had believed to be greed and lies, was actually something much more unsettling.

The powers of the Oracle were real. The Deities had to be real too. And Clio was running into this uncertain world, stripped of all the beliefs on which she had so long depended. Beliefs that had made her who she was.

She ran because it was all she could do. Because she could no longer be the girl who had climbed into that tree to hide from the world. She was the Oracle.

CHAPTER SEVEN

Everything was deathly silent except for the pounding in Clio's head. As she made her way past the palace and down the stifling city streets, she tried to put together all the pieces that had been jumbling around since her first Vision. Recalling it sent shivers down Clio's spine.

She had never anticipated this, never been prepared for it. The Oracle must have known somehow that something was going to happen to her. She couldn't see her death, but she must have had some idea because she made sure Clio got the Sight. But why didn't her mother teach Clio anything about how to handle these powers? A rush of anger rose in her chest. If only her mother had thought to give her some advice on what to do with the Sight if she ever inherited it.

But Clio knew she never would have listened to her mother if she had tried to explain everything. Clio had never even believed in this. And the Oracle had allowed that. Resentment boiled in the pit of Clio's stomach. Her mother had pushed Clio away until Clio had felt so alienated that she had rebelled against everything. If only her mother had thought to bring Clio into the secrets of the Oracle. Maybe Clio would know what to do now. Maybe she would even embrace this new power. Maybe she would know enough to save Ali.

Ali, who had been sent to Morek in Clio's place, blinded of the Oracle's powers, completely helpless. Why wouldn't her mother give the Sight to Ali? Maybe the Oracle knew Mannix would have killed Ali immediately. Maybe she knew that Clio was the only one with a chance to survive. Clio stopped running.

She realized that her mother had let her run away.

Her family didn't know when they were going to be attacked, but they had some idea about it. Their silence and reserve—it wasn't because they couldn't be bothered with Clio, it was because they were driving her away. No one chased her down because they wanted her gone.

They had saved her.

Pain flared in Clio's chest. She didn't know how to feel about her family anymore. Maybe they saved her because they needed someone to carry on the Oracle's powers, or maybe because they cared for her. Everything she had believed about her mother had been turned upside down this evening. Maybe what Clio had always thought to be indifference was actually something much more complicated.

Clio started running again. She couldn't stop to work this out. Ali needed her.

She reached the city perimeter and headed in the direction she knew the sun to rise. Clio had spent too many sleepless nights watching the sun come up not to know the right direction. The cliffs seemed to stretch to the ends of the horizon, and the city of Morek was somewhere behind them. She'd never be able to find a way around those mountains, not like this, not on foot with hardly any supplies.

She ran for what felt like ages, exhausted in every way. She had vomited up everything in her stomach when she had the Vision, and unless she timed her stride to hit with the pulsing in her head, the pain was too much to bear. Her head felt like an open wound. The tiniest pressure sent shock waves of pain rippling through her body.

Her foot slipped in some mud, and it wasn't until then that Clio realized it was raining. No stars were in sight, obscured by black rainclouds. She tripped over a rock in the dirt and cried out as it tore a long gash in her ankle. Mud rushed up to greet her, invading her eyes and nose as she collapsed.

Spitting the muck from her mouth, she tried to pull her arms out and raise herself up, but they felt as heavy as stone. She had no choice but to turn over and lie there for a moment as waves of exhaustion rolled through her. It wasn't long before she felt tears streaming down her cheeks.

She was so confused. So unsure of who she was supposed to be. Her family was gone, and they hadn't been the stone creatures Clio had always thought them to be. But what did it matter if she realized they cared for her more than she thought? That wasn't going to bring them back. She was completely alone.

Ali.

Everything within Clio pulled her toward her only family left, but her body gave out. Deep down, she feared that Derik was right, that she had little chance of doing anything to help Ali.

All because of Mannix. Everything came back to him. He gave the order to have her family killed; he took Ali and then gave her away, and because of him Clio was burdened with the Sight. Part of her didn't even care if he found her. Maybe it would have been better if she had died along with her family. A quick and silent death like that would be better than whatever she was about to face in Morek. Maybe she and Ali could enter the afterlife together. The world had never been kind to them, so why was she fighting so hard to keep them both in it?

She couldn't help wondering whether she could have stopped it all had she had been home. It was a ridiculous thought, she knew that. If Clio had been there, then Ali would have been killed instantly, and Clio would be in Mannix's hold right now. Her sisters must have been more capable than she was when it came to fighting. The Oracle would have trained them if the Vessels' duties involved killing.

Why Mannix wanted Clio so badly, why she should have been kept alive…that was a mystery Clio didn't have the strength to pursue yet.

She closed her eyes and let the rain fall down her face, mixing with her tears until it was impossible to distinguish which was which. It would be so easy, peaceful even, to remain there, savoring the feel of the warm raindrops lightly pelting her skin.

A soft shuffle crept over the land to her ears. Clio turned her head to see where it was coming from, hoping that it wasn't some beast come to devour her. A string of red flame torches floated along the horizon. It was too dark to make out the men who carried them, but Clio didn't need to see them to know who they were.

The Untouched.

Only they would risk drawing attention to themselves with flames in the middle of the night. Her heartbeat picked up, hammering so hard in her chest that she feared it might echo across the ground to them.

The Untouched were cannibal tribes, savage in every possible way. They roamed the hollow lands searching for wayward travelers and foolish tribes. Without loyalties, organization, language, they should have been easy to defeat. The Emperor's forces should have been able to eradicate them ages ago. But somehow the Untouched lived on. Too subtle, unpredictable and wild to be pulled into a trap. The tribes that they came across were worse than destroyed. The healthy were butchered and eaten, the children were taken captive. The sickly, if they were lucky, were killed for sport. If they were unlucky, they were raped and left to watch as their families were consumed. Any survivors took their own lives as soon as the Untouched moved on. Some tried to go after their children, but no one ever found them.

Clio held her breath as if that would stop the sound of her pounding heart, only letting it out when she saw the last of the flickering lights fade into the darkness. She was lucky. If they had found her, she would have suffered in the worst way imaginable.

She wondered why they were here, only a day's travel from Sheehan. They weren't supposed to be this close to the city, but clearly Sheehan lacked the force necessary to keep them at bay. When Sheehan perished, the beasts would come for her carcass.

The city—Derik. She couldn't let him find her body here tomorrow. When she rescued Ali, she would have to go back to Sheehan. She had to help him. He was alone too, trapped under the rule of Mannix. Her blood boiled at the thought of Mannix sitting on the king's throne and giving orders to Derik. Or worse, imprisoning him. Derik needed her. He had helped her, and she wasn't going to repay him by giving up. She made a promise a long time ago to Derik that she was going to remain herself for as long as possible. That she would fight. She couldn't give that up now.

As long as she had the slimmest chance of helping Ali, she had to go on.

Slowly, she pulled herself up and began to search through the bag that Derik had given her. In it she found water, fruit, and a tunic. She set to cleaning out her wound, tearing the tunic up and using it to wrap her ankle and stop the bleeding. While Morek was within walking distance, it was far, and Clio knew that in her current state she wasn't strong enough to make it there. She stared at the glistening red fruit, grimacing at the thought of putting something in her stomach. In the end, she nibbled away at half of one as she walked.

Surprisingly, it stayed down and even quieted the drumming in her head. Clio could make out the soft glow of the sun rising in the distance and began to feel she could do this.

Then she saw it.

Morek, the mightiest city in the lands below the Great Sea. A city with pyramids that rivaled mountains, with gold enough to pave its own streets. Its armies weren't made up of scared farmers and young boys. Instead, warriors were trained from birth in the art of killing. They had no mercy because they were raised believing that to bring back the head of an enemy was the highest honor one could achieve. A city that had shed so much blood that it had managed to conquer every city it reached.

One look at its faint outline made it clear why no army had ever managed to breach the city walls. Morek wasn't behind the mountains that Clio had seen from her bedroom. It was *part* of them. Situated dizzyingly high atop a sheer cliff face, the city was absolutely impenetrable to invading armies, let alone to a weak and tired 15-year-old girl.

CHAPTER EIGHT

She sat watching as the sun peeked out behind the mountainous city, spreading its growing rays over the golden rocks and dirt below. The city had only one entrance from this side, and it was treacherous to say the least. A path not wide enough to fit two people side-by-side wound its way through switchbacks up to the city wall. No one could march up that path unnoticed and gain entry to Morek.

Clio racked her brain for a way in, but nothing was coming. She looked up to the sky and muttered, "Well, this would be a good time for a Vision, don't you think?"

But the Deities remained as silent as always. No Vision came. Actually, Clio had no idea how Visions worked. The only part of an Oracle's duties that Clio had ever been privy to were the blessings that she'd helped her mother bestow. She tried to remember as much as she could about the ceremony, as if it held some clue as to how she was supposed to use her gifts, but all she could remember were the faces of those innocent girls headed to a new life in Morek.

Then it hit her: headed to *Morek*.

A group of that size would have traveled slowly through the day and would have had to camp through the night. The only reason she hadn't seen them on her own trek to Morek was the storm clouds that had swallowed up the moonlight. They were headed into the city, and what was one more young girl to them? They wouldn't notice a stowaway, because who in their right mind would stow away on a slave train?

Those girls were being delivered directly to the temple. Clio had to laugh. The Deities were not without their sense of irony—run away from her temple only to end up in another. She would escape, though. She would have to. Ali's life depended on it.

She retraced her steps back toward Sheehan, and it wasn't long before she found their camp. No one seemed to have woken yet, but she didn't have long.

She caught her reflection in a pool of rainwater and stifled a gasp. She didn't look like herself. She had forgotten about her hair. It only came down to her shoulders now, and it was the purest white. She would have to do something about that. Her eyes were wide and wild. The strings of beads that had hung from her woolen tunic had broken off during her desperate run to Morek. Everything from her skin to her clothes to her hair was mud-splattered. Dried blood coated her foot below the gash in her wrapped ankle.

The mud gave her an idea. She knelt before the pool and dug her fingers to the silty bottom. She came up with a dark brown mud, which she used to cover her hair. She would look just like all the other street urchins who hadn't had a wash in ages.

She had to say goodbye to the supplies Derik packed her; slaves weren't allowed to have possessions. It was just a leather bag, but it was hard to part with nonetheless. As she buried it in the bottom of the pool, she wondered whether she would ever see Derik again. She had just gotten her friend back, and it hurt to say goodbye to him.

When they were kids, Derik had said to her that one day the two of them would be married. He told her that was what boys and girls did who liked each other very much. Clio hadn't had any idea of what marriage was. She didn't even know that men and women could live together. It wasn't until she was much older that she started to wonder about what he said. Of course it was impossible. He had been only a boy when he said it, and Clio carried no illusions that he had fully understood or even wanted it. But still, after all these years, the thought was not unwelcome. All she had of him now was the bloodied and dirt-stained bit of his tunic wrapped around her ankle. She used the remainder of the material to bind her hands together like the other slaves.

As quietly as possible, she made her way to the camp and stepped past sleeping guards. All the girls were in the center of the camp, each tied to the wooden beam they carried on their shoulders as they walked.

One of the guards was stirring. A fly buzzed around his nose, and he groggily swatted at it with his eyes closed. Clio scanned the girls, hoping to find some room on the beam, but the slavers had assembled a full offering. She could tell none of the girls were actually asleep; they were all too still in their uncomfortable postures.

They didn't give her up, though. A lifetime as a slave had taught each girl to watch out only for herself.

At the back of the train, one girl's eyes opened and fixed right on Clio. With as little motion as possible, the girl gestured with her head for Clio to join her. It was the one without hair, the one who had stubbornly wiped away the anointing oil. It felt like millions of years ago that Clio was helping her mother dole out blessings, but it was only yesterday. Quickly and quietly, Clio made her way to her.

"Let me untie you," Clio whispered, keeping an eye on the sleeping guards.

The girl only shook her head.

"Come on, I know that all these other girls"—she paused as a guard shuffled in his sleep—"want to be here. You don't."

Clio could see a slight glimmer in the girl's eyes, but when she spoke, her tone was decisive. "Too far from the city. I...wouldn't make it." She covered her mouth as she fought to stifle a fit of coughs. The guard let out a groggy moan.

They had no time to argue. Clio looped her hands around the beam, just barely getting into the same awkward kneeling position as all the other girls when the guard finally woke.

By the time they reached the top of the winding path up to Morek, Clio's thighs were burning, and her shoulder felt as if it would never recover from the weight of the pole she had to bear. A seeping trickle down her ankle let Clio know that the exertion had opened up her wound. The blood loss wasn't doing much to help her up the summit. More than once she felt she was about to trip and tumble off the edge of the cliff, taking all the girls tied to the pole with her. The girl in front of her did her best to carry some of Clio's weight, but Clio could hear her labored breathing.

In fact, none of the girls looked like they were suffering during the climb as much as Clio was. They were all tan, and Clio could make out the carved muscles in their calves, evidence of the hard work to which they were accustomed. Clio was pale, and her life in captivity had made her relatively weak. Every muscle in her body ached, unused to the extreme demands she had placed upon them.

But somehow she made it to the top. One of the slavers went ahead and conversed with a Morekian guard. As the great doors to the city creaked open, Clio got her first view inside Morek.

It was like nothing she had ever seen. Not a single building was made of clay. Everything was stone. This city screamed permanence. While the clay homes of Sheehan would wither away in coming winters, these homes would last until the end of time. Generations could live here with little effort. But the stone held none of the warmth, none of the life that burned brightly within each fleeting clay home in Sheehan. Some stone even looked to have been carved from the mountain itself, as if Morek had written over nature.

Despite the immovability of it all, Clio could not deny its splendor. Winding streets snaked through rows of colorful homes. Each home was made out of a different granite. Clio's eyes went wide as she took in the yellows, pinks, blues, and greens around her. Some homes were even gilded in gold, and when the sun beat down, it was reflected in such a bright gleam that Clio had to cover her eyes. The city was absolutely breathtaking, a city worthy of Deities rather than mortals. Clio was so overwhelmed by the feeling of power and wealth inscribed in every stone that she forgot why she was there.

But when they reached the heart of the city, there could be no forgetting. The pyramid. A structure so great, at least three times the size of the one in Sheehan, that it seemed to rival the mountain's own peaks. Clio couldn't even make out the top, but what she did see was enough to make her blood run cold.

They had to push their way through a sea of sweaty people. At the base of the pyramid, under a layer of buzzing flies, lay a tangled mess of bodies. Sticky coarse hair peeked through the grayish flesh. A trail of blood ran all the way down the front of the pyramid and pooled in a dark brown spot under the bodies. The rank stench of decay was unbearable. Clio had to cover her mouth to stifle the bile that rose up her throat.

It was horrifying, and everything in Clio shouted that she should get as far away from this as possible. But it was too late.

Crowds swarmed around them, chanting and yelling, eagerly trying to get a better view of the pyramid.

"No," the girl without hair gasped as she looked up the pyramid.

"Wha—" Clio started. She saw what had everyone's attention.

Someone was being led out on top of the pyramid. Whoever it was was obscured in a thick escort of guards. A man in amber robes with a brightly colored headdress stood waiting behind the altar.

A sacrifice was about to be made.

Clio had never seen one, and she had never wanted to. Sheehan couldn't afford to make such offerings to the Deities, and the city's forces weren't strong enough to conquer a city and capture slaves. Over the decades, Sheehan's priest moldered away like his unused pyramid while the Oracle's power grew. But in Morek, there was no Oracle, and each victory would bring this city countless sacrifices. The Deities needed to be thanked with the blood of the defeated. Men who had watched their brothers die in combat, seen their cities go up in flames, their women and children slaughtered, were all brought back to Morek and slaughtered atop this very pyramid.

The man in the amber robes, who must have been the priest, was talking, but Clio couldn't hear what he was saying over the roar of the crowd. She was about to move on when the sacrifice emerged from the throng of warriors. It was no conquered warrior. Trembling, a girl was shoved before the altar—a girl with gleaming black hair and clear white eyes.

Ali.

"No!" Clio yelled, but the multitude swallowed her voice. She pushed forward, but her bindings held her back.

The priest held up a gleaming black blade. Clio cried out for her sister, feeling a strange power course through her veins. She pulled on the ropes so hard that they splintered and snapped. Breathless, she rushed to the front of the crowd. The world around her melted away. All Clio saw were her sister and the black blade that beckoned to her.

All her life, Clio had felt as if she never had any control. As she watched that blade hover closer and closer to Ali's pink skin, she knew she had been wrong. This moment—*this* was what it meant to be powerless.

Something collided hard with her head, making the world go white and forcing her to her knees. Dazed, she turned to find a slaver. In his hand was a thick club, fresh blood dripping from its broad surface. Hers.

By the time she could look up again, it was over. Ali was gone.

She heard a shrill screaming nearby, a cry that held all the pain and anguish of the world. It was only when she saw everyone's eyes fall on her that she realized the scream was her own. She couldn't get up, couldn't move. Her cry had emptied her lungs, and Clio didn't have the will to breathe. Something hit her back, knocking her to the ground. She wanted to lie there, to let the crowds trample her, but rough hands pulled her up. She didn't have it in her to fight them.

The slaver forced her on her feet and back to the group. Her mind was a blank. Somehow her legs moved her forward, but Clio didn't feel connected to them anymore. She trudged through the throng of people who had witnessed and cheered for her sister's death, and rage slowly filled the emptiness. Rage at these people, at Morek, but most of all, rage at Mannix. He consumed her thoughts.

She would escape, and he would pay for this.

They were led around the pyramid and stopped at its entrance. Warriors stood guard, but these warriors bore no resemblance to the ones in Sheehan. These men truly looked like the warriors of the sun Deity. They wore pure gold breastplates over the traditional leather gear of the Sheehan warriors. Glistening cloaks of different colored feathers flapped in the breeze, signaling their rank. But what drew

Clio's attention most were their weapons of black obsidian.

One of the girls up front spoke up. "Is this the way to the temple?"

A warrior answered, "The temple? No, you are to be taken into the pyramid."

Clio could feel panic stirring in each girl—each girl except the bald one before her. She just looked up at the pyramid's façade with an expression of fatal resolution, as if she already knew this was to be their final destination.

"No, I think you are mistaken. We are here to become temple maidens." Fear pitched the girl's voice higher and higher.

The warrior laughed. "We don't have temple maidens in Morek, slave. The priest doesn't allow women in his Temple. You are here as a sacrifice."

There was no more discussion. One by one the girls were marched into the gaping maw of the pyramid, a path that only had one ending—amongst those rotting bodies at its base.

CHAPTER NINE

The warriors took the girls from the slavers and led them down a dark and twisting stone corridor. The flames from their torches cast hulking shadows that seemed to stretch to the ceiling. Clio didn't know what happened to sacrifices in the days before their deaths, but this corridor did not make her eager to find out.

She moved slowly, as if being dragged through mud. Everything around her seemed to be happening too quickly. Ali was dead, and somehow Clio was expected to keep going. But the world had no momentum without Ali. Clio would find Mannix, she would kill him, but what next? Beyond revenge, the world was empty.

Much too soon they reached a long room with cells lined up in two back-to-back columns that ran down the center. The gates were made with thick wooden logs. Even from the entrance, the fetid odor hit Clio.

If there was a worse place to be, she couldn't think of it.

She heard more approaching guards. Their accents lilted in a way Clio had never heard before.

Each guard came forward, untied a girl, and shoved her into a pen, locking the gate behind them. Clio did her best to sink as far back as she could.

A young guard grabbed the hairless girl. Clio was surprised to see that he couldn't have been much older than herself. Even under the gleaming breastplate, Clio could see how broad his chest was. He stood taller than the rest of the men, and moved faster too. Everything about him was brown, even in this lighting. He had brown hair that was cut just below his ears, and it fell almost like a mane, casting a shadow across his face. His eyes were a dark brown, and his skin was tanner than the other warriors. He looked like he was made out of earth, like clay baked in the sun.

His face, though, was anything but warm. Under his eyes, a strong jaw line and sharp cheekbones looked like they were carved from stone. A scar so thick and jagged that it looked like his head had once nearly been ripped from his neck wound around his throat. He was completely unreadable. He reached Clio in the line-up and raised an eyebrow when he noticed that she had been staring at him this whole time. The young guard led the hairless girl to a pen.

Then it was Clio's turn. A beast of a man hulked forward, tipping and swaying as if he had had too much to drink. He grabbed her arm with a hand that was sweaty and covered in dirt and began to pull her toward a pen.

If she was locked up, she would never escape. She couldn't give in to the people who had dragged Ali through this hallway. She resisted, fighting with all the energy she had left.

She should have been spent; every muscle in her body had been screaming at her in the ascent. But her legs gained an unnatural strength, foreign, as if placed inside her by some outside force. She didn't question it.

Bracing herself with everything she could muster, she twisted out of the guard's slimy hands. His eyes widened in shock as he lost his hold, stumbling until he was left on all fours. She didn't look back as she put all her strength into sprinting toward the exit. The cries of the other guards followed her down the hallway.

She was fast. Much faster than she had ever been, much faster than the guards on her tail. This was going to be easy. The alien energy pulsed through her body, sending a thrill of power through her system.

She was halfway down the tunnel when she was thrown, tackled to the ground. Her elbows hit hard on the stone beneath her, shooting pain up her arms. She tried to roll over, to kick her attacker away, and was surprised to find the young guard with the grisly scar. His arms formed a cage around her, pinning her to the ground.

She looked into his eyes and spat in his face.

"Truly?" he growled as he took one hand off her to wipe his cheek.

She didn't miss her chance. Squirming from beneath him, she broke free.

He rolled to his feet in a blur of movement. She managed to get to her knees when his hand grabbed her arm, pulling her back. Unable to throw herself forward, she used her momentum to swing her leg backwards in an arcing kick that connected solidly with his face.

He let her go. Surprise and something like awe flitted across his face as he rubbed his jaw where her foot had been. She expected him to pull out his blade, but for whatever reason, he didn't. Instead, he waited calmly. She would have to make a move in order to get past him.

Guards were approaching from behind. She didn't have much time. She took a deep breath, pulled back her arm and threw a hard punch. He caught it as easily as if she had tossed him a ball and pulled her into him, eyeing her as if she were some kind of curiosity. His arms locked behind her back, forcing her body up against his.

She struggled against him, but all that accomplished was rubbing herself much too intimately against this stranger. All of a sudden, she was conscious that their bodies were lined up, toe to tip. His arms were wrapped around her in a way that under other circumstances might have been an embrace.

She tried to use her head to butt his face, but he ducked to the side, letting out a soft chuckle.

"Don't struggle." His voice was deep, sending chills through her as it echoed through her ears. "Believe me, you won't fare much better out there."

She stilled in his arms, letting the hands that had been beating so furiously against his back and shoulders fall limp.

"That's better." He let his grip on her relax a fraction, giving her room to breathe.

She smiled sweetly at him and kneed upward as hard as she could. He swore loudly and dropped down onto his side. She got only one satisfied look at him before something hard smashed into the side of her head.

She fell to the ground beside the writhing boy and looked up to find another guard, the big man from before, looking down at her.

She heard the boy wheeze behind her. "No, she's mine."

But it was too late. The meaty fist of the hulking guard swung toward her. She felt the punch for only a second before she lost consciousness.

CHAPTER TEN

Clio woke to a painful stinging in her ankle. Her eyes shot open and she saw the young guard she had fought leaning over her, dressing her wound.

She looked around and was relieved to find that she was not in a cell. Instead, she was lying on a feathered mat in what must have served as their infirmary. A fire burned in the corner, smoke rising up a stone chimney. She felt stronger. Despite the blow, her head had stopped pounding.

He must have noticed she was awake, because he spoke to her without turning his head from his work. "You know, for someone with such a severe infection, you really put up quite the fight." His eyes flashed up at her for the briefest of moments. "I can't say I approve of that move you pulled back there, but it was doubtless effective. A lesser man than myself might be concerned about his potential for progeny."

Arrogance. Clio narrowed her eyes. "Then clearly I didn't hit hard enough."

He laughed, and the way he flashed his grin in her direction made it clear that he thought himself good-looking. Which he was, Clio couldn't deny that, but the obvious pride he took in himself made Clio want to slam her fist right into that wicked smirk. He was young and vain, probably puffed up because he had just become a warrior. But she wouldn't stand for his self-importance, not when every guard here had to pay for what they had done to Ali.

She tried to pull her feet away from him to get up, but he held them tight in his hands.

"Like I said, you have an infection."

Her eyes followed his to make sense of what he was saying. Bright red veins spidered out from the deep gash in her ankle. She groaned. *Great*, she thought, *I don't have time to be sick.*

"What are you doing?" She struggled to sit up, but he laid a hand on her shoulder, pushing her back down.

"I'm trying to clean out the wound. Stop moving."

"Why?"

"Well, because it will hurt more if you don't keep still. But you choose."

She shook her head. "No, I mean, why are you trying to clean it?" To him, she was no more than a slave, a sacrifice. It couldn't possibly matter if she had a fever and was delirious with infection while they cut her heart out.

He dipped a cloth into a basin at his side and went back to cleaning out the wound. The pain made her eyes roll back into her head.

"Because," he answered, "there's no need to suffer while you are here." His words surprised her, and the way he said them, so genuinely, didn't make any sense.

"Isn't suffering kind of the whole point?"

"No. It's not." His tone was firm. "Sacrifice and suffering are not the same thing."

"Oh, so I won't suffer when I have my heart cut out?" Her voice carried a sharp edge.

"No, that's not—what I mean is suffering without sacrifice, like letting these wounds fester, is meaningless. The suffering in sacrifice has a greater purpose."

"Well then, you need to cauterize that." She sounded surprisingly strong despite the dizzying pain.

The guard looked up sharply. "Usually, the slave doesn't give the orders." His voice was hard.

"If you don't know how, I can do it. Give me a heated blade."

"And now the slave is demanding a weapon. After your near-escape earlier, I don't think that would be wise."

"You afraid of a girl, a slave?"

"It's a foolish man who pays no mind to desperation, especially armed desperation." Their eyes locked for the first time. She felt at a loss of for words.

"Plus, I know how to cauterize a wound. I just don't think that such pain would be the humane thing to do in this circumstance. It's too much."

"I'm telling you that the pain is not too much." She sat up and grabbed his hand. "I'll die within the week without it."

"You'll die in three days."

"Just do it. I'll need my leg if I'm going to escape."

He stared at her. "You know, you really shouldn't be so forthcoming with your plans."

"At least give me a fighting chance. It would be the honorable thing."

"You are as foolish as you are arrogant."

Clio ground her teeth. That was rich coming from him. "Come on. I'm sure you can handle one girl. You are what, third rank?" She craned her neck to get a look at the plumage on his cloak, but he turned to keep it hidden.

He picked up a blade and walked over to the fire. "Out of curiosity, what were you before you were sold? You are much stronger and quicker than most slave girls."

Clio searched her mind for an explanation that would make sense without drawing attention to herself. "I have always been a slave." It wasn't wholly a lie. "Do you make it a habit to ask personal questions of girls being led to the slaughter?"

"No, I try not to. You intrigue me, is all. I've never been taken down by a girl before...by anyone, really." He pulled the knife out of the flames and headed toward her. She flinched slightly, a reflex. He must have seen it, and stayed his hand. "Not as brave as you thought."

"I intend to live. Do it."

She had once sat at Derik's side when he needed an infection burned away. They had been only children and he had fallen from their tree. The smell of burning flesh had been enough to make her feel sick. But this time, she didn't smell anything. She was too busy crying out. She put everything she had into not passing out. She needed to stay conscious for as long as possible if she was going to escape. Agonizing minutes went by, but finally he was done. Instantly, her leg felt better.

He turned to clean the blade, but she caught his wrist. "Thank you," she breathed. He froze. The muscles in his arm tightened, then relaxed. He was so warm under her fingers.

They were like that, her hand on his wrist, their eyes locked together when another guard, older, burst through the door.

"Sir? Is that you? Why—what are you doing in here?" The man's eyes flashed between them.

Clio dropped her hand. *Sir?*

The soldier spared her a glance, one eyebrow raised, before he turned to address the intruder. "Everything is fine, Hul. You are dismissed." His voice was commanding, and the older man bowed his head in submission.

As the young guard turned, Clio got a glimpse of his plumage. Her spirits sank. Gold. The highest rank. Rank was based on how many enemies a man had captured for the sacrifice. "How many men does it take to get first rank here?"

His response was flat, emotionless. "Ten." The scar stood out pink and raw against his brown skin.

Ten men. This boy, barely older than herself, had captured and brought back ten men, ten warriors, from foreign tribes. Even she knew he was not to be trifled with.

"How old are you?"

"Now, who is the one asking personal questions?" He eyed her. "I'm 17, and also the commander of the Emperor's forces."

Her mouth dropped open. "How?"

"You know how. I presented the priest with ten warriors for sacrifice."

She sat stunned.

And Ali. He had been in charge when Ali was brought through these corridors, when the priest sank his dagger into her chest. This was not a boy at all. He might have been helping Clio, but he stood by when Ali was sacrificed.

He was the enemy, and Clio wanted him to suffer for what happened to Ali.

"And he saved the Emperor's life," Hul added from behind.

The commander shot an irritated look at Hul. "I thought I dismissed you."

Hul nodded and made his retreat.

Clio tried to get up, but a wave of dizziness overcame her.

"Whoa there, maybe not so fast," the commander said. His arms caught her in a steely vise.

"No, no, I'm all right," she said unconvincingly as she tried to right herself. She couldn't stand the gentle thrill that his touch carried. She slid out of his arms, desperate to get away from the man who had given the order for Ali's death. "Really, I feel—" Pain shot through her head. It felt as if a knife stabbed behind her eyes, and with it came an image—

Mannix stood outside the entrance to the pyramid. It was broad daylight, and he was speaking to the commander.

"I'm looking for someone…a fugitive. A young girl, 15 years old, with white hair. Do you have her?" Mannix asked.

The commander shook his head. "You mean an Oracle," he said. "If we found someone matching your description, she would be dead by now."

Mannix grimaced. "Please, if I could just look through your slaves—"

But the commander cut him off. "We don't have her. If we do happen upon her, I guarantee you will hear about it."

It was over as soon as it started. A Vision. Not as painful as the first one, but still. She was able to come back to reality much more quickly this time.

"Sorry, I must have gotten up too quickly." But her voice was distant, and he noticed the change. As much as she wanted this man to suffer, she needed to tread very carefully. Turn him away and he would have her sacrificed, get too close to him and he might discover what she was and hand her over to Mannix. She did her best to meet his eyes, trying to mask who she really was.

He was eyeing her suspiciously, but he must have believed her because his face softened.

"Time to get you to the cells." With that, he ducked his head out of the door and called to the guard. "Hul, escort this girl to the cells."

"Wait," she called before he took his leave. "You saved my life. Can I at least know your name?"

He turned back, barely looking at her over his shoulder. "My name is Riece, but you should stick to calling me 'sir.'"

CHAPTER ELEVEN

Riece.

Her newest enemy had a name. Mannix, Riece, and the priest who had actually done the killing. Clio had nothing left to fight for except retribution against these three. Ali's death left a horrible emptiness in Clio, an emptiness that threatened to consume her. But as long as these three men lived, as long as Clio could think about revenge, then that resounding emptiness was quieted. Just for a while.

As Hul led her to the cells, Clio made sure to note exactly how many paces and how many turns they were taking. The belly of the pyramid was a network of tunnels, but Clio didn't have any problem remembering that the cells were two lefts and a right turn from the infirmary. The better she knew her prison, the better her chance at escape.

The cells were eerily silent. Girls lined the walls, clinging to the stone like dead vines. Hul held Clio's arm tightly and painfully. The squeak of the wood gate was the only sound that echoed in the stone hall.

Hul tossed her in with as much force as he could. Her face collided hard with the back wall. Clio ran her tongue over her lip, tasting the coppery tang of blood.

Riece might not have wanted her to suffer, but this was a reminder of why she was truly here. She was a slave, and no one was going to treat her differently.

As she slumped to the ground, she heard a faint rustling in a dark corner of the pen. Another slave girl crawled out of the shadows. The same girl from before, the one without hair. Seemed fitting that they would die together. Ever since Clio had seen the girl disdainfully wipe the Oracle's blessing from her forehead, Clio had felt a kinship with this girl. They were both trapped, but neither one was going to embrace their fates.

"I had hoped you'd escaped," the girl said.

"So had I." Clio rubbed her jaw, trying to ease out the sting.

"Where did they take you?" The girl's voice was soft.

"My wound was infected. The commander treated it."

"You mean the boy you knocked over when you tried to escape?" The girl smiled, and for a moment Clio got a glimpse of who this girl might have been.

"The very same."

"I wonder why a commander took on those duties."

Clio hadn't realized that. It was odd that a first-ranking warrior would take the time to tend to a slave, and it had seemed as if he hadn't told his men what he was doing. "They don't want us dying in here. Where's the fun in that? But it doesn't matter. I don't plan on dying at all. And I got a good look around."

The girl smiled. Clio could read this girl's desire to escape written in the lines of her grin, and she smiled back.

"What about you? How far away is the entrance from here?" Clio asked, trying to keep her voice down.

The girl shook her head. "Too far and too well-guarded. Was there any way out from the infirmary?"

"Maybe. Plenty of blades. And a chimney."

"We probably don't have much time—a couple days, I'd guess. I'm Maia, by the way."

"Clio."

"You serve in the temple, right?" Of course Maia recognized her.

"Shhh," Clio hushed as she knelt beside Maia.

"Why are you here?" Maia spoke in lowered tones.

"It's not safe to talk about here. If anyone in Sheehan or Morek finds out who I am, they won't wait to kill me. Like they did my family."

"You are the only one left?"

Clio nodded.

Maia's eyes widened in understanding. She obviously knew the lore of the Oracle.

"If you are killed, then the Deities can't help Sheehan."

Clio was surprised to hear such loyalty from a girl who clearly hadn't been treated very well by Sheehan. "Back in the Temple it didn't seem like you believed in any of this."

"Oh, I know the Deities to be real, but there's nothing they can do for me now. I made my choice already."

Clio wanted to ask more, but the way Maia's gaze sank to the floor made it clear she didn't want to discuss it.

"Well, if the Deities want to save Sheehan, I doubt their only choice is through me," Clio said.

Maia threw Clio an annoyed glance. "You are their eyes among mortals. They need you as you need them."

"I hope they are enjoying the view," Clio said as she let her eyes feast upon the hideous display of the rear end of a bulbous and greasy guard.

They spent a while inspecting their cell for a way out, but there was none. The night stretched on, and finally they decided that they should get some rest if they were going to have any hope of making a break for it the next day.

Lying on the hard floor, Clio finally had a moment to think about her latest Vision. Mannix was looking for her, that much was clear. Was Mannix still in Morek? If anyone found her out as the Oracle, she would be killed, no matter where Mannix was. All she knew was that somehow she had to escape and stay out of Mannix's grasp.

Her Vision had shown her that the commander held a fair amount of power, if he could turn Mannix away like that. If she could gain his trust, she might be able to use him to get out.

A wet cough echoed through the cells, disturbing the silence. In the torchlight, Clio could make out glistening beads of sweat rolling down Maia's forehead. Maia lay there, her chest heaving, as if breathing were an almighty struggle, as if her lungs could not expand at all.

Clio sat up and leaned over to help, but Maia firmly shook her head, halting Clio's advancement.

"Nothing to be done..." A wet and heavy wheeze carried across the silence. "...It...will pass. Always does."

Maia lowered herself until she was flat on her back. It seemed to help somewhat, and Clio nodded off to the steady pulse of Maia's labored breathing.

When she awoke, she found a new guard patrolling the cells. It was the big beastly man who had clubbed her upon her arrival.

He was going from cell to cell. Each time after he went in, Clio heard a mumbled command, a series of rustling sounds, sometimes the heavy thud of a blow and the ensuing moan of an injured girl.

Maia was still sleeping in her corner, obviously exhausted from the battle with her lungs the night before.

Finally, the man made it to Clio's cell. He pulled open the wooden gate, his hulking shoulders filling the entire frame. She slid back a bit farther away into the shadows. Something about the way he was looking at her wasn't right.

"Lie down on your back." His voice was a gruff grunt.

"No." Whatever it was this man wanted, Clio was not going to lie down for it.

"Lie down on your back, or you get the club."

"I'll take the club, thank you."

A sick thrill lit the man's eyes. He stalked closer to her, his fingers running up and down his club in a twisted caress.

"I was hoping you'd say that."

He raised the club above his head. As the air whistled with the approaching blow, Clio dodged to the side, faster than any normal girl could have moved.

The beast cried out as the club hit uncompromising stone, sending a shock wave through his arm. The club clattered to the ground, and Clio dove onto it before the guard could realize his mistake.

Unarmed and embarrassed, the beast ducked out of the room and slammed the gate shut behind him.

"Hard to get, are you? Well, maybe I'll just have to introduce you to my *other* big club."

"Only if you want to lose that one too," Clio added defiantly.

She grinned down at the weapon she held firmly in her hand.

"Know how to use that thing?" Maia rose weakly from her mat.

"I'm a quick learner."

Footsteps echoed down the hall, drawn by all the commotion. The commander rounded the corner, his mouth pulled and serious. When his eyes landed on Clio and the club, he cocked an eyebrow.

He turned to the beast. "And how did a slave manage to disarm you?"

"She tricked me, sir." The beast bowed his head in shame.

"Not the first time, and unfortunately won't be the last. Go clean out the washroom, and try not to lose any more weapons today."

When the beast retreated, the commander approached the pegs of her cell. He brushed his long, thin fingers along the gate.

"Hello again, Riece." Clio grinned as she lightly tapped the club against her leg.

"I thought I told you to call me 'sir.'" He was smirking while remaining outside the pen. This one wasn't dumb. He wouldn't open the door and give her an opportunity to escape until he had a plan.

"You did, but I see no reason to do so. I've yet to treat you as a slave should treat her captor, and it's worked for us so far." She threw in a wink and was rewarded when his eyes went wide. "Plus," she added, "I have a big club now." She would kill him. Lure him in, disarm him with petty flirtation, it would be easy.

"So you do. Now that you're armed, I think it is only fair if you tell me your name."

"Clio."

"Clio." He said her name softly, as if he were testing it on his tongue. "Well, Clio, I'm afraid I am going to have to come in there and take that away from you."

"I was hoping you would." She tilted her head back and bit the corner of her lip in what she hoped was a seductive invitation.

Slowly, he unlocked and opened the gate. They stood frozen, sizing each other up and assessing their options.

In the blink of an eye, the commander lunged at her, pinning her into the wall. Clio swung the club, but his arm shot up, blocking the blow, while his other hand snatched the club from Clio.

It all happened so fast. Clio stood stunned that he had managed to disarm her in two beats. This would be harder than she had thought.

The commander grinned as he stepped back, his smile giving his face a new warmth. He looked so young, so kind. No lines on his face hinted at the truth: he was a killer.

Maia tried to rise during the commotion, but she fell, landing hard and with a cry. Her breath left her in another wet cough.

Clio moved to her, but the commander held her back.

"How long have you been coughing?" His voice was authoritative again. He still held Clio's wrist hard in his hand.

"It's nothing new," she wheezed. "Was born with weak lungs."

The commander nodded but looked unsure. "All of the girls have to be checked for signs of fever and coughing, something that my subordinate was in the process of doing before he got—well, you know." His eyes fell on Clio.

The commander released Clio and moved over to Maia, who was still struggling to sit up. Gently, he laid his hand on her forehead. "No fever." He lowered his ear to Maia's chest, and his brow furrowed at whatever it was he was hearing. "Is there anything that can be done for your ailment?"

"Yes, you could let her out of here," Clio snapped.

Maia laughed at that, or tried to.

"You know I can't, but I will do whatever I can to make your final days as comfortable as possible." The commander stood up, straight as a blade.

Maia spat at his feet. "Keep your half-hearted kindness."

He nodded and turned back to Clio. "I think it's safe to say *you* are in fine health, but I should check on that wound."

He motioned to her to lie down.

The thought of his hands on her, now that she knew what he had helped do to Ali, made Clio hesitate a moment longer than she should have.

But she needed to keep him close.

He knelt before her and pulled her leg toward him, gently skimming her calf with the tips of his long fingers. She didn't need to fake the shiver that his touch sent up her spine. He saw; one side of his mouth raised in a thin grin. She should have been disgusted, but her body clearly didn't feel the same way as her mind. Clio couldn't stop herself from reacting, it was better that he thought she was affected—at least that was the excuse she told herself.

Without a word he pulled fresh bindings out of a bag that Clio hadn't even noticed, and proceeded to rewrap her ankle tightly. He kept his other hand on the back of her calf to steady her leg. His fingers were rough, calloused, but his hold was soft and tender.

"Do you do this for all your slaves?"

The smallest of hesitations at the word "slave" slowed his hand on her ankle. "No," he said, sharp, clipped. "No. Out of all the slaves that have ever come here, you have caused a particularly impressive amount of trouble."

She couldn't meet his gaze, afraid of how her body might respond to it. "Just admit it." She tried for teasing, but the war of emotions within her brought out a more ragged edge. "You just can't stay away, can you?"

He laughed. "Don't flatter yourself."

"Oh, it's not me who is doing the flattering. Your actions speak volumes, Riece."

He trailed his hand down her leg as he set her foot down. She tried to fight the heat rising in her cheeks.

"Your blush speaks volumes, Clio." His mouth curved in that sly grin again.

Clio tried to ignore the way he looked at her, the way her cheeks burned.

The commander rose, collected his things and headed to the gate. On his way out, he bent to scoop up the club, which lay heavy on the stone floor.

Clio's heart sank as she watched that club swing away from her, the man who carried it departing with yet another sliver of Clio's hope.

CHAPTER TWELVE

"So that was...interesting." Maia sat up, her back against the wall. Her breathing was steadier, but Clio could tell that the girl had been seriously weakened by the journey to Morek.

"What do you mean?" Clio's eyes flashed.

"Tell me that you are making nice with the commander so that you can play him into some kind of escape plan."

"What else could it possibly be?" Suddenly, Clio felt defensive.

"Well, you are a very convincing performer, blushing on all the right cues, batting those heavy lashes of yours. The boy is absolutely drawn to you. And it doesn't seem one-sided."

"Good. Then he's falling for my trap." Clio stood up, hiding her eyes from Maia's questioning gaze.

"Clio, he is the commander here. He may be lusting for a slave girl. I'm sure it's not the first time, and it certainly won't be the last time, but stay realistic. This man is smart, and more importantly, he's a killer. To get those pretty gold feathers, he had to spill a lot of blood. And blood stays with a person, stains them. He's not going to have a change of heart just because one pretty slave smiles at him."

"I know exactly what he is. That girl we saw sacrificed when we brought in—that was my sister. Don't think that for a moment I will forget how he contributed to her death. I'm not a fool." But Maia's words stung, biting into her skin. Clio was using the commander, but Maia had seen what Clio had tried so hard to ignore. She was drawn to the commander. As much as she hated him, and as much as she wished him pain, there was something about him.

"Good. Just, you don't know what it's like to be a slave. You still expect others to see you as a person. But you aren't. Not to them, and not even to him. And you never will be."

Clio's hands balled into fists at her side. "I don't need a lecture from you about what it means to be seen as a thing. Even if I get out of here I will be subject to whatever control the Deities have over me. I'll never be just a person again."

"I'm sorry about your sister." Maia's eyes softened for a moment as she dropped her gaze, but when she looked up again there was a new hardness. "Don't count on people. Not on anyone. Everyone is only out for themselves." Tears welled in Maia's eyes. Her chin quivered, fighting back a sob.

It was obvious that Maia felt her words with more conviction than Clio had ever seen before. As gently as possible, Clio approached as she would a wounded animal, not knowing whether the beast would lash out for getting too close. Maia had started to shake when Clio wrapped her arm around her small shoulders.

The soft flesh of Clio's arm brushed up against Maia's back—

skin pulled tight over the sharp dramatic angles of rigid bone. The girl was made of nothing but the barest essentials needed to stay alive. Her skin was rough, like leather left out in the sun, and her back was covered with hard protruding scars. This body told a story, one of pain and suffering and despair so black that Clio recoiled.

Clio's hands gently kneaded Maia's back, trying to get her breathing to slow and her body to relax. After several silent moments, Maia's breathing matched the rhythm of Clio's hands.

Clio didn't know what to say. This girl was alone, but she didn't have to be. "We'll get out of this together, Maia."

Maia smiled through the tears that slid down her face and off her chin. Her smile was so soft, like a breeze gently kissing the water's surface, spreading ripples in its trail.

"I don't have much longer to live." Maia's hand rose and rested on her hollow chest. "My lungs...I...it's why I'm here."

"What do you mean?"

"To die. I'm here to die." Her hand curled on her chest.

"We're all here to die."

"No. I'm dying. My tribe knew it. My family knew it. They have nothing. Children are starving, and well..."

"They sold you." Clio pulled the frail girl closer to her. She was so cold.

Maia nodded. "I understand it, I do. I was going to die anyway. What does it matter if I die as a temple maiden, or a slave, or even just a girl? This way, my death maybe can help someone there stay alive. But I still wish, I just wish that I could die in peace. Not like this, not with my heart pulled out before my very eyes."

"We are getting out of here before then."

Maia's head slumped down into Clio's lap. Clio's hands gently ran up and down Maia's thin arms. They stayed like that until nightfall, neither one wanting to remove herself from the other. Clio couldn't help but be drawn to this girl and her story. They had each been given up by their families in different ways to serve some kind of higher purpose. Just the feeling of Maia's shallow breaths reminded Clio that the world still had some life in it. Even without Ali, there was still someone worth fighting for.

Clio would get them out. As soon as they were taken out of this pen, Clio would get them out. She had to. If only the Deities would give her a Vision of something useful, of some way that she could get out of here. For the thousandth time, Clio wondered why they only showed her events that she had absolutely no way to influence.

At the changing of the guard, the commander was back patrolling the cells. When he walked by their cell, his eyes pierced through the hazy dim and found hers. Maia was still nestled in Clio's lap, getting what must have been her first sound sleep in many days. Riece saw this, nodded his head once, and moved on.

Maia slept so deeply, she didn't stir when Clio gently laid her head on the ground. Clio couldn't wait for a Vision to tell her what to do.

"Riece," she hissed, rising shakily. She didn't have a plan beyond getting his weapon. He needed to come in, and he needed to be distracted. Without hesitating, she raked her fingers down over her scabbed wound, biting down on her lower lip as her blood flowed out. She should have built up more trust with the commander, broken down more of his defenses. But Maia didn't have the time for it.

In the span of what felt like numberless heartbeats, the commander was back.

"What now, Clio?" His face tried to remain stone, but Clio could see the slight glint in his eye.

"I—" She cleared her throat. "I need you to check my wound."

He came up to the bars. "I saw it this morning. It's fine."

Clio swallowed hard and moved to meet him at the gate. She brought her hand into the flickering torchlight so he could catch the red gleam of fresh blood. "It's opened again."

He looked around, clearly wary of something. No one was nearby though. It must have been the middle of the night.

"Stand back against the wall," he ordered.

Once she was safely away from the gate, he opened it and stepped inside. His hand rested on the blade at his waist. He was still on guard. Clio knew she would have to work harder.

Before he could ask, Clio slid down until she was sitting up against the wall. He came over and knelt at her feet.

"You've only nicked it. It's fine. See? It's already stopped bleeding."

Before he could rise, Clio grabbed his hand. The touch sent unwelcome pleasure through her arm.

"How many days do I have left, Riece?" She didn't have to work as hard as she would have liked to sound vulnerable.

His gaze fell. "One."

She needed him to come closer, to comfort her. "But when we came in a girl was being sacrificed. Why wasn't she saved to be killed with the rest of us?" Tears stung in her eyes. He would think they came from fear.

"She wasn't a sacrifice to the Deities. She was executed at the Emperor's command." His tone was flat. He felt nothing about this. Not a shred of remorse.

Hatred surged through Clio's blood.

"She was only a child." Her voice had a dangerous edge.

"She was an Oracle witch." The commander shrugged.

"You felt nothing when you watched this girl die?"

"Of all the girls I've sent up there, hers is the death I least regret."

He was just making this easier for her. She had only to pull him in, and then it would be a pleasure to drive his blade into his chest.

"Will you regret mine?" she asked, looking up at him from under her lashes. She lifted her chin and arched her back, bringing her lips closer to his.

"I thought you were planning to escape." Whether it was conscious or not, he brought his face down to hers.

"I am, but..." Her words trailed off as she slid her hands up his arms, following the line of his body until she reached his chest.

Before he could bring his lips down on hers, she had the blade between them.

"Come any closer and you're dead," she said with a victorious smirk twisting her mouth.

He surprised her by laughing. "Clio, Clio." He clicked his tongue. "You think I am so easily fooled? Not to say you aren't a great actress but I know when someone is playing me."

Clio threw her head forward, butting his and sending him sprawling onto his back. In the blink of an eye she was crouched over his chest, the blade firm against his throat. She felt something sharp against the inside of her thigh.

"So many people go for the neck," he said, clearly unafraid of her knife. "If I cut you here, no one will be able to stop the bleeding." He pushed his hidden blade into her thigh enough to hurt without drawing blood.

"I don't care if you kill me." As she moved to sink her blade into his throat, her vision flashed white.

The commander was fighting dozens of men robed in red. He spun to parry the blow of an approaching figure. Clio could make out a sea of red behind him.

The Vision lasted only a moment. Not long enough for the commander to tell there was something wrong with her, but enough for him to throw her off him. Her side hit hard against the stone floor, knocking the wind from her lungs.

"Don't play with me again, Clio." He picked up the blade she dropped in her fall and left the cell.

He stood there for a moment, just outside the gate. "I think you are strong. Stronger than most here. But this wasn't your moment. If I am around, I have no choice but to stop you. I like you, but not enough to die for you."

With that, he was gone.

CHAPTER THIRTEEN

One day.

All night that number echoed around the corners of Clio's thoughts. One day, and the Deities had stopped Clio from killing the commander when she had the chance. That was what her Vision was—an interruption. It had served merely to prevent Clio from doing something that went against the Deities' wishes.

So the Deities didn't speak directly to the Oracle. Clio had figured that much out. But they communicated with her through the Visions. She wouldn't be allowed to go through with anything that they didn't like.

Fine.

She'd find a way around that eventually.

The contents of the brief glimpse of her Vision were puzzling, though. The commander seemed to be battling Mannix's men. The red robes could only mean that. Perhaps Clio was meant to guess that Mannix would eventually try some kind of attack in Morek.

Clio must have fallen asleep, because she woke to Maia gently shaking her awake.

"Clio, get up," Maia whispered. "I think they are doing something."

Clio bolted upright. Girls were being led out of their cells. But the sacrifice wasn't supposed to be until tomorrow. Panic instantly woke every muscle in Clio's body.

Riece passed by their pen. Clio refused to look at him. She had ruined that strategy. There was no way Riece was going to fall for any more of her charm.

It was better that way. At least now she didn't have to pretend to like a killer.

"Mealtime," The commander said, reading the panic in Clio's eyes.

A guard Clio had never seen before opened her cell.

Something was going on. There was no reason for the guards to take them out of their cells to eat. Clio laid a hand on Maia's shoulder, holding her back.

The commander sighed. "You can put up a fight, but you'd just deny her," he nodded toward Maia, "her last good meal."

"And why should we trust you? Last time we willingly went with your men, we were promised lives as temple maidens, now—" Clio gestured around them.

"I never told anyone they were coming here to be anything but a sacrifice. What your *Oracle*," he said the word with obvious disgust, "might have told you is her own lie."

Clio remained silent, but her posture relaxed somewhat. There were no sounds of girls screaming down the corridor, no evidence that this was some kind of trick. One look at Maia and Clio knew that she needed the meal. If Clio was going to be strong enough to escape and take down some of these men with her, then she was going to need the sustenance too.

Grudgingly, Clio nodded at Maia to let her go with the men. Riece let out a short laugh before continuing down through the cells. He was clearly still entertained by Clio. For what reason, Clio didn't know. But the thought of any part of her giving this man any pleasure whatsoever made Clio angry enough to stay in her cell.

But she didn't. Mostly because she didn't trust Maia alone with the guards.

As it turned out, they didn't have far to go. Disappointingly. Clio couldn't get a better glimpse of the labyrinthine passages of this pyramid. The room beyond the cells opened up into a wide oval. Girls were crouched along the walls, holding pieces of fruit in their stained fingers.

As Clio and Maia entered the room, they were handed some kind of yellowish fruit that Clio had never had before, as well as a small piece of bread. Before they had made it two strides inside, Maia had devoured her bread and was biting greedily into her fruit.

With a bashful look on her face, Maia shrugged. "Most likely the commander is right—this is my last meal. I'll take a full stomach into the afterlife over manners."

Clio couldn't help but laugh. Without thinking she passed all her food to the starving girl. Maybe it would be enough to keep Maia alive until they could escape.

They were allowed to stay in this open room while they ate. It was still captivity, but the lack of latched gates and damp corners had the girls in considerably higher spirits. Maia was talking to Clio about all the brothers she had back home. Clio tried to listen, but her attention was drawn toward the commander making his way through the girls. Every so often he would stop and offer a girl more food or water. His expression was oddly sincere.

"Clio," Maia said, "Clio, are you listening?"

"What?" Clio's gaze snapped back to Maia. "Sorry. It just confuses me. He's responsible for every one of our deaths, yet he looks like he actually cares about them all."

"Maybe," Maia said. "It doesn't change anything. He isn't stupid. He's not going to risk his neck for one of us."

Just then the commander made his way over to Clio.

"You didn't eat." It wasn't a question. He must have watched her from across the room.

"No," Clio said simply before turning her back on the commander to face Maia again.

Clio could feel the room's eyes on her. She had just disrespected this man.

"Yes, you are right. Maia seems to need more," the commander said calmly, turning to Maia as well, as if Clio hadn't turned her back on him but was merely directing him to the girl. The room instantly relaxed.

He pulled out two more loaves of bread and handed one to Maia and Clio each.

"I don't want your food," Clio said, handing the loaf to a girl beside her. Her stomach, however, loudly disagreed at that moment.

"How many days has it been since you had a real meal? Take it."

"You don't understand. I don't want any special favors from you."

His expression darkened, and Clio found herself pulled almost painfully behind him as he stormed back into the now empty cells.

When he released her, Clio felt the angry imprint of his fingers on her arm.

"I'm *not* giving you any special treatment. But you have got to stop pushing your luck. There is only so much longer that I can cover for you." He had turned away from her while he spoke so Clio couldn't read whatever was going on in his expression.

"You mean to tell me that you personally attend to the wounds of all the slaves that come in here?"

His head snapped toward her. "I see to it that all these girls get the care they need."

"But you don't personally tend to them, do you?"

"No." He looked her dead in the eyes. "That was a mistake. But from then on, you have been given no special favors. The food—I would have given it to any girl who hadn't eaten." He ran his fingers agitatedly through his hair. "I don't understand why you insist on making this harder for yourself. Why deny yourself anything in these days?"

"Because I couldn't live with myself for accepting anything from a man like you."

"And what kind of man do you think I am?"

"You are a killer. You are responsible for my—for so many young girls' deaths." She had been so close to mentioning Ali. "Anything that comes from you is stained with all the blood you have helped shed. I want nothing to do with it."

Regret seeped through the lines of his brow, catching Clio up short. The scar on his neck stood out painfully red.

"You don't know the first thing about what kind of man I am. You are right, I do have blood on my hands. I feel guilt you can't even conceive of. But none of it comes from them," he gestured to the girls just down the hall. "These girls—I do everything I can for each and every one of them. You don't know what these days could have been like for these girls. For you. You think previous commanders let you eat? Let you keep your honor? Every day I stop some entitled animal from coming in here to spend a couple hours of pleasure among the slaves. Yes, you will all die. But I—I do what I can."

Clio wanted to hurl something back at him. To accuse him of killing her sister. To be able to have someone answer for all of the pain of the last few days. Instead, she just stood there, speechless.

"So when it finally sinks into your thick skull that I'm not the villain here, eat this." He shoved the loaf back in her hands before the tide of girls and their guards swept over them both.

The rest of the day passed rather quietly, with Clio's thoughts endlessly circling around a way out. The commander didn't come back. Clio was glad about that. His presence would have just brought out too many confusing and mixed emotions. She hated him, or at least she thought she did. But what he said about trying to do his best for all the sacrifices—she didn't know how true that was. Maybe part of her should be thanking him for keeping his men away from Ali. Maybe he had spared her so much extra suffering.

But none of it really mattered. Or at least, she kept telling herself that. If Clio wanted to escape, she had to be prepared to harm the commander in some way. Worrying about the kind of person he was wasn't going to make that any easier. He was the enemy. Maybe he wasn't the worst kind, and maybe she didn't *want* to hurt him, but that didn't change that he was standing between her and her revenge.

She had until tomorrow to find a way out, and not a moment could go to waste. Night must have fallen outside because there were only a couple of guards patrolling the cells. Clio was occupying herself with memorizing their patterns when a new pair of footsteps clacked down the halls, interrupting the steady pulse of the guards' rounds.

"What are you doing here?" The commander's voice rang out from down the hall.

"Just wanted to get a look at the girls before the big day." This stranger's voice sounded somehow damp, as if it had been kept far from the sun's rays. It made Clio shiver in the stuffy heat of her cell.

"There really is no need for that." Was that disgust coloring the commander's voice?

Clio got up and walked to the front of her cell, sticking her head out between the pegs as far as possible. In the flicker of the torchlight, Clio saw the commander's glorious gold cloak. He was standing at the head of the cells, trying to block another man from coming in.

"No, there is no need for it," the man agreed even as he slid by Riece. He was wrapped in amber robes. Clio could only make out the sharp point of his nose, jutting out like a dagger between the heavy folds of his hood.

The priest.

This was the man who was going to cut all these girls' hearts out tomorrow. The one who had killed Ali.

CHAPTER FOURTEEN

The commander was striding alongside the priest, his arm twitching as if he wanted to pull the priest back. "If you don't leave now, I will be forced to report this to the Emperor," the commander said.

The priest limply waved the commander away. "Yes, yes. Go report me. I will have gotten what I want by the time you get back."

Slowly, shakily, the commander raised his hand, letting it hover ever so closely above the priest's shoulder, but the priest only sneered at it. "Commander, let me remind you, touching a man of the Deities is an offense of the highest order."

The commander pulled his hand away and bowed his head. "My apologies."

Satisfied, the priest walked around the perimeter of the cells. He peered into each one, sometimes simply nodding, sometimes stopping to get a closer look.

"Sheehan always sends us crops from the bottom of the barrel, don't they?" The priest sighed in disappointment.

The commander remained silent, leaving the priest's question hanging in the thick air.

Finally, the priest came to Clio's cell. The man was tiny. It was hard to tell from a distance because the substantial folds of his robe engulfed his frail frame, but up close, Clio could make out the thin, spindly ankles that stuck out in an almost comically unbalanced contrast.

Maia was resting against the back wall, but Clio had not moved from her place at the front of their cell. The priest spotted her, and his lips pulled back into a nefarious smile, filled with sharp teeth whittled down by years of evil deeds.

"Perhaps I spoke too soon."

Dark blotches stained the wrinkled folds of his forehead. The priest was a very old man. Clio couldn't even guess at how long he had been looking at girls in her position. His eyes were slate, no doubt deadened by snuffing out countless lives.

Clio stared into those lifeless eyes, refusing to break away from his gaze. She filled her glare with all the hate she felt for him, as if a look could burn.

"Ooh, yes. Commander, was this one too taken from Sheehan?" He broke away from her gaze so that his eyes could roam freely over her body. Still, Clio refused to flinch.

"Yes, but Sire, I really think it is time to move on now. This one is sick; she carries some kind of disease." The commander moved up in an attempt to step in between Clio and the priest. The priest simply brushed past him, stepping up to the gate of Clio's cell.

"I am a man of the Deities. I am not concerned."

Clio's hands gripped the pegs of the gate, steadying herself. Still grinning at her, the priest pulled her hand into his. His touch was like a slime that slowly spread across her skin. He uncurled her fingers so that he could get a good look at her palm.

"Well, you don't look like a slave. I've never seen such smooth hands from a Sheehan."

The commander couldn't stop himself. Curiosity drove him to step forward to get a closer look. Surprise and maybe suspicion flickered across his face.

Clio snatched her hand back, retreating to a dark corner of the cell.

If these men didn't believe that she was a slave, if they figured out who she actually was, they wouldn't wait to kill her.

"Commander," the priest finally pulled his eyes away to address the commander, "open the cell. I'd like a closer look at this one."

A closer look? Clio didn't need the Sight to know that this man would discover her secret if he got a closer look.

"You let this man in here, and he's not coming back out." Clio tried her best to adopt a confident demeanor. She widened her stance, arched her back, and kept her arms loose and ready to move as soon as that gate opened.

"Girl, it is not your place to address the commander so casually." The priest turned to him. "You allow this?"

The commander's expression was pained. "No, Sire."

"Then open this cell, do your job, and discipline the slave."

For the briefest of moments, the commander locked eyes with Clio. His gaze was an apology even as his hands undid the heavy lock. For the first time, Clio saw only the boy, Riece, without all the trappings of his position. He didn't want to do this.

The priest trailed in Riece's shadow. Clio found herself backing up until she bumped against the stone wall behind her. Out of room.

"Slave," Riece's face was unreadable, "you will call me 'sir.' If you fail in this again, you will be beaten. Understood?"

She quickly nodded. Clio felt a rush of gratitude toward Riece.

Riece turned back to the priest. "We are done here."

"No, Commander. I heard about what you did for that Oracle bitch who came through here. She should have been made to suffer in everyway imaginable for her crimes—degraded until she could no longer pretend to be a human being. But you stepped in. You can't this time."

Clio's gaze flew to Riece.

"Slaves don't learn from warnings. They learn from consequences." The priest stalked closer, accidentally kicking Maia who cried out in pain as she curled into a ball and struggled to regain her breath. The priest was surprised to see her there. His gaze had been so fixed on Clio that he hadn't even noticed Maia. He looked down at her, regarding her as if she were filth soiling the hem of his robe. Disgust flared his nostrils and narrowed his eyes. Clio had never seen anyone look upon an innocent human being with such loathing.

Without thinking, Clio knelt at Maia's side and gently stroked her, hoping it would help relax her and ease her pain.

The priest only chuckled.

"Commander, punish her insubordination."

"I may not be able to touch you, but that does not mean that you can give me orders. Only the Emperor himself has that privilege." Riece bent down to help Maia.

"Very well." The priest reached down and pulled Riece's whip from his belt.

It all happened in the blink of an eye. Riece tried to grab the whip, but without being able to touch the man, he could only do so much. Clio reacted before she even registered the descent of the lash. She rolled out of the way, letting the lash crack sharply on the stone where she had just been.

"Ooh, this one has fire. I do always like that in a sacrifice." Instead of being enraged by his failure, the priest's eyes flashed with excitement. "You see, their hearts beat so hard for so long, even when in my hand." He delicately rolled the whip back up in his hands, twisting the leather between his bony fingers.

Every line in this man's body whispered his barbaric tastes. Clio had no doubt this man took a sadistic pleasure in butchering young girls.

"Still, you must be punished." Before anyone realized what he was doing, the priest let the whip uncoil and thrashed it brutally onto the defenseless Maia.

Her scream carried more agony than Clio thought a person could withstand.

In that moment, in the slash of the whip that ripped into Maia's skin, in the scream that followed, Clio saw the glint of a blade brought closer and closer to Ali's chest. In front of the pyramid, Clio hadn't heard her sister cry out, but she heard it now in Maia's agony. As the priest brought his hand back to his side, Clio couldn't help but see the flash of a black blade dripping with her sister's blood in his hand. The flickering firelight obscured the priest and his weapons, casting a dark shadow over the horror at Clio's feet. It was so easy to see the faces of all the girls the priest had hurt written into the nameless black. But nothing could hide the pain.

The pain that Maia was feeling—it was what Ali had felt in her final moments. Looking down at Maia's face, for one moment, one fleeting flash, Clio saw the face of her sister.

Maybe some of Clio's rage at Mannix heated her blood. Maybe her lust for vengeance was all for the priest. It didn't matter. She hated one as she hated the other.

"You are sick," Clio spat.

"I only did what the commander here could not."

Riece stood to the side, his jaw pulled tight in anger.

"She didn't do anything!" Clio shouted as she tried to staunch the flow of blood from Maia's wound.

"You are a slave. She is a slave." The priest motioned to Maia, who cried silently on the floor. "Act out again, and you will face consequences. It doesn't matter to me which one of you pays for your actions. Slaves are all the same. And you will all die the same. "

He turned to go, shoving the whip into Riece's chest as he

passed him.

Clio stared at the back of that man with the burning hatred of every girl whose life he had ended, every girl who had watched this man cut out their own hearts before their eyes.

Clio knew with more certainty than she had ever known anything in her life that she had to kill this man.

She would kill him, and she would be happy to do it.

She would kill him for the dead girls whose faces she had seen emerging in the shadows, and she would kill him for her sister. And maybe she would forget that she was a girl just like all the rest. Because that was the fear Clio didn't want to acknowledge. Becoming the Oracle had made Clio the target of these men. But the truth was, Clio wasn't in danger just because she was the Oracle. She was in danger because she was a girl, a girl with no name, with no family, with nothing to go back to. So maybe, if she killed these men she wouldn't be afraid anymore.

But maybe it would only whet her appetite.

It didn't matter.

It didn't matter that killing him would make her a murderer, would make her into the very thing she had run away from, the very thing she accused her sisters of being.

She would kill him and she would lose part of herself, but that price wasn't too high. Not too high for this man's blood. Even to become like her sisters—broken by the things they had done for the Oracle—like the hard statues Clio had so hated. It would be a price worth accepting.

"I wonder how many times your heart will struggle to beat once I've removed it from your chest." The priest turned and smiled, his sharp teeth catching the flickering light. "Oooh, I think your heart will pump two, maybe even three times in my hand." He licked his lips. "Until then." He nodded his head in a mock bow and made his way out of the cell.

Before he could leave, another image slammed into Clio's head, behind her eyes.

CHAPTER FIFTEEN

She stood at the base of the great stone pyramid in Morek. A girl's body tumbled lifelessly down the steps, landing with a fatal stillness in the tangle of rotting corpses.

The crowd cheered and cheered.

Then, they stopped.

Silence descended, a silence so thick that Clio could hear her own blood pumping through her head.

The people around her were all gaping at something at the top of the pyramid, horror and shock etched deeply into every eager pair of eyes. But to Clio, the top of the pyramid was lost in a grey haze. She could see the guards. She could even see some of the other girls she recognized from her trek here, but for some reason she couldn't make out the altar.

Everyone let out a stunned gasp, but Clio couldn't see the cause of it.

She strained her eyes, but it was no use. She could not penetrate the fog that swallowed whatever was occurring on the pyramid's edge.

Finally, a shape emerged. A body. It tumbled as the others had. Only this time, the crowd remained silent.

Something was wrong. The body was a blurry streak of red and amber.

When the crumpled mass finally got close enough for Clio to make out, she sucked in her breath in satisfied shock.

The lifeless eyes of the priest stared unseeing right where Clio was perched. His mouth was open in a final tortured cry of surprise and pain, and his chest was a ragged, bloody mess.

Clio tried to look up to the top of the pyramid, tried to see who had done this, her eyes couldn't find a focus on whoever had dealt that fatal blow.

When Clio came back to the world around her, she smiled. A dry chuckle escaped her lips. The priest halted in his exit, turning back to face her.

"What could you possibly have to laugh about, slave?" he demanded, spittle flying from his lips.

"Nothing, sir." But her smile remained fixed.

He eyed her uneasily. Her gaze was steady, confident. Her eyes shone brightly with knowledge.

"WHAT?" he raged.

He couldn't scare her. She had seen the future. And she knew that he would die a horrible death, a death he deserved. Justice would be served on him, and it didn't matter what he did to her. It wouldn't stop his fate.

"It will be a glorious day indeed. I only wish I could see it." Her voice was otherworldly, ethereal, ringing with a truth that came from the Deities themselves.

The priest fell back, as if instinctually uncomfortable with something in her manner.

"See what?" Riece asked, also eyeing her uneasily.

Without taking her eyes from the priest, she said, "His death."

She laughed. Even as the priest rushed forward and backhanded her across her face, she laughed. None of this mattered. She had Seen his fate. And Clio knew better than anyone else that fate would have its end.

Desperate, he shouted into her face, "Tomorrow, before the entire city, I will hold you down, cut into you and pull your heart out before your very eyes. That is all you will be seeing!"

Clio was still smiling as he left the cell.

Riece followed the priest out, no doubt to ensure that he really did leave. As he passed Maia, bleeding and struggling on the ground, he stopped and rummaged beneath his cloak. He pulled out a small leather pouch slung across his broad shoulders.

He eyed Clio suspiciously. "I have to go. See to her wounds." He tossed a bundle of bandages at Clio, who caught them effortlessly.

Locking the gate, he spoke to Clio across the cell. "I don't know what stunt you thought you were pulling, but it was foolish. That man…is not to be trifled with."

Before Clio could respond, he was gone.

Clio knew he was right. Of course he was.

She turned to Maia. Her tunic was torn where the whip had lashed her skin. Blood blossomed from the deep gash that parted her flesh and ran all the way along her abdomen.

Maia's chest shuddered and spasmed painfully with each breath she fought to take. Clio laid her hand on the girl's forehead. Her skin was burning to the touch, and Clio's hand came away drenched in cold sweat.

"Maia…" Clio knew this wasn't good.

Maia wheezed, her eyes screwing up with pain.

Clio felt the sting of warm tears leaking from the corners of her own eyes. Maia wasn't going to get out of here. Clio had failed her, and it felt as if she was failing Ali all over again. Clio's own lungs felt like stone in her chest.

All Clio could do was tend to Maia's wounds and try to ease her pain. As she pulled the shredded fabric to the side, Maia's hand caught hers.

"No point."

"I'm not going to give up on you, Maia. It's not fair, all your life…and this is how it ends?" Her hands started to shake. This girl, given up by her own family, sold so that others might live, was going to die abandoned in this horrible place. Her death wasn't going to be easy, either. It was slow, and she was suffering.

"I am grateful," Maia said with a weak smile.

Clio almost laughed. All Clio could think of was how unfair this girl's life had been, and here Maia was saying she was thankful? It was so wrong, and part of Clio wanted to convince Maia of her own injustice. But she couldn't take away whatever peace this girl had stumbled upon. Clio would carry Maia's injustice for her, and that would have to be enough.

"I am," Maia continued, her voice stronger. "I thought…I

thought I was going to die alone, but the Deities have given me something I never even thought to hope for." Her hand squeezed Clio's. "It is a blessing to have you here with me. I do not have to pass over alone."

She had spoken too long, and her lungs protested violently. Huge, wet, wracking coughs erupted. Clio put her hand on Maia's chest in a foolish attempt to stop them, as if her hand could take away the cruel disease hidden inside.

When the fit finally passed, Clio knew it would be her last. Bright blood seeped out of the corner of Maia's mouth. Clio wiped it away with her fingers.

"You…I know you will save all these girls. You being here, it is a reward…for the sacrifice I made for my tribe." Maia words came out in a strained wheeze, ending in a timber barely above a whisper lost in the wind.

The way Maia was looking up at Clio with almost rapturous devotion made Clio want to pull away. She had only seen that look on people who had visited the Oracle, people who had believed wholeheartedly that the Oracle could bestow the Deities' own blessings. Clio didn't want that. She didn't want to be some kind of savior, especially when there was nothing she could do. She wasn't responsible for saving all these girls.

Maia could no longer speak, but her eyes fought to keep from rolling back into her head.

Clio pulled Maia into her lap, running her fingers through the wisps of fine hair left on her head. Clio's tears dripped from her face and mingled with the beads of sweat that coated Maia's forehead, but Maia was beyond feeling them.

Clio felt when Maia's pain passed. Her eyes flicked up to Clio, holding the relic of a smile that could no longer reach her lips. Her body released a sigh of utter relief, exhaling back into a state of total peace and serenity. Clio saw that her wounds were no longer bleeding and felt Maia's heart stop its painful struggle.

As she closed Maia's eyelids over her unseeing eyes, Clio felt a bitter satisfaction at the thought that Maia's heart would remain in her chest. Her body would be whole even though her life had not been.

When Clio cried, her tears were for Maia and for Ali both.

Clio had not had the chance to mourn her sister's death. Being catapulted from one catastrophe to the next had made her numb to it all. But Maia's death violently reopened the wound, and it bled the tears that Clio had held back.

Tenderly laying Maia's head down and placing her hands on her chest, Clio was given the chance to tend to her sister's body. Nobody had given Ali the burial that she deserved, but with this simple gesture, Clio felt she was paying respects to both of them.

It would be a lie to say that Clio didn't feel for the rest of her family. She mourned the girls her sisters used to be, the girls they could have been if they hadn't been sacrificed to the needs of the Oracle. And wasn't Maia sacrificed as well? Even her mother—Clio couldn't know what she had given up. To be the Oracle, Clio had already discovered, came with few choices. Maybe her mother had been forced to do all the awful things for which Clio had always hated her. Clio would never know who her mother had been before it all.

She cried for them all, and her tears washed away the dirt that coated Maia's face, bringing back a glimpse of the girl she had been before all the tragedy. Before the sacrifice.

She was beautiful.

CHAPTER SIXTEEN

It was only when Clio stood that she realized how violently her legs were shaking. Unsteady, she had to rest a hand against the wall in order to take a deep breath and regain her balance.

The stone was gritty, and her hand came away coated in a thick layer of dust that had accumulated from the countless girls who had spent their final days there. The air they breathed, the sand they tracked in from across the land, the dirt they carried on their bodies, even the blood that was spilt in this pen, all of it came together mingling in the layer that coated the walls of this grave.

That was what it was. A grave. And now, with Maia's cooling and lifeless body, it was impossible for Clio to ignore the suffocating feeling that constricted her chest.

She looked down at the dust on her hand, took a breath and tasted it in the air, stale and thick. Every breath Clio drew took in a little piece of each and every girl who had been here.

Her eyes would never forget the sight of death stealing through Maia's body. Her hands would forever feel the ghost of those shuddering, halting breaths, and even worse, the sheer stillness that descended when her body gave up its futile attempts to keep going.

Clio was alone. It was in the calm of the air, a consummate lack of movement. No breaths stirred, no chests moved, no sounds parted the stale atmosphere. None but Clio's. The puffs, the breeze, the exhale, everything from Clio alone, echoing soundlessly through the space and through her mind.

Maia was gone forever, but Clio would not die here. This place of dust and ash and blood, this place of stone would not be her grave.

Their cell was long and narrow, only wide enough for two people to stand side by side. Maia's body lay right in the middle. Clio didn't have a plan, not yet, but she knew she would need space.

She had to move Maia as far back as possible. When she bent to lift Maia, she realized that her left hand still clutched the bandages she had never used. A smile tugged lightly at the corners of her mouth. This was good. This was something she could use.

As gently as possible, Clio opened Maia's hands, hands that only moments ago had held onto Clio with all the passion and tenacity that life could inspire, now cold. Clio would live. She would live, and Maia's sacrifice would never be forgotten.

To get out of here, she had to make her body stone. She welcomed the hardness into her. Her muscles quivered beneath the surface, ready to spring at whatever stood in her way.

"Guards!" she yelled as she shook and pounded on the creaky pegs that formed her cage.

CHAPTER SEVENTEEN

The only response was some murmuring in the distance.

"Guards!" she repeated, this time throwing any panic, fear and tears she felt into her cry. She kept the hate, though, and the anger. Those she still needed.

A pair of footsteps clamored down the hall. For some reason she hoped they didn't belong to Riece, that she wouldn't have to hurt him to get out of here.

Clio backed up, falling into the shadows in the back of her cell.

She wasn't shaking anymore.

She was stone.

A guard she had never seen before came up to the cell and peered in hesitantly. It didn't matter that his face was foreign. He was the same as every man who was keeping her here.

"What is it?" The guard gripped his club tightly in his hand. Obviously, he had been warned about her propensity to cause damage.

"She's dead." Clio pointed toward the body behind her.

"So?" He stepped in closer, trying to penetrate the darkness in the back of the cell. His eyes darted to each side, clearly unsure of what he should do.

"So get her out of here."

The bandages were balled tightly in her fist, hidden behind her back.

"Your commander won't be pleased to know you left a body to rot in here overnight. That stink doesn't come out easily."

"Puq!" he called out behind him. "Give me a hand with this. One of the girls died."

It was the beast who came running up. He was fat, breathing heavily with the strain of running a few steps. Clio had to smile. The shadows hid the glint of her teeth.

"Hold out your hands," the beast ordered.

The beast and the guard eyed each other nervously as they unlocked the gate. "Be ready," the guard said.

Clio pressed herself against the wall, making herself as small as possible. She cradled the bandages between the curve of her back and the stone behind her so that she could hold her empty hands innocently in the air.

The guards smelled of wine and smoke as they squeezed past her into the darkness of the back of the cell.

They hoisted Maia up between them. The guard led the way out, holding Maia's head and shoulders. The beast was behind, carrying her legs.

Clio stood idly by as the first guard passed her.

When the beast was within an arm's length, Clio sprang.

Deftly catching the bandage behind her, she wrapped it tightly around his thick neck. The air was forced from him before he could even scream.

She stared at Maia's limp form, tumbling to the ground in all the confusion, as she squeezed. The man had fallen back on her when his legs gave out from lack of air. He was heavy, and she was pinned. But it also meant that the other guard could not get to her through the cramped space.

He was tangled in Maia's limbs, desperately shoving aside her brittle arms, which were unrelenting in the finality of death. Panic shook his body, making his struggle more and more futile. Even in death, Maia was doing everything she could to help Clio.

As the heavy mass that weighed her down ceased its flailing, Clio felt the beast lose consciousness. The other guard finally freed himself from Maia's grip and bolted to the door in a rushed frenzy of terror and alarm.

He struggled with fumbling hands to lock the gate of her cell. If he managed it, all of this would have been for naught.

She had moments to get to the door. The unconscious beast was heavy, but she managed to scramble out from underneath him, shoving his meaty head to the side.

With her newly powerful legs, she crossed the cell in gaping strides.

She didn't slow down when she reached the gate, choosing instead to barrel straight into it. The heavy wooden gate, made of thick logs the size of a man's thigh, collided hard with the guard behind it.

But it didn't take him out. He managed to keep hold of the key, and as he held the gate shut with one hand, he furiously continued to try to lock it with the other.

Straining with all the will she had—the will to get out of here, to burn this place to the ground—she threw herself against the gate. Slowly, it was giving way.

She reached through the opening and grabbed the guard's hand that held the keys. She yanked it toward her, between the heavy gate and the wall.

Before the guard could realize what was happening, she slammed the gate hard on his arm. The sickening crunch of bones breaking was quickly followed by an agonized scream and the give of the gate as the man fell to his knees.

The keys clattered to the ground at Clio's feet.

Scooping them up, she jumped over the guard, who huddled on the ground cradling the bleeding and mangled mess that had been his hand only moments earlier.

A swift kick to his back pushed him into the cell, where the beast was slowly coming to.

"Your turn," she called as she turned the key in the lock, sealing them into the dusty grave they deserved.

It wouldn't hold them. Someone would hear their screams, and they would be on her tail with the entire guard and an arsenal of weapons.

She had to work fast if she was going to make it out of there before that. Girls lined the cells around her, but there was nothing Clio could do for them. "The priest will die," she said as if it were some kind of apology. But they were silent, and Clio turned to go.

She sprinted through the hallways, following the mental map she had made of the tunnels. Gasping and out of breath, she reached the infirmary where Riece had treated her wound. It was empty, thank the Deities.

But the rising din of echoed voices chased her into the room. Someone had already found the men.

Sweeping the room, she found what she was looking for—the knife that Riece had used to cauterize her wound. She grabbed it, then snatched up a strip of cloth used to pack wounds and tied the knife to her thigh, a makeshift sheath hidden under her tunic.

A cauldron sat in the hearth. Flipping it over, she used it as a step to launch herself up into the dark flue of the chimney. Steeling herself, she used her hands and feet to climb up and up. The walls were slippery with all the soot, but strength and sheer desperation held her in place. She was halfway up when she heard angry shouts from below.

"She's not at the entrance."

"How do you know?"

"Because none of the guards are dead or unconscious over there!" Clio smiled at this. These men were scared of her. Finally, they knew a tiny fraction of the fear they doled out everyday.

The voices lowered to a murmur too quiet for Clio to make out.

They must have realized that screaming was giving away their own location.

But nothing could muffle the sound of their approaching footsteps. They were there, in the room.

She froze and looked down, her gaze following the descent of the soot she disturbed with each movement and the sweat that dripped from her body. A timid face finally appeared below, its body out of sight as it craned to get a look up the chimney.

Clio scuffled up higher, and in the process sent another shower of soot and debris down onto the intruding face.

"In the chimney!" the voice coughed below.

The man was pulled out of the way as another face replaced him.

"Well, get the flint then."

Clio's blood ran cold.

She couldn't watch what was going on beneath her, but she heard them drag the cauldron out, and then the sharp clicks of flint followed by the crackle and pop of flames.

They had lit a fire. Beneath her.

Only one choice now. She climbed up the chimney as fast as she could.

The air around her grew thick and dark. Smoke billowed around her, suffocating her as each breath forced ash into her starved lungs.

Sparks shot up, licking the heels of her feet. The heat was unbearable. Eyes watering through the pain, she strained to make out the top of the chimney through all the smoke. Her breaths came in strangled gasps as the smoke caused her throat to swell and convulse.

Losing her footing, she slid several painful lengths downward. She cried out as her newly scabbed ankle opened up in the descent. But she forced herself onward.

Every muscle in her legs started to quiver and shake in their attempt to hold on despite the now slimy soot coating her feet.

"What is going on here?" It was Riece. She could barely make out the top of his head through the dark swirling clouds of smoke between them.

A moment later, she heard his voice again, this time angry. "We do *not* flay people here!" A pause, she couldn't hear the response. "I don't care how she got here. She never should have gotten out in the first place!"

Only an arm's length from the top, Clio was able to get some much-needed gulps of fresh air. With shaking hands, she reached her fingers to the rim of the chimney. As she pulled herself up, she felt a dull pressure behind her eyes and Saw:

It was the top of the pyramid. The priest held his blade to a shaking girl lying on his altar. With expert precision, he plunged the dagger into her chest and pulled out her still-beating heart, holding it up for the bloodthirsty crowd.

"Any more?" he called to the guards behind him.

"No, Sire. That was the last of them."

He walked to the edge of the pyramid and looked down on the tangle of new bodies coloring the steps below. A chilling smile parted his lips as he addressed the raving crowd below.

It didn't make any sense. Just moments ago, Clio had watched him die, and now...? How could the future have changed so drastically in only a few short hours? If only she knew who had killed the priest in her first Vision, but that hazy fog had kept the scene incomplete.

Nothing was different. Except for Clio. She realized it as she heard the chirp and cry of birds flying above her. The peak of the pyramid stretched up high above her, as if to point to the open expanse of sky filled with glittering starlight. She was going to be free. And now the priest would live.

She had had the Vision of his death only after she recognized within herself the desire to take his life with her own hands. While she didn't know how the Visions worked, it must have been that decision, that want, that had sparked what she saw.

The fog—it must have been Clio herself at the top of the pyramid. She wasn't allowed to see her own fate. It was the only explanation that made sense. And Mannix had known—he used it to ambush her mother. It was what he had said to Ali in Clio's Vision. The Oracle couldn't have Visions of herself, but Clio did know one thing: if she left now, the priest would live. If she didn't, he would die.

She would kill him, but would it cost her own life? That she could not foresee.

What was more important, her life or his death?

She wanted to pick her life. She wanted to leave and never look back. But if she did, those girls would die, and many more after them. She was the Oracle, and the only one with the power to change fate.

A dark part of her heart told her that that wasn't the whole truth.

She wanted to save the girls. Of course she did. No one had ever helped them. Each one was like Maia, each with her own equally tragic life. She could fix that.

But she would be lying to herself if she said that that was all she wanted. Darkness in her called for the man's blood. She wanted him to die. And it horrified her to admit it, but she wanted that man to die just as much as she wanted those girls to live.

The Deities were sick. Clio had a choice. She did make her own fate, but in Seeing the consequences of her actions, what free will did she have? She couldn't act of her own volition without knowing all the repercussions like everyone else, and so her decision had been made for her. The Deities wanted her to save these girls, and they put Clio in a position where she had to do their will. She hated them like the stone walls of her prison.

From below, she heard the splash of water poured onto the fire. The sparks subsided, and the smoke cleared. With the calm around her, she knew that she had to drop down. She took a deep breath and mumbled, "You owe me" to the Deities. Then she let loose her footing and slid down the chimney, scraping her arms and legs as she plunged, until finally she landed in the sopping wet pile of kindling.

CHAPTER EIGHTEEN

Looking up, she found four guards and Riece staring at her with wide eyes. Riece's expression quickly changed from surprise to anger. No, rage. Grabbing her by the arm, he pulled Clio to her feet and nearly dragged her down the hallway back to the cells. She passed by dirty faces and wide eyes peeking out at her between closed bars.

Riece shoved her into another cell, adjacent to her old one. A girl so small she looked to be merely a shadow on the stone sat huddled against the back wall. Dark, greasy hair obscured her face.

"Hold your hands out to the side." He was so furious that he wouldn't even look at her.

Clio remained still, unsure how to deal with this Riece.

He did it for her, pushing her arms out until they were extended flat against the wall.

"The knife. Where is it?"

"I don't know what you are talking about." But her tone was all wrong, going up at all the wrong times, not convincing in the slightest.

"Clio, despite your opinion of me, I'm not a fool. I know you took the knife. Now tell me where it is, or I will have to strip you."

His eyes held none of the playful sparkle she had grown accustomed to. She never would have thought that this was the man who had healed her so tenderly.

"Tied to my thigh." She burned with anger, shame, and frustration as he gruffly lifted her dirt-crusted tunic and ripped off the makeshift sheaf.

She watched as he took away her last defense.

"Please, don't." He turned to go. "Sir."

He stopped, no doubt hearing all the defeat that that word carried.

"*Please.*"

"What, Clio?" He turned on her, his face a mask of rage. "Let you have a weapon so you can hurt more of my men? I can't let you do that. I've made a mistake with you."

She was stunned. *His* men?

"You send countless girls off to their deaths, and yet you worry about your *men?* Your men—" she spat the word, "—are the ones keeping us here! You know, for a moment there you had me fooled. I actually thought that you were decent. But the truth is you would rather stick your neck out for a bunch of murderers than for innocent girls."

She knew there were so many words he wanted to say to her, but he was so mad that they got stuck, trapped in a mouth that was gaping at the audacity of the girl in front of him.

"You have *no* idea what you are saying," he growled.

"I know that I would sooner kill every man here than let one of those girls walk up to that altar."

"Would you? Would you kill Hul? He's only just become a man. His brother died last moon, and Hul joined the Emperor's service so that he could provide for his four nieces. What about Victer? He works here because his daughter was born so wrong she'll never be able to talk, let alone marry. And Esso, I looked his wife in the eye and promised her no harm would come to him. You don't know anything about these men. You think any of us asked for this job? You think it's easy to have to watch young girls come in, hear them cry at night, knowing there's nothing we can do for them, then watch as they climb those fatal steps?" His words tore out of him. With each sentence, he came a step closer to her until he was nearly pinning her against the wall.

"Telling me about their families doesn't change anything. All of these girls, they have families too. You don't care about that because you don't know them."

"I *can't* know them, Clio. Deities, can't you see that? There's nothing I can do but ease their suffering. I can't free them because I'd instantly be killed and they would be caught. I can't leave my post because the next one to take it could share the priest's lust for cruelty. I'm trapped here, and as long as I have no choice in that, forgive me for wanting to maintain my sanity by not getting to know my prisoners. I've already made a mistake getting to know you."

"You don't know anything about me." Clio glared at him.

"No? I know you didn't fall down that chimney by accident. You came back on purpose. I'm guessing because you have some imprudent dream of killing the priest. You are going to die just so that you can kill one man. But let me tell you. It's not worth it."

"You're right. I am going to kill him. If you know anything about me, then you know that I am capable of it."

"Deities, you are so foolish."

"Do *not* address me like some stupid girl. Am I foolish for wanting to actually change all this?" She took a step away from the wall. They were so close now she could feel the heat rolling off him, and her skin responded, tingling in anticipation.

"You *are* foolish. You are going to get yourself killed over guilt."

This stopped Clio up. "Guilt for what?"

"Come on. You feel responsible for Maia's death. The priest was trying to punish you and it resulted in her dying. But Clio, she wasn't making it out of here anyway. You didn't bring down the whip. Do you hear me? You can't carry the evil of others on your back."

Tears stung behind her eyes, but her anger desperately tried to fight them from spilling down her cheeks.

"What a convenient philosophy for you."

"Perhaps. Maybe I should accept more responsibility, but you, you are faultless in this. You fight against everything. And if it had been possible, you would have fought to save Maia." He looked her right in the eye, and Clio felt as if he were staring into her. "And I don't know who you lost before you came here, but I know that you shouldn't carry around guilt for them either."

She let go at his words, letting the tears stream freely down her face until she found her head pressed into the crook of his neck.

Her skin lit up, the tension that had built up in the tiny space between them finally relieved. A sense of weightlessness descended on Clio as she felt his arms hesitantly wrap around her.

His touch was so warm, like the ground at the end of a sunny day. Clio felt the sun on his skin, and her body ached for more.

But he pulled away, confusion in his eyes. He held her at arm's length. Clio wondered if he had felt it too, that spark that was growing, that any moment could erupt into an all-consuming blaze. She searched his gaze but couldn't glean anything from his brown eyes. The red jagged scar was pulled tight across his neck, as if he were holding himself back from something.

The moment passed, leaving the room altered permanently. The anger burned away, leaving behind something that was too raw to be felt or understood. Clio took a step away from him, unsure.

"I'm not going to try to stop you tomorrow when it comes to the priest. But after that, I can make no promises. You go for my men, and I will cut you down. I can't give you the knife back." Out of the corner of his eye, he was tracking the pacing of guards in the distance.

"I know." Of course he couldn't.

"I also have to stand guard over you all night." His eyes snapped back to hers. "You're too problematic, and obviously I can't trust any of my men to keep a proper eye on you."

A dry chuckle broke through her tears. She was surprised to find the ghost of a grin spread across his face in response.

Stowing the blade in his belt, he left the cell, locking it behind him. She heard the rustle of his cloak and the soft thud of him sitting down against the wall outside her cell.

Clio slid down the wall as well. They rested against the same stone, each on a different side, out of sight of each other.

"This really isn't necessary. You know that I won't make my move until I have the priest within my grasp, and that won't be until I'm on that pyramid tomorrow." Clio felt certain that she could tell Riece everything. She had seen the way he looked at the priest—with hate.

"I know, but I can't exactly take your word for it. Not after everything you've done."

"Well, in that case, you are in for a long night, my friend."

He laughed.

"How will we pass the time?"

"You could sleep and make my job a little easier. Won't you need rest to pull off your big plan, anyway?"

She waved his question away, but of course he couldn't see it. "I don't think I could sleep if I tried."

"No, I suppose not."

Tomorrow, Clio would either be dead or she would be a murderer. Or most likely both. It wasn't exactly going to be easy to kill the priest in front of Morek and get away with it. Not by herself, anyway. Clio didn't care though, she wouldn't be giving up much if she died. She never wanted to be the Oracle. She could never return to Sheehan. She would never see Derik again. Her life was worth much less than this man's death.

But if she did live—if somehow she managed to escape after killing the priest. To have the same kind of blood on her hands as her murderous family—that would be harder to live with. At least, Clio hoped it would be hard to live with.

"Riece?"

"Yes?"

"How…I mean, who did you kill?" Her voice was unsteady, raw with all the fear, doubt, and pain that were battling in Clio's mind.

He didn't need her to explain the question. He must have known it was weighing heavily on her mind. After all, he carried the same burden tenfold.

He sighed, and in it, Clio could hear the echo of all the anguish she felt.

"The men I killed…the world is better without them."

"So they weren't just enemy warriors you came across in battle?" Over the last decade, Morek had expanded its empire, stretching out to lands that Clio had never even heard of. She had expected the men whose lives Riece took to have been casualties of conquest. Maybe even men from Sheehan who had fought so long to maintain Sheehan's independence. It had all been in vain, of course. Sheehan was now just another beaten kingdom within Morek's empire.

"In a way, they were." He wasn't going to say more.

"Why did you do it?"

"We were ambushed. I couldn't give up. I made a choice—I

would spill as much blood as I needed in order to get back to my sister. I'm all she has left in this world."

Clio's heart sank in her chest. He killed in order to survive, in order to come back home. An honorable kill, no one could argue with that. But Clio craved the death of the priest. She yearned for it, and she wouldn't have peace until his blood was shed. She was wrong, maybe twisted in as perverted a way as the priest. While the priest was by no means innocent, he was still a living being, and surely Clio shouldn't enjoy taking anyone's life. Surely she shouldn't look forward to the moment her blade would sink into his chest, to when the light in his eyes would die away. But she did, and that made Clio nearly hope that she wouldn't make it off that pyramid tomorrow.

Riece continued, pulling Clio away from her spiral of guilt. "I understand, you know."

"Understand what?"

"Why you have to do it. I've felt it too, that aching, gnawing you get knowing that person is alive, as if every breath they take cuts you a little deeper, makes it that much harder for you to give up and walk away and live a normal life. I've been there. I spent years of my life dreaming of another's death."

"Did you...get him?"

She could hear him shake his head, disturbing the dust that coated every wall in here. "I was too young, and by the time I would have been old enough to do it myself, it was too late."

The mysteries of this man, this young commander, were coming to the light. He was hard, the kind of hard that could only come from true suffering early in life. Clio knew the murder he carried with him cut away at him at a young age, and nothing would ever fill the deep gouges of that burden. He wasn't stone like her sisters—he was broken. Although he was out of her line of sight, Clio felt that she was looking upon Riece with more clarity than before.

Clio smiled. She was broken too.

"What did he do to you?" It was a personal question, but Clio knew he would tell her. They were the same. She wouldn't judge him because he hadn't judged her.

"It was a she." This caught Clio up short. "She was responsible for the death of my family. My brothers and my parents, all were killed because of what she did."

"She...?"

Riece chuckled darkly, and Clio became aware of the flickering light around her.

"She wasn't an ordinary girl. Do you know what an Oracle is?"

Clio froze, her hairs standing on end. Unconsciously, her fingers dug into the grooves of the stone below her, gripping so hard that she could feel the fresh sting of blood.

She waited to respond until she was confident she could control her voice. "We have them in Sheehan."

"So you know, then. Creatures of deceit and manipulation, willing to sacrifice anyone who stands in the way of their agenda. My family stood in the way of something she wanted, and they died for it.

"I swore I would kill her for what she did, but I was only seven. A couple years later, even the Emperor had learned how evil she was. She was executed atop this very pyramid so that everyone would know that she had betrayed all of Morek."

Clio gulped as she found herself pulling her hair behind her back, keeping it as out of sight as possible. She had to change the subject. Anything to make him stop talking about the Oracle.

The worst part was that Clio couldn't blame him for hating her kind. She spent her whole life hating the Oracle, and now...now she didn't know anymore. Hate like that didn't die easily.

"Yours is still alive, right?"

"I think so, but I'm really not the one to ask about that."

"They are all the same. One of your king's advisors brought in a Vessel the other day, so I wondered if the rest were dead. Maybe one day, I can help Sheehan get rid of their Oracle, get a tiny piece of my revenge back." He laughed, but instead of his laugh warming Clio, she felt chilled to her bones.

Anything, anything at all to change the subject. "Have you been to Sheehan?"

"No, I have to stay here for my sister, Tirza. She is everything to me, the only person I have left."

She nodded. She knew what that was like. Derik was the only person she had left in the world. The only one who even cared about her. He must be looking for her, but what girl would he find when he finally reached her? Clio could barely recognize herself. She had failed in her promise to herself and to him never to change. She failed when she vowed to kill the priest. The old Clio would have recoiled from that. The old Clio would never have been capable of such hatred.

The old Clio ran away from that.

She knew with a frightening certainty that she wasn't that girl anymore. Everything she saw, everything she'd been through, couldn't be undone.

She was like Riece, broken. And tomorrow, she would either be a killer or she would be dead. It didn't even matter which. All she knew was that she could not live while that man was still breathing.

Actually, she knew one more thing. It wouldn't stop with the priest. Mannix had to die as well. He had to die for Ali, for Vire and Mira, her mother, and maybe most of all, he had to die for herself, for taking away that old Clio and replacing her with something broken and vicious.

And as much as she wanted to believe that she could stop with the priest—with Mannix, even—once she crossed that line, she would be capable of much more. She would turn to stone just like her sisters—turn off all the feelings that make killing abhorrent. The Deities would show her who needed to die and there would be nothing left in Clio to shudder away.

Maybe that was what it meant to be an Oracle. It was certainly who her mother was. It was not enough just to See what was to come. The Oracle had to change it. Clio couldn't run away from her Visions of the priest, she had to do something about it. In the end, the Oracle was a killer, and Riece was right to want her dead.

CHAPTER NINETEEN

She must have drifted off to sleep. When she awoke, Riece was gone. Whatever had passed between them last night, whatever understanding that they had come to, it wasn't enough for him to help her, or to even say goodbye.

It would have been wrong for Riece to help her. If he had really known her, known the truth about her, he would have killed her in a heartbeat. He'd said as much.

It was good that he was gone, that she didn't have to lie to him anymore, didn't have to hide who she was after he had exposed everything to her.

Inside the cells, Clio could feel a buzzing energy. It hummed in her ears and made her hair stand on end. The girl whose cell she shared bolted upright, and Clio could see a restless agitation in the way she curled and uncurled her fingers.

Clio didn't need to see the other girls to know it was the same with them. She could feel it, taste it even, in the air. Today was going to be it.

They hadn't given up. If Clio could give them the opportunity, they would run, and they would fight.

In the front of the cells, she heard a guard, "All right, men, let's get this going. The priest is ready."

More guards than she had ever seen made their way around the cells, opening cells and dragging girls out.

The girls were placed single-file. Their eyes were cast downward, already refusing to witness the spectacle that was to be their death. Clio briefly made eye contact with a nameless girl. Her gray eyes were puffy from a night of crying. Clio hadn't even heard her in the night. Her forehead was marred with the black of the Oracle's blessing—an ugly reminder that the Deities had somehow found her lacking. But in her jaw, Clio could see a deeper strength. Her face was Maia's. Her face was Ali's. But Clio couldn't do anything for Ali or Maia. For this girl though, Clio would kill.

Clio winked at the crying girl as she passed her in the line-up and took her spot at the head of the line, surprised to find that she wasn't nervous, not in the slightest. Clio had seen the future. She would succeed.

But how? a voice in the back of her head whispered. *You didn't see what happened next.*

They were led through a maze of tunnels, deeper into the belly of the pyramid than she had ever imagined possible. All of the labor it must have taken to build this titan, this megalithic slaughterhouse, all so that the priest would have a glorified spot to act on his sick will, so that the Emperor could claim to honor the Deities. It all made

Clio want to destroy it, to take it apart brick by brick. But she knew that something this big could never be destroyed, could never be unmade. It would stand to the ends of time, a monument to its people's barbarity.

The air was stale, rotten from sitting stagnant in this pit so deep inside the pyramid. Without warning, the winding corridor finally ended at a cramped set of stairs, which circled around above, a spiral that rose out of sight.

Higher and higher they went, until the stairway was only big enough for one person to pass through at a time. Every time Clio thought that they couldn't possibly make another turn, couldn't possibly go any higher, they continued on. The hallway became so narrow that Clio's elbows bumped against the sides. Everything was black. Each girl felt only the guard's hand on the nape of her neck as guidance, pushing them ever higher. Clio's toes bumped against the stairs in the dark, and every once in a awhile, she could hear a girl behind her trip and fall only to be pulled up again and pushed onward into the darkness.

The walls continued to close in on her as she ascended the stairs. It was so constricting, so suffocating that it would make anyone, even someone heading to the chopping block, eager to reach their destination and end the infernal pressure. Like a morbid birthing canal, squeezing them ever tighter until suddenly, the stairwell spilled into light.

Going from blackness to brilliant sunlight was temporarily blinding. Clio found herself squinting and shading her eyes with her hand in order to see the scene before her. They were greeted by several robed men whose faces were hidden by the black folds of their hoods, but Clio knew that they must have been the priest's men.

There, at the edge of the pyramid, the priest stood wearing the same amber robes from before but with an added golden and ivory headdress that cascaded down his back, catching the sun's rays and throwing them into Clio's eyes. Her pulse quickened.

They were so high up that Clio could barely make out the figures below. One giant mass stood at the base of the pyramid, a single body made up of countless human parts all strung together by a common lust for bloodshed. A dull roar travelled up to her ears—a multitude of voices crying out in a discordant harmony.

Clio had never seen so many people in her life. It was a staggering sight. Thousands of men and women and children crowded into one place, all cheering in anticipation of the gory spectacle. So many people, and not a shred of humanity amongst them.

The High Priest held up his hand, quieting the masses below. As he began to speak, projecting his voice over the crowd, Clio focused on the altar at his side, where a row of black obsidian blades was laid out.

The priest's words caught her attention. "WE OFFER UP THESE SACRIFICES IN THE NAME OF THE EMPEROR. IN HIS WISDOM, HE SAW THROUGH THE LIES OF THE ORACLE AND TAUGHT US THAT ONLY BLOOD COULD BRING THE DEITIES' FAVOR. HAVE WE NOT SEEN THE

PROOF WITH OUR OWN EYES? MOREK STANDS MORE POWERFUL THAN ANY OTHER CITY BECAUSE OF ONE THING—SACRIFICE."

Thunderous applause greeted his speech. The stomping of the eager voyeurs carried all the way up the pyramid, reverberating against the stone, culminating in a shudder so violent that the knives rattled on their dais.

The priest took his place behind the altar and turned so that Clio could see what the crowd could not—a perverse sneer that stretched his features to extremes. With horror, Clio watched as he almost licked his lips while his eyes took stock of his victims. He was getting a sadistic thrill from the anticipation.

When his eyes fell on Clio, there was no mistaking his excitement. She thought he would pick her first, but when he motioned to one of his hooded men to bring another girl forward, Clio knew that he wanted to save her for last. Prolonging her life, making her watch the others girls die would heighten his own pleasure. If Maia had still been alive, she had no doubt that he would have killed her first.

Anger consumed every fiber of her being. She had to get to the front. From back here, without a weapon, she was helpless, and that girl was going to die. She made to approach the altar, regardless of the priest's intentions, but she found herself held back.

While she had been watching the display before her, one of the priest's men had grabbed her shoulders and held her firmly in place.

She struggled against him, straining with everything she had to free herself from his iron grip. But he was strong, much stronger than a priest should have been. She tried to elbow him in the gut, but met unrelenting flesh. The priest must have ordered some extra brawn to ensure that Clio wouldn't make a break for it.

As Clio struggled, the girl was walked up to the altar. The priest's hand danced above the row of obsidian blades until landing on the thinnest and sleekest of the bunch. He held it up before the crowd, but it caught none of the sun's light, remaining purely black.

The priest swept out his arm, imploring his trembling victim to approach him.

Clio called on that unfamiliar strength that seemed to be a part of her now. It rose, beckoned by her will, and coursed through her veins, lighting a fire within her. Moving faster than she expected, Clio jabbed her elbow as hard as she could up into her captor's face. He had no choice but to release her as he tried to stay the flow of blood that was cascading from his broken nose.

In a flash she darted forward, pulling the man who was escorting the sacrifice back so hard that he fell to the ground. She stepped in front of the terrified girl and defiantly stared down the priest.

"No! You won't be taking anyone's life today."

A dozen men grabbed her, overpowering her.

Undaunted, Clio turned to the girls. "We can't just let him kill us on this altar! You need to fight!"

Whispers of surprise and confusion rippled through the slaves. Should they fight? Could they?

The priest's eyes narrowed as if he could sense the hope Clio was instilling in the girls. He grimaced and motioned to his men to bring her forward.

As Clio was placed on the altar, she wasn't afraid. She didn't resist the men who held her down. Her face was set in rigid determination.

The priest started to speak, giving an incantation to the Deities. He leaned over her, grinning wickedly. Her arms lay limply at her sides, hands balled into fists.

His hand began that same dance over the row of blades. He looked at her as he picked the largest of them. The corner of Clio's mouth flicked up in a sly smile—he had picked the very weapon she had been hoping for.

The priest raised it above her chest as the men held her head down and to the side to constrain her. But she didn't need to see the blade to know exactly where it was. She felt it in the air, in the shift in the breeze above her, broken by the thick blade.

He called out to the crowd, and finally Clio could hear what he was saying to them. "AND WHEN I TAKE THIS HEART, IT WILL BE A SACRIFICE FOR ALL OF US, AND THE DEITIES WILL SMILE UPON US FOR WHAT WE HAVE GIVEN UP."

Her head was pinned down, and as he was talking all she could see was the roaring crowd below. Clio shut her eyes and focused on the space above her.

With a jerk so fast, so sudden, and so sure, her hand shot out and clamped down hard on his wrist. She heard the collective gasp of the audience, just as in her Vision.

Her eyes remained closed. She didn't need them for this. All of her attention was channeled into the hand that held the shaking wrist of the priest. All she needed was that hand, and so that was all she was. She couldn't feel the rest of her body as she sharply yanked and twisted his wrist. Her hand absorbed the crack that resounded as his wrist fractured under her grip.

As the blade dropped from his now useless hand, the rest of her body sparked to life. In an instant, her other hand shot up and caught the blade, its edges digging into her flesh. She welcomed the pain. It awakened all of her senses, all of her muscles, preparing her body for what had to come next.

She opened her eyes. Still squeezing down on the priest's broken wrist, immobilizing him with pain, she flipped the blade, catching it by its hilt, and plunged it deep into his chest.

She didn't think. She didn't feel. She moved at an unnatural speed. It all happened so fast that even the guards stood shocked.

But no one was more shocked than the priest, who gaped at Clio with the stunned realization that this slave girl had just stilled his heart.

CHAPTER TWENTY

Everything was silent, as if the entire world were caught between inhale and exhale—that empty weightlessness of total and utter balance that couldn't last longer than a heartbeat, but held all possibilities within a single instant.

Nobody moved, save for Clio. She got to her feet, wielding the knife. The men stepped back, incredulous.

She stood on the altar and yelled to the crowd below, "THIS DEATH IS NOT A SACRIFICE. IT'S RETRIBUTION!" She looked down at her hand and only then felt the sticky heat of the priest's blood leaching down her arm. Blood mingled with ash and dirt. It was only a couple days ago that she had washed away the same stains from her sister's skin. Then, it had horrified her. Now, she felt nothing.

She dragged the priest's body to the edge of the pyramid, and with a nudge from her foot, sent him tumbling down the steps that descended to the ground.

In the silenced crowd, every crack of his bones echoed and rang throughout the square. Every pair of eyes was fixed on the unnaturally bending and breaking body. When it finally hit the ground with a resolute thud, it crumpled into an inhuman shape. The spell was broken, and the entire world came to life in one shared instant.

She expected to feel relieved. The weight of that butcher's life, a weight that had been squeezing the breath out of her, should have been lifted, leaving her free to be herself again. She had accomplished what she swore to do.

But she felt no different.

Killing this man didn't dull the pain of everything she had lost. All it did was teach her what she was capable of—murder. That burning rage still threatened to boil over under her skin.

As she turned to look behind her, a heavy black mass hit her. One of the priest's men had tackled her to the ground. She held the knife in her bloodied hand.

But she couldn't use it.

She didn't have to be a ruthless killer. At least, that was what she told herself. If she killed this man now, for nothing more than that he was in her way, then she would be living up to everything Riece had said to be true of the Oracle.

But the screams of the girls behind her told her that she had to do *something*, or they would all die and her destruction would have been for nothing but revenge.

The man kneed her in the stomach, knocking the wind out of her. He had her pinned beneath him as he tried to pry her fingers from the blade. Taking her free hand, she tried to push his head away. Her movements were clumsy as she struggled to regain her breath. Instead of getting ahold on him, she shoved her fist into his gasping mouth. He tried to bite down, but her hand was too much, filling his mouth. His throat convulsed around her fist as it tried to gag away the intruder. Choking, the man had no choice but to get off of her.

As soon as her legs were free again, Clio kicked at his knees. Losing his balance, the man staggered backwards and slipped off the edge of the pyramid. He rolled down only a couple of the pyramid's steep steps, but it was enough for Clio to get back to the more important struggle behind her.

She had only moments to assess the situation. Three of the girls had taken advantage of the confusion and slipped out of the perimeter made by the cloaked priests. Clio could make out their blurry figures scuttling down the backside of the pyramid.

The rest were still struggling to free themselves. A common spark had ignited in each girl, flaring into a desperate desire to live. Each breath they took in the battle for their freedom fed that spark until it erupted into flames.

Clio rolled to her feet, grabbing another blade from the altar. This one was long and heavy, but it didn't feel unnatural in her grip. Something in her body hummed and came to life at the feeling of its golden hilt in her hands. A blade in each hand, she watched as guards poured from the mouth of the tunnel. Their long blades glistened in the light.

Clio found herself grinning. She could do this.

Without hesitation she rushed head-on into the skirmish, wielding the obsidian against their spears. She slashed through shields, twirling and spinning, careful not to inflict any fatal wounds. She cursed Riece under her breath for what he had told her.

Several guards fell to the ground, blocking others from getting to her. From behind, she heard a girl scream—one of the other priests had grabbed her. Ducking under the blow of a club, she rolled over the altar until she was abreast of them. She could kill the priest so easily. Her blade would slice through him like water. She even knew what it would feel like to do it, how his heart would shudder and stop beneath her hand.

But something in her recoiled from the thought. It was something that her sisters, the warriors that they were, would undoubtedly do. She had to be different. She had to stop herself from falling off the edge into the black gulf that had claimed her family.

I will not lose myself to this. She flipped the blade and slammed the hilt into the back of the man's head. He dropped instantly, losing consciousness. The girl looked up at Clio, gratitude etched across her face.

"Go," Clio urged. She placed one of her blades into the girl's trembling hands.

All the guards were focused on Clio. The longer she drew their attention, the more time the other girls had to get away but the less chance Clio had of making it off the pyramid alive.

With the blade in her left hand, she ran and slid across the ground, scooping up a club from a fallen guard. She came up a blur of motion and fought as if she had done so a million times: her body knew every step, every correction it had to make to stay out of harm's way while maintaining balance. It was intoxicating, a heady feeling of exhilaration and power. She wasn't growing tired. In fact, with every move, she felt herself loosening up. She felt muscles awakening that she had never used before.

That was, until a searing pain sliced through her torso. Her club clattered to the ground as her hand reached to her side. It came away wet with blood. Five guards were descending on her, surrounding her. She tried to deflect their blows with her blade, but there were too many of them, and the pain tapped her concentration.

She looked up at a blade raised above her, descending much too quickly for her even to think of rolling away. Squeezing her eyes shut as if that would stop its fall, she heard a dull thud as the blade came in contact with a shield above her. A rustle of robes swept around her as her savior bent over her frame.

It was one of the cloaked priests. Clio's first thought was of Derik. Somehow he had found her and saved her. The hood covered his face, but clearly he could see because he fought off five armed guards single-handedly. He battled with every inch of his person. The way he wielded the shield was almost as lethal as his blade. He missed no opportunity. He saw every opening and used it to his advantage. With a sure kick, he sent a club at his feet flying into the stomach of a guard, knocking him to the ground.

Still, he never went for the kill although he could easily have massacred every man there. Instead, he put them down only long enough to get away. As he bent to Clio, he sent his shield flying over her head. She heard the muffled grunt of it colliding with a guard.

Next thing she knew, he was pulling her up into his arms. She clung to his neck as he ran to the back steps of the pyramid. Each step he took down sent a ripple of pain through her body. She was losing too much blood. She knew it. She could see the trail she was making along the backside of the pyramid.

What she couldn't see was whether any guards were following them. The world was losing its color and focus. With their final step onto solid ground, it went black.

CHAPTER TWENTY-ONE

Clio woke to sunlight streaming across her face. "Finally!" a high-pitched, melodious voice chirped.

She looked around. She was in a bedroom of some kind. A washbasin stood in one corner, and she lay in a pile of colorful furs and pillows. The padding underneath her was made with feathers softer than she had ever felt. The walls were painted a somewhat burnt-looking cream. To Clio it looked the very color of comfort. She had never seen the inside of a house colored—in Sheehan everything was the grays and browns of stone and clay. The ceilings were high, and large archways opened to a private courtyard that let in swaths of sunlight that cut across Clio. For the first time since the night she'd run away, Clio actually felt warm.

A girl stood in the far corner of the room. Her skin was a rich brown, and her hair was piled on top of her head in tight black spirals. She was young—13 or so—and wore a shimmering yellow silk dress that somehow seemed to glide against and hug her skin.

"Who...? Where am I?" Clio's tongue was dry and cracked.

"I'm Tirza." She paused as if she expected Clio to know who she was. "Riece's sister? He said that he had told you about me." She was annoyed.

Riece! "How did I get here?" All she could remember was that priest carrying her down the pyramid. That priest who had fought amazingly well...

"He rescued you, remember? Carried you all the way here! He was in a disguise, though. Couldn't have anyone knowing that the commander of the Emperor's guard was helping a fugitive escape. He just always has to be the hero." Her tone carried sarcasm, but her eyes shone with devotion and admiration.

"Where is he?" Clio's voice sounded overly eager even to her ears. She owed this man everything. But he had to have had a reason for saving her. She knew that. And she knew that whatever that reason was, Clio couldn't stick around to find out.

"He sat by your bedside for two days, but the Emperor called him away today. He left me to look after you, and I think the first thing you need is a serious washing. I would have bathed you earlier, but you are too heavy. Riece wanted to help carry you, but I told him that no lady wants a man to see her naked while she is unconscious." Her words came out in a flurry.

Clio blushed.

"I was right, yes?"

"Yes. I mean no! I don't need to wash, really." Her heart skipped a beat at the thought of washing away all the dirt and soot and blood that was hiding her snowy white hair.

The hair that would give her away as the very thing that Riece hated above all else. No, she couldn't stay here long. The budding trust between the two of them would never survive the truth.

Tirza laughed. "You really are wild! I've heard stories about how people in Sheehan live in the dirt, but I never thought that it was true! Don't be ridiculous, though. You are filthy. If anyone were to see you like this, there would be no doubt of where you came from." She eyed Clio seriously. "Everyone is looking for the Sheehan girl who killed a priest and set a bunch of slaves free. People have taken to calling her the Shadow. We don't want you to match that description, do we?"

"Tell your brother that I really appreciate what he's done for me, but I can't stay." Clio rose to stand, but crumpled when pain shot through her abdomen.

"You can't leave like that. You were stabbed, remember? It has healed remarkably fast, but still you have to take it easy. And as long as you are here, you absolutely must bathe. You smell foul." Tirza wrinkled her nose in disgust. "You really have no choice in the matter." Tirza walked over to the washbasin.

"Fine. I'll bathe, just let me do it by myself. Please?" Clio needed to be alone. She needed to find a way out of here.

Tirza sighed. "All right, come on, lean on me." Gently, Tirza helped Clio to her feet and over to the basin as if she had done it countless times before. She probably had, Clio realized. When Riece came home from his warrior duties, Tirza was the only one there to help him recover from his battle wounds.

Every step pulled on tender muscles and tendons, but the pain was a reminder of how much worse it could have been if Riece had not been there.

"I owe your brother my life." Clio couldn't understand it. There was no reason that he would risk everything to save her, and yet he had. There had to be something he was hiding. The back of her mind whispered that maybe he knew what she really was and wanted the pleasure of exacting his own revenge for his family.

Tirza giggled. "Join the club. But you'll have to get in line behind the Emperor."

She knew she shouldn't pry, but she had to know. "How *did* he save the Emperor?"

Tirza brightened. She really did idolize her brother. "Well, it was his first duty in the Emperor's service. He was part of a party escorting him south. A day into the trek, they were attacked by a tribe of Untouched."

Clio shivered. The Untouched were known to eat any travelers they came across.

"He doesn't talk about what happened. There was a whole new moon by the time Riece returned, carrying the Emperor on his back."

"That's when he got the post of commander?" No one ever escaped the Untouched. The only clue to their nature was the occasional horrifying story of a traveler coming across the devoured body of one of their victims.

"Yep. Youngest commander ever, but after saving the Emperor from such a fate, no one has ever questioned it."

The men Riece had killed, the ones who got him his gold cloak, they were Untouched. He didn't kill innocent men. The blood he had taken belonged to savages. She couldn't blame him. She had killed a man for the same crime.

So he was more honorable than Clio had thought. But his story also told of a young warrior so loyal to the Emperor that he would use all his strength to save the man, most likely putting himself at great risk in the process. That man would never disobey the Emperor and help a fugitive escape.

Finally, with a few agonizing steps, Clio reached the washbasin. "Tirza, I'm so grateful for all that you must have gone through to help me. I can manage from here. Could you just bring me some clean clothes and a scarf?"

"All right, but if you fall over and can't get up, you better call for me before you bleed all over our floor." She left, and finally Clio was alone.

Clio craned her neck to get a look through the archway and into the courtyard. It wouldn't be too hard to leave through there. In the middle of the night she could slip out without anyone seeing her, scale the wall, and disappear in the streets of Morek.

But the slightest movement brought paralyzing pain to her gut. She had no way to climb a wall like this. Not yet. Until then, well, she would be at the mercy of Riece and whatever agenda he had for her.

Only until she was well enough. As soon as she could, she had to leave.

The water stung her skin. She had to scrub so hard that she felt as if she was taking off a layer of her own flesh with all the dirt and soot. When it came to her hair, she ended up dunking her whole head into the basin and running her fingers through it under water.

The water was brown with all the dirt, but Clio could still make out a dim reflection. Who she saw was a stranger. Her cheeks were gaunt and hollow, her lips were cracked, her eyes hung too large in her wasted face, and worst of all, her hair shimmered as if in sunlight.

She looked like her mother. Like an Oracle.

She left her bloodied hand for last. A glove of caked blood clung to her skin, marking the priest's final struggle. She thought it would repulse her—scrubbing away the gore, as it had when she had scrubbed away Vire's—but it was easy.

Tirza left the garments outside her door. As Clio was tying her hair up into the red silk scarf, she heard a commotion.

"You're back!" Tirza chirped in that way of hers. "What did the Emperor want?"

"Just preparing for a royal envoy from Sheehan. How is she doing?" His voice was urgent.

"Oh, she woke up! She should be—" but whatever Clio should have been was cut off by Riece parting the curtain and ducking into Clio's room. They both froze in the instant their gazes found each other.

His eyes were wild, running over her entire body, searching for any sign of injury. His chest heaved as if he had been running a great distance. Once he saw that she was all right, his eyes locked with hers.

And Clio couldn't breathe. The relief she saw there, in that warm brown look, was almost more than she could take.

He took a hesitant step toward her. She knew she should step back, but her body was drawn toward him. He raised a timid hand to her face in the whisper of a caress, letting it hover above her skin for only a fraction of a heartbeat but long enough that Clio thought her flesh would combust if he didn't pull away.

He did, letting his hand fall to his side.

They stood like that, neither sure what to say. And there was so much to say, so much that should be said. He opened his mouth, drawing in a breath as if to speak, but she cut him off.

"I know that you rescued me, but you really should knock."

He stood there, grinning at her. He shrugged. "Nothing you could show me I haven't seen already."

Suddenly, she was very much aware of the thin silk that covered her skin, still glistening from her bath. "It's common decency, Riece." Her voice shook.

"You look...clean."

Clio laughed. The way his eyes were roving up and down her body let her know that she looked much better than just clean. "High praise!"

Was that a flush on his cheeks? She took a step toward him. "Really, though—I can't thank you enough for what you did back there."

He raised an eyebrow, "Oh, I'm sure you can think of

something…" Now it was her turn to blush. He continued in a more serious tone, "I've never seen anyone, not even warriors, fight as bravely as you did. I couldn't let it go to waste."

"But why?" Clio felt her body shift onto the defensive.

"Why what?"

"You're the commander. Your sister told me how you saved the Emperor's life, you're obviously very loyal to him. Why would you risk it all to save me?"

"Why do you think I would save you?" Riece narrowed his eyes.

"I truly don't know. You've never rescued any other girl. And you're still the commander."

"Killing the priest didn't break the whole system. The Emperor still depends on sacrifice for the city's prosperity. A new High Priest has already been appointed."

"Right. So why did you go through all the trouble of rescuing me? You clearly don't have any real qualms with the system."

The scar across his neck tightened in that way Clio had learned to mean Riece was holding back some strong emotion. Usually anger.

"Deities, Clio. You are insufferable."

Definitely anger.

He threw his arms up and walked away.

"You can't expect me to simply accept what you did for me. I'm not a fool. You risked too much, there had to be a reason." He couldn't know what she was. There was no way. Unless he recognized some resemblance to Ali. She needed to get him to say it.

"Why does there have to be a reason for everything with you?

Why can't you just accept kindness from others?" He was pacing across the room.

"Because you are the commander of Morek's forces! You order the deaths of Sheehans and girls for a living!"

He stopped moving. "I keep my city safe."

"Call it what you want. It doesn't fit with rescuing a poor Sheehan slave."

"First of all, I never for a moment believed you were ever a slave." Clio stilled. "Second..." but his voice trailed off in his gaping search for words. "Deities, Clio, just drop it, all right?"

"No. What are you going to do with me?"

"Do with you? I'm not going to *do* anything with you." He looked genuinely puzzled. "Clio, I rescued you because I didn't want to see you die. I mean, I never want to see any of those girls die, but with you—something just...I just couldn't let it happen. And yes, you are right—I am still the commander. I am still loyal to my Emperor. But for the time being, I am also the man who didn't want you to die. I don't have any plans for you. I didn't even know what to do with you when I brought you home. If anyone found out you were here...I haven't thought two steps ahead, but I do know that I can't see you on the pyramid again. You are the one who told me I have the responsibility to take action when I can, so I did. So you can distrust me as much as you want. You've probably already planned the best escape from this room and that's fine. Please go and return to whatever life you came from. I just didn't want you to die."

He didn't even wait for her to respond before storming out of her room.

Clio stood there paralyzed as the dull thuds of his footsteps echoed in her mind. He cared about her. He had helped her simply because he didn't want her to die, not out of any concealed agenda. It could have been funny—only days ago, Clio had been planning to flirt her way out of that pyramid, and now that was exactly what she had done.

But...it wasn't funny anymore. Somewhere along the way things got so tangled that Clio didn't even know what she thought about this man anymore. First he was merely the commander, but now, now he was Riece. And there was so much that came with Riece, so much that Clio couldn't let herself consider.

Because if he ever found out what she really was, they would be back exactly where they started.

Tirza came in at regular intervals during the day to check in on her, but each time Clio feigned sleep. A new emotion had settled in the pit of Clio's stomach: guilt. Concealing who she really was and imposing on Riece's kindness was a nauseating combination.

The worst part was that Clio knew she was treating him as a real Oracle would. As Riece knew the Oracle would. He had saved Clio's life twice, and she was paying him back with lies. Whether she cared for him or not—a question she didn't want to dwell on—she owed him the truth. A part of her was even willing to accept the inevitable consequence of it. It would be easier to hate him again, to see him as the enemy.

A soft knocking announced Riece before he stepped inside. The sun hung low in the sky, stretching his shadow far across her room as he made his way over to her bed.

"You're still here," he said, sitting down on the edge of her mess of pillows and furs.

"I can't exactly move yet. I'll leave when I can walk." She peeked at him.

His gaze had been fixed on the floor, but swept up to hers for a moment. "Don't do that," he said.

"It's easiest that way."

"Do you even have anywhere to go? Sheehan?"

She shook her head. "I can't go back there. Not now. I'll be fine, though. I can take care of myself, and you can go back to being the Emperor's commander."

"And what if I don't want to go back to just that? What if I want you to stay?" He was looking at her now.

She stood painfully, as if that could help escape the weight of his searching eyes. "You don't know who I am. You wouldn't want me here if you did."

"How about you let me decide that? I know you like to give orders," he gave her a quick smile, "but for once can you just let me decide?"

"Riece," she began, "I'm—" but all of a sudden she stumbled as her senses were assaulted with another Vision.

She was in a dark stone corridor, but Riece and her current surroundings were somehow distantly present, as if she was looking in a reflection on water's surface to see the rocks and sand below. Mannix was leading a group of men dressed in his signature red robes down a narrow corridor. Between them, they carried the limp form of a girl.

He was speaking to them as he went, but Clio was too far away to catch his words. She found that she could move forward and follow these men inside their world. Her footfalls carried no sound and disturbed no dust. But when she looked past the reflection into the depths, she could see that she was nearly walking into Riece.

"We will have the girl soon, and this is where she will be kept. It is absolutely imperative that you not let anyone in or out of this room besides myself," Mannix said to the men over his shoulder as he led them into a darker room lit only by torchlight. By the time Clio entered the room, the girl had been put down on a thin blanket in a row of other sleeping figures. Clio nearly gagged when the stench of the room hit her nostrils. Human feces, blood, and something else, something rotting. From the corners of the room, weak moaning rose from a crumpled and misshapen figure. Clio took a step forward to look and had to stifle a scream.

It was girl, a common slave girl. Recognition tugged at the corners of Clio's mind. Something about the girl was so familiar. She bore that same demeanor Clio had seen of all the girls in the pyramid—a will to fight despite overwhelming forces. Firelight caught gray on her forehead—the Oracle's mark. She had been one of the slave girls who escaped the pyramid.

Now her face was gaunt, and her skin was a pale gray in the flickering light. Flies buzzed around a deep wound in her abdomen. Every sense in Clio's body was telling her to turn away, but she had to see. She focused on the wound, not the girl. This way, it was almost possible to convince herself that this ravaged flesh didn't belong to a person who had a home and a family and a beating heart. Because if Clio really let herself see the girl beneath all the horror, it would be too much, and she would have to shut her eyes to it all. But Clio couldn't close her eyes, she couldn't look away. The Deities were showing her this for a reason. She had to be strong enough to learn everything she could.

Thin leather straps served as some kind of stitching, but they weren't keeping the wound closed, they were holding it open. Nothing, absolutely nothing hid the slow pulse of blood through organs from the outside world.

Mannix knelt by her side and whispered in her ear, "Will you tell me everything now?"

Clio didn't think the girl was even conscious of Mannix's presence. It was all she could do to keep up her uneven, ragged breathing.

Mannix rose, an expression of disgust on his face. "This one is nearly dead. Do what you like with her." He swept his hand out, offering the dying girl to the men at his side. Their eyes seemed to sparkle in the light.

"But," he continued, "when we have the Oracle, you mustn't touch her. She is mine, completely."

The reflection was gone, and Clio found herself back in her room with a very confused Riece staring at her with gaping jaws.

"What is it, Clio?" Riece was looking at her, concern furrowing his brow.

"Nothing," she said weakly. "It's just still hard to stand, makes me dizzy."

He suspected nothing.

"What did you want to tell me?" His hands clasped her arms lightly, steadying her.

She could still tell him. But that girl—Mannix was doing something unspeakable to her. Clio knew it was probably too late to help her. By the time she got back to Sheehan, the girl would be beyond saving. But there would be more. She knew it with a fatal certainty. She would be shown more people in trouble, more suffering, and if she told Riece what she was, if she exposed herself, that would be it for all those people. Maybe he would forgive her, but most likely not, and it wasn't just her own life hanging in the balance. She was the only one who could do something about Mannix.

Without her, Mannix could continue to do this, hurt people. She could stop him, but not if she was imprisoned.

It wasn't her choice to make.

She needed to get strong so she could go after him.

And she needed to take advantage of Riece.

"I wasn't a slave, but I have nothing to my name now. I can never repay you for what you are doing for me." She tried to fire those words with the real truth in them.

"I don't care about that. Please stay."

She couldn't meet his eyes as she nodded.

"You shouldn't be on your feet." He swept her up as if she were as light as a small child and gently lowered her onto the tangle of pelts and pillows that had been her bed. With a smile so genuine it touched his whole face, Riece looked at her one last time before sweeping under the curtain.

CHAPTER TWENTY-TWO

She must have fallen asleep. Before she knew it, she was opening her eyes to find her room shrouded in darkness. Night had fallen, and only the faint shimmer of delicate moonlight cast a subtle gleam on her surroundings.

Slowly she stretched out, testing out the tenderness of her injuries. Somehow, in her brief respite, her body had nearly finished knitting itself back together. She found that she could stand with only moderate discomfort.

The quiet hum of voices drifted into Clio's room. She saw the flickering golden light of a fire around the edges of the hanging pelt that closed off her room from the rest of the house.

Riece and Tirza. Clio's hand drifted to the scarf wound tightly around her head. She moved to the pelt curtain and hovered there, her hand outstretched ready to lift the pelt and join them, the warmth from the fire and the smell of something cooking enticing her to take that one step forward.

But she couldn't bring herself to do so. The thought of

pretending, lying to them, made her stomach turn. She recognized that she couldn't leave just yet, she needed a plan, but she also knew she wanted to face her hosts as little as possible. Her hand fell to her side, and she took a step backwards out of the faint glow of light and into the dark. A cool breeze flowing through the archways that opened to the outside disturbed the fabric of her tunic, chilling her skin underneath.

Whenever she had felt trapped as a child, her instinct had always been to step outside, to taste the fresh air. Clio smiled—at least that hadn't changed. She grabbed a large brown fur from the ground, wrapping it around her shoulders, and stepped through the arch to the courtyard beyond.

The size of the mountain peaks in the distance threw her. She had been expecting the flat landscape of her home, if she could even call Sheehan her home anymore. Sighing, she leaned against the wall, wondering how she could stop Mannix.

She had to get back to Sheehan; that much was clear. Mannix knew she was alive, and he would be coming for her. But without Derik, she didn't know where she could go. If only she could talk to him. Together, they could figure out where Mannix was and find a way to stop him from hurting anyone else. Even without the threat of Mannix, Clio just wanted to see him again, to escape into their world together at the top of their tree. No matter how much had changed below.

"Hey." Riece's voice surprised her, making her jump and drop her makeshift wrap. "What are you doing out here? Escaping?" He stepped forward, swooping down to pick up the pelt that had fallen to the ground.

"Just thinking," she mumbled, unable to meet his eyes.

"Here." He wrapped the fur around her, letting his hands gently linger on her shoulders.

Without warning, he grabbed her hand. She looked up and found a crooked smile slowly spreading across his face.

"Come on, I want to show you something." She looked down at their intertwined fingers. Touching him wasn't like touching Derik. With Derik, she had felt so comfortable, completely at peace and secure. With Riece, it was the opposite. Nothing was steady in the world while her flesh touched his, as if at any moment the very air around them could erupt into a blazing conflagration, consuming them until nothing was left.

He led her farther out into the courtyard. Her bare toes scraped against loose pebbles and stones.

With his free hand, he untied the cloak from around his neck, letting it fall in a golden pile on the ground. Only a thin woolen tunic covered his dark skin. He knelt to the ground, still holding Clio's hand in his, and pulled her down beside him.

When her eyes adjusted, she saw that they were at the edge of a shallow pool. He slipped his sandals off and dipped his feet into the water. She did the same and was surprised to find the water warm.

"How?" she asked him incredulously.

He smiled, and the glint of his white teeth caught the moon's light. "It comes from the ground. See the steam?"

She saw it, twirling and spiraling into the open night air.

With a heavy sigh, he leaned back so that he lay on the dirt ground. "Before, when you were trapped in that cell, I thought you might like it out here. Look."

She leaned back beside him, their arms almost touching, and looked into the night sky. It was as if she were seeing it for the first time. Above her twinkled a blanket of stars. She saw hardly any black—every corner shone and sparkled in a way that was so perfect it was unnatural.

She had always stared up at the sky through the ceiling in her home in Sheehan. But that sky had been dark, only the moon's light reaching down to her.

"In the mountains, the air is a lot clearer than it is in Sheehan." His voice was so soft, barely above a whisper. "I'm sorry I couldn't get you out sooner, before…"

She sat up, pulling her hand from his. "You are the one who got me out of there. You don't…I owe you everything." She looked into the pool, at their reflections. All she saw of herself was the scarf hiding her white hair. She kicked the water, trying to dispel what she could never change.

He sat up next to her, his hand brushing against her cheek as he tucked a stray lock of hair back into the folds of the fabric. She froze, but the night kept the strands' color shrouded in darkness. She leaned away all the same.

"You saved all of those girls, you know." His voice glowed with admiration.

"Not all of them."

"The sick girl, she was your friend, wasn't she? What was her name?"

"Maia. I don't know if we were friends, but neither of us had anyone else."

"And what does that make me?" His voice was teasing. She had to smile.

"You are the commander. I couldn't have hoped that *you* would help me."

"It's a good thing I did. You broke my nose, by the way."

"I did not!" She protested, horrified.

"You did," he laughed, and in the moonlight, Clio could make out a slightly crooked notch in his strong nose. It should have been ugly, but it was more endearing than anything.

"When?"

"I was the one trying to hold you back, trying to stop you from doing something stupid. Turned out it was a foolish move on my part. I should have known nothing could stop you."

She blushed scarlet in the dark.

"That makes how many times now that you've hit me? Do you always make a habit of punching the boys you know, or am I just special?" He raised one eyebrow teasingly.

"You, Riece, are special." She jabbed him lightly in the side.

He caught her hand, refusing to release it, a sly grin crossing his face.

"I'm going to need that back," she said. It was so easy to let all the guilt, all the fear fall to the back of her mind. He made her feel normal.

"Are you, now? Well, I don't think you can have it back until you promise not to unleash it on me anymore. Of course, I wouldn't be opposed to some more gentle action—a massage, perhaps? My body is awfully sore after all the beatings."

"I warned you," she teased as she brought her free hand down on his chest. He caught that one too, and she could barely move. She squirmed, trying to get free, and they collapsed onto the ground, just as she had the first time they met.

"You know," he said, "I am having the oddest sensation. It's as if we have been in this very position before."

"Yes, and how did that end up for you?" Clio asked, still struggling. "Think your *progeny* can take another beating?"

His eyes widened. "You wouldn't." He rolled over, pulling Clio with him. They were getting dangerously close to the pool, but Clio couldn't see its edge. She tried to kick away from him and ended up pulling both of them into the warm water.

The water felt heavenly. She had never experienced anything like it. It sent warm shocks of pleasure through her body, waking up every nerve it came in contact with.

She came up sputtering, holding the sopping-wet scarf in place on her head.

He laughed. "I have to say, you brought this entirely upon yourself."

She stayed submerged in the water, aware that her thin tunic was now all but transparent.

Tirza stuck her head out of the house. "What is going on out there?" she called.

"Nothing, Tirza. Just Clio being impossible."

"Well, it's late, and Riece, you have to be at the market at dawn tomorrow. So why don't you leave Clio alone and let her come in and eat something?"

"Yes, sister. Your advice, as always, is spot on."

Without hesitating, Riece climbed out of the pool. Clio had to shut her eyes quickly in order to avoid catching a glimpse of his translucent garment.

This only made him laugh. He walked over to the abandoned cloak and wrapped it around his waist. "You can open your innocent eyes now."

She did, to see that he had slicked his wet hair back, and his tunic clung to all of the lines of his chest.

"Don't worry, I won't look," he said. He held out the pelt she had been wearing earlier and turned his head to the side.

Grateful, she climbed out and wrapped herself in it.

"See you tomorrow, Clio." And just like that, all the laughter and all the teasing were gone from his face. He turned around and headed inside.

She ducked back into her bedroom, where Tirza was busy setting down a platter of olives and freshly baked bread. She smiled sweetly at Clio before heading out. "I'm glad you are here. Riece is so different around you. I hope you aren't planning to leave us soon."

Clio returned a weak smile to the girl before she left Clio alone with her thoughts.

She changed into something dry, then sat down on her mat and nibbled at the food in front of her. She was starving, but she couldn't bring herself to enjoy it.

In some ways everything was still the same between them—Clio was still hiding the truth and she was still trying to escape. But in every other way, everything had changed. Little by little more of the real Clio was coming through. He was bringing it out of her. Just when Clio had thought she was in danger of slipping into the cold stone of her sisters, Riece was there to pull out her warmth, to make her laugh and to make her feel. Something about being with Riece was so raw, so exposed, like a tender nerve. Maybe it was because she knew it couldn't last. It was only a matter of time before she had to leave—or worse, before he found out what she really was. Every look, every laugh was numbered.

For the first time, Clio recognized how much it was going to hurt to leave him and how much she wished she could be Clio—the girl, not the Oracle—so that she could let herself fall in love with him.

As if she had any choice in the matter.

CHAPTER TWENTY-THREE

Her dreams were haunted by images of Mannix and girls who had been cut up and were bleeding. Clio ran through rows and rows of brutalized girls that stretched on forever. Sometimes they had the faces of her sisters, sometimes Maia. When she reached the end of one row, she looked down at a girl, but her head was turned to the side. She felt an uncanny pull to this girl, as if she knew who was going to be there. Clio reached a shaking hand out to turn the girl's chin toward her and found that the girl was herself—except instead of white hair, the girl had Clio's old long black hair billowing around her face.

She woke with a start, sweating and gasping for breath. She got up and splashed her face with cool water from the basin on the other side of her room. She passed by the archways. The sun burnt low, a dull pink glow spreading high into the sky.

Sunrise. Riece would soon be leaving for the market. Was he thinking of her?

She shook her head. She couldn't afford to think of him like that. She had to focus on finding a way back to Sheehan, on preventing the horrors she knew were coming. Her wound was well enough now that she couldn't put it off any longer.

She could get out. Easily. With Riece out of the house, it wouldn't be hard to sneak away.

She looked around the room. She should gather supplies. But it didn't feel right. She couldn't take anything from Riece, not anything more than she already had. All she really needed was the thin red scarf to wrap her hair in.

As she was finishing the knot at the back of her head, another Vision smashed into her sight.

She was looking at Riece. Behind him, the sky was streaked with the pink and gold of sunrise. He was walking lightly toward her, a lilt in his step. Clio smiled when she made out the faint sounds of him humming something under his breath, a slight curl on the corners of his lips. He was getting farther and farther away from the house, walking past cramped alleys and streets cloaked in shadows.

Out of one of those spindling alleys, movement caught Clio's eye. Riece continued unaware.

"Hey, Riece, you forgot your blade!" Tirza called from their house. "Honestly, you've all but lost your head since you brought that girl home." She smiled endearingly at him.

At the exact moment when Riece turned to jog back and collect what he had forgotten, the shadow emerged from its hiding spot, and a man wearing a deep red cloak stepped behind Riece, sealing off his retreat.

Riece never heard him; the man moved silently, his robes nothing but the trickle of water in a gentle stream.

Clio watched helplessly as the man took out a long, curved, black blade. Tirza cried out, but it was too late. Moving like the shadow he was, the man swept up to the defenseless Riece and gutted him where he stood.

Clio came back to reality gasping for breath, Tirza's cry still ringing in her ears. Pain lanced her heart at what she had seen, as if she had been the one stabbed.

A cold sweat broke out on Clio's skin. She looked to the sky. Gold was beginning to tinge the edges of the pink glow, just like in her Vision. Riece would be leaving soon. She didn't have much time if she was going to save him.

If. There couldn't be an "if" in this. And yet there was. *If* she went out there and saved him, she would undoubtedly expose herself.

No, she would make this choice for herself. If she let Riece die, she would truly be everything he hated—a manipulator only using people as long as they were convenient. She cared about him, more than she was able to admit.

"I'm still Clio," she mumbled out loud.

The man in her Vision had been hidden in shadows, but when he stepped out, the red of his robes had caught the sunlight. No one but Mannix and those who served him donned that red.

Mannix must have sent that man to kill her, which meant that he knew where she was. Riece was going to die because of her. Because he was in the way.

That power that was growing more and more familiar surged and bubbled in her veins. This Vision was useful. Something she could act on.

Footsteps pounded down the hall, and Tirza emerged breathless in the doorway. Clio realized she must have cried out.

"What is it?" Alarm sparked in her eyes.

"Is Riece here?" Clio asked urgently.

"He just left," Tirza answered slowly, confusion furrowing her brow.

"I don't know how much time we have. I need a weapon, now." Her voice was uncompromising, her body and her features hardened to stone. She could do this, for Riece.

"What? Why? What's going on?" She backed away from Clio, doubt flitting through her eyes.

"By the Deities, if you don't give me a weapon, Riece will die."

Tirza's eyes widened in shock. "I don't understand—how do you know Riece is in danger? He's only gone to the market."

"Tirza, we don't have time for this! Any moment now, he is going to be attacked. He forgot his weapon. Let me help him."

The girl was scared, but Clio didn't have any more time. She brushed into her on her way out of the room and into the main living space. Tirza had lit a fire in the middle of the room, and something was roasting over it. The ceiling was domed, with the middle of the roof left open to let the smoke out. Several archways led out to other rooms in the house, including one to the same courtyard from last night. She didn't have time to check them all. She glanced around, hoping to find the blade that Riece had forgotten.

Panicked, she hurried to the center of the fire pit and dug through the bowls lying at its rim, carelessly throwing things to the side until she found what she was looking for—a thick knife used for cutting meat. It was dull, but it would do.

A heavy black fur served as the entrance to the house. Somewhere beyond it Riece was about to walk into a trap.

"Stay inside," Clio called to Tirza over her shoulder. She sprinted out into the sunlight.

Riece was approaching the place where she knew the assassin to be hidden. A red rustle of cloak flicked out into the light.

"Riece, watch out!" He stopped and turned to her, confused. She barreled onwards, her eyes searching for the man hidden in the shadows. She lowered her voice. "There is a man here to kill me."

Instantly alert, Riece reached for the blade that wasn't at his side, his hand coming up empty. He looked back to the house where he had forgotten it.

Just then, the man leapt from the darkness, brandishing his wickedly curved blade.

Sure that the assassin would jump straight to her, Clio prepared herself for the battle, but it never came. Instead, the man lunged for Riece.

"Um, I don't think he is here for you," Riece huffed as he ducked and dodged the long swipes of the blade.

Odd—why was Riece the target when she was in full view?

Unless, of course, Riece actually was his target. Clio had no time to think of why Mannix might want Riece dead.

Riece slipped as he bent back to avoid a vicious stab. He came up, throwing fistfuls of sand into the eyes of his attacker. "Clio, behind you!" he yelled.

Seemingly out of nowhere, Clio felt something hard collide with her feet, yanking her off her balance, sending her sprawling onto the ground and knocking her knife from her grip and out of reach. Sand slammed down her throat, into her nose and blinding her eyes. Before she could roll over and face her attacker, he was gone, the sound of his pounding footsteps reverberating as he flew toward Riece.

She tried to rise and retrieve the knife, but her feet were tied in something: a thin cord with weights tying both ends down—a bola. Clio recognized it as the weapon used to take down cattle. The weights had tangled the cord up, making it impossible to move her legs.

Wiping the sand from her eyes, Clio could make out Riece fending off two assassins with no weapon. He was fast, a constant blur of motion that Clio could barely make out.

"Boys—" he addressed them casually but out of breath—"Are you aware that by attacking an imperial commander, you are declaring yourself an enemy of the Emperor himself?"

The attacker's only answer was a blade swiping dangerously close to Riece's head.

"I'm guessing that's a 'yes,'" he said under his breath. He took quick steps back as he feinted to the side, drawing their blades wide.

But he was running out of space, and the men were closing in.

Clio desperately worked her fingers, trying to untie the knot, but her eyes kept flashing up to Riece and the danger he was in. Finally, she got the knot undone. She sprang up, scooped up the knife, and darted to help Riece. Grasping the knife firmly in her hand, she jumped one of the men, taking him down from behind. She slammed his face into the sand until he was too disoriented to fight.

Taking advantage of the surprise, Riece slid under the other man, grabbing his blade as he did. He immediately dove into the offensive, slashing down on the assassin, who blocked each blow with a small club.

Clio didn't have time to watch Riece fight. The sounds of his struggle rang in her ears as she straddled the assassin beneath her. Placing the knife on the back of the assassin's neck so he could feel it she yelled, "Why are you here?"

No response.

She slammed his head back down again. "Tell me who your target is, or this is going straight through your neck!" She added some pressure onto the knife in her hand. "Who did Mannix send you after?" she demanded.

Still nothing.

The man rolled to the side, trying to throw Clio off of him. He reached back and grabbed her arm, raking her skin with his nails. Pulling and twisting at the same time, he flipped their positions, and suddenly she was the one on the ground.

To her surprise, he made to get up and just leave her there, but she still held on to a fistful of his robes. As he struggled to get to Riece, who was still trading blows with the other assailant, Clio was left no choice. She sunk the blade deep into the man's chest and kicked him off her before she had to watch the light die in his eyes.

This time, she didn't want to feel the shudder and stop of the heart she had pierced.

It was too late, though. She was already stained bone deep with his blood.

Holding back tears and trying to catch her breath, she turned to Riece. The world had fallen silent in the wake of so much death. In one final slash and a flash of bright red, Riece's assassin fell in a puddle of his own blood. Riece stepped swiftly over the fallen body toward something behind him.

Tirza had run out of the house, bringing Riece's blade. Riece held his sister behind his back, ready to protect her, his face a mixture of confusion and surprise.

Without a word, Clio dropped her knife and fell to her knees next to the body of the man whose life she had just taken.

She couldn't hold back the sobs anymore as she looked upon his face. She had had no choice, she knew that. It was her second kill, and the number hung heavy on her chest, making it hard to breathe. There was no disputing that she was a killer, just like the rest of her family.

The man's mouth fell open in that silent scream of the dead, but something about it was off. Clio peered closer and recoiled at what she saw—

The man's tongue had been cut out.

CHAPTER TWENTY-FOUR

She was shaking, covered in blood, and weeping. Weeping for the man she had just killed and for the thing she was becoming. Weeping because she didn't have many choices left. She couldn't escape killing as long as she was the Oracle.

A blanket was wrapped around her, and she looked up to find Riece staring down at her, his expression one of concern. Blood speckled his face.

"Clio, what...what's going on? Who were those men? How did you know where the first one was hiding?"

She couldn't speak. It was all over. Everything.

Riece turned to Tirza. "What happened? Did she say anything to you?"

"She only said that you were going to die and that she was the only one who could do anything about it," Tirza said, her voice shaking.

Riece and Tirza were only blurry shapes in Clio's teary eyes.

"We should get inside." He came closer, kneeling to help her up.

But Clio scuffled away, unable to take advantage of any more of his kindness now that the truth was nearly out.

"No, I can manage." She put her arm out, holding him at a distance. Blinking the tears from her eyes, she shakily rose to her feet and retreated into the house. She walked straight into her room and took a moment to prepare herself for what was going to come next.

When she turned to Riece and Tirza standing on the threshold, it was with a look of fatal determination.

"Riece," she started, "I knew what was going to happen because I Saw it."

He shook his head, "What do you mean you saw it? You hadn't even left the house. There's no way you could have known where that man was hiding." Skepticism was creeping into his voice, draining the color from his cheeks.

"No." She looked him right in the eye. "I Saw it in a Vision."

He almost smiled. "Stop, Clio. This is absurd. It's not the time to be joking around. Who was that man?"

"He was sent by Mannix, the man who is trying to kill me, the man who ran me out of Sheehan."

"And why is this Mannix trying to kill you?" He was running his fingers through his hair, beginning to pace side to side.

She sighed. "Mannix is trying to kill me because I am the last Oracle." Clio had imagined telling Riece what she really was countless times since she arrived. She imagined feeling relieved, feeling scared, feeling uncertain. She imagined every possible shade of expression from Riece. What she didn't foresee was that saying it out loud would make her feel strong. She didn't want to be this thing, she hated everything it had done to her life, but she couldn't deny the strength that came with the power.

He stopped short. "No, you aren't. That's impossible." His voice was cold, even, only a faint tremor in his hand betraying uncertainty.

Tirza gently interjected, "Riece, she knew something was about to happen. She was in her room, alone, and then she just knew. And she knew that you didn't have a blade on you. How else can you explain—"

But Riece interrupted her. "Stop it! Both of you. This is insane."

Deliberately, without the slightest quiver, Clio raised her hands to the back of her head. He wouldn't believe her, not until she shoved the proof in front of his eyes.

She undid the knot in two quick pulls, letting her snowy white hair cascade around her shoulders.

CHAPTER TWENTY-FIVE

She heard Tirza gasp in astonishment, but Clio's eyes were fixed on Riece, on the horrible exchange of emotions running across his face. First surprise, then anger, then finally and worst of all, hurt and betrayal.

"Please just let me explain. I—I've wanted to tell you." She tried to touch him, as if that could communicate what her words could only clumsily grasp at, but he knocked her hands away.

"Deities, how foolish am I?! I should have known. Should have seen you for what you are. You played me just like that witch played my mother." He turned away from her, but not before Clio caught a glimpse of the hatred hardening his features.

"No, Riece, I promise it's different! I didn't want to lie to you!" Tears stung her eyes, blurring her vision. She wanted to approach him, to run her fingers down his shoulders. She hadn't realized how much she wanted to touch him until now, until she had lost the opportunity altogether.

"And to think I actually...I am such a fool. When were you

planning to use me? Or did you already get what you wanted? Using me to help you escape?"

"No! I swear I wasn't using you. I would never—"

He rounded on her, closing the gap between them like a beast on its prey. For the first time, Clio was afraid of this man. "Would never what, Clio? You lied to me! You pretended you were someone you weren't! Pretended to like me, all just to use me, just like the rest of your kind." He was shaking with anger.

"I didn't tell you the truth about who I am, I admit that. But that's all I lied about. I'm not pretending to like you! Please believe me." She had backed up as she spoke until her foot got tangled in the mess of pelts and blankets that had been her bed. She fell hard onto the floor.

He grabbed her wrists much too tightly and pulled her up to him. His grip burned her skin. "You disgust me. I should turn you in for this."

Tirza came forward, placing her hands on his shoulders. "Riece, please. I think you need to calm down."

Painfully, he released Clio. She fell to the ground, a pathetic puddle at his feet.

No, she would not fall apart. But the revulsion in his eyes was like a club to the gut. She picked herself up. "You won't turn me in."

"Oh, see that in a Vision, did you?" he spat the words at her.

"No, Riece. I don't need a Vision for that. I know you, and you aren't a killer."

"Really?" he scoffed. "I think your second sight has made you a touch blind. Did the man outside slit his own throat? Tell me, what color is my cloak?" He held the glistening gold plumage up to her. "Don't you ever forget that I earned these feathers with the blood of ten men. What's one small girl compared to that?"

"I saved your life."

"Excuse me?" He stepped closer to her.

"I saved your life back there, when I didn't need to."

"You were the reason it was in danger in the first place!" he roared.

"I was planning to leave. To go back to Sheehan, to prevent the things I have Seen there. I didn't need you anymore. The only reason I did what I did for you was out of—"

"Out of what, Clio? What could have possibly motivated someone like you to help me?"

"I—*I care about you, all right?*"

He stood stunned. Clearly he hadn't expected her to say the words. "Oracles don't care about anything or anyone. All they want is power."

"Power? I've been powerless my entire life! The Deities know that all I have *ever* wanted was a normal life, away from all of this. But I never had a choice in the matter! I've never had a choice in anything. I didn't choose to become this!" She pulled her hair. "I don't get to choose what it is they show me! What I do get to decide is how I act on it. Today they showed me your death, and I made the choice to stop it.

"So fine, turn me in for it. It doesn't matter to me. All it will be is another thing I have no control over." She raised her hands, offering her wrists to him.

"Riece, stop." Tirza pushed Clio's prone hands down.

"You were too young when she took our parents from us, but I remember everything! I remember trying to comfort my scared baby sister every night when I knew that they were never coming back." He was staring at Tirza, and Clio could see all the unresolved pain that swam in his eyes. "Our mother served that woman all her life. Even when the Oracle was blind and had no powers whatsoever, our mother did her bidding. And for what end? The Deities weren't speaking to her anymore, and yet she still had our mother do her dirty work. The Oracle put *our* mother in danger rather than risk her fragile and precious daughter. Isn't that how it's supposed to be?" He turned to Clio. "The Oracle's daughters are her Vessels, right? They spy and kill for her."

Clio nodded, not wanting to hear the rest of this story.

"But the Oracle's eldest daughter died and her second was too weak for killing, so the Oracle had to find someone else for the job."

"Riece, please don't. I know what happened." Tirza had a foreign coldness in her voice.

"I'm not telling *you* all this. It's for her." He nodded at Clio. "So she knows just how familiar I am with her kind. So she understands why I'm going to leave her for dead with the only regret that I should have let her die on that pyramid."

He wasn't looking at Clio as he spoke, and Clio was glad for it. The unadulterated hate in his words cut deeper than any blade. She wanted him to kill her there. It would be better than having to hear this.

"So what happened next, Tirza?" Riece asked venomously.

But Tirza wouldn't answer.

"Our mother found something out about the Oracle. Found out about a great crime she had committed against the Emperor. And the Oracle had her, our father, and our older brother killed when she found out that our mother had gone to the Emperor. She would have killed us too if the Emperor hadn't gotten to her first."

Tirza had tears silently streaming down her face. "That Oracle is dead, brother. Do not let the sins of one stain another."

"You don't understand." He was breathing heavily, and his foot kicked agitatedly into the sand below his feet.

"Look at Clio. Really look at her! Do you see a heartless manipulator? Because all I see is a scared 15-year-old girl. A girl who just saved your life! You haven't let anyone into your heart since our parents died. And that's fine, I understand. You had to grow up too much, too soon. But since you met Clio, you have been different. Don't pretend it's not true. I know you, Riece. Better than anyone. And I know that if you in any way cause harm to this girl you will be broken forever."

His face softened as she spoke.

"I'm a killer, Tirz. It's what I do." But he was looking at Clio with an unendurable rawness in his voice that made her tremble. His long fingers fidgeted with one of the gold feathers coming loose from his cloak.

Clio knew that look. It was a perfect reflection of the remorse that she herself felt.

"But with her around," Tirza gestured to Clio, "you are so much more than that."

He fell silent, and Clio took her chance to explain.

"Riece, I inherited the Sight only days before I met you. I grew up in my mother's temple, but she never taught me anything about being an Oracle. I watched her my whole life, and believe me when I say that I have always hated Oracles more than you do. I didn't even believe in her powers until I was given my first Vision. I was made to watch as my sisters went out to do horrible things for her. I had to watch as they were so torn apart by it all that they came back hollow and faded. I know what it is like to lose someone you love to an Oracle.

"But none of that kept me from becoming one. I hardly know what to do with what I See. I could barely admit to myself that I had become the Oracle—that I was now going to have to act on the very things I hated my mother for doing. So how could I have told my captor I was the Oracle, no matter how much I might have liked him?" She could see the rage dimming in his eyes, the willingness to believe what she was saying beginning to grow.

He studied her, then dropped his head into his hands. "I just can't…" he mumbled.

"If you turn me in now, it won't only mean my death, but—" she stopped, unsure how say it now that he was listening. "Riece, I am given Visions of horrible things that are to come. Like your death,

I've seen other people in danger, and I am the only one who can do something about it. If you turn me in, I can't do anything to stop Mannix."

"What is this Mannix doing that you have to stop?" Riece looked up to meet her eyes. Something flickered in his gaze, a gentle light.

"I have been Seeing him doing...horrible things in Sheehan."

"Like what?" Tirza asked.

"I don't know. It's hard to—well, I don't yet fully understand these Visions. I saw him take a girl. He did things to her, unnatural, inhuman things. I don't know what he is planning, but I think he wants me—the Oracle—probably to torture and then kill. And he will continue to hurt people, so I can't ignore it. I can't just sit by while a man like that has control of Sheehan."

"Clio, why didn't your mother prepare you for this?" Tirza asked.

"We don't start training until we are 16 years old, and I had three older sisters. I was never supposed to inherit the Sight."

"*Had* three sisters?" Riece looked up from his hands.

"My mother and two of my sisters were killed the day before I met you. That's why the Sight passed to me. My first Vision was Seeing all of them get their throats slit in the night." Her voice was surprising still.

Sympathy finally broke through in his gaze, but the anger was still there too, boiling just under the surface.

"Why did you come here?"

"My third sister, Ali. Mannix took her and brought her here. You must remember her. I had no choice. I had to try to find her and save her. But she died atop your pyramid. I could do nothing as that priest cut out her heart for your city to watch.

"Mannix slaughtered my family, and now he is the king regent in Sheehan. He would have had me killed too if he had found me alive. I Saw him come here, to your pyramid to ask you about me. I think he knows I'm here, or at least he has a pretty good idea." She shivered as she remembered her last Vision of him.

"But the only thing I absolutely know for sure is that he wants me dead. It was sheer chance that I wasn't home when he had his men butcher my family. That's why I thought that the assassin he sent today was for me, but obviously, he was ordered to kill you. I don't know why. I haven't been able to make sense of it yet."

"For someone who can see the future, you certainly seem to run into a lot of trouble," Riece spoke almost in his old teasing way.

"Like I said, I'm new to this. Fumbling in the dark, so to speak."

"How can you be sure he was one of Mannix's men?" he asked.

"It's his color. I've never seen anyone but his court wear those robes. But I never knew that he cut out their tongues."

Riece stiffened. "What did you say?"

"That guy, his tongue was cut out. It's why I couldn't get him to answer my question."

"Where does Mannix come from?" Riece was pacing again, agitated.

"None of us know. He showed up in Sheehan a couple years ago. Why?"

"Because in all of my travels, the only men I have known to cut out their tongues are the Untouched."

"But…But Mannix couldn't be Untouched. He speaks our tongue, he is well studied, he can even read and write…"

"I'm not saying he is. I'm just telling you what I know."

"Maybe Mannix buys his men. Is that even possible? Buying the Untouched? I thought they didn't value gold."

"They don't. All they barter in is flesh. It's the only thing that means anything to them."

"I saw him give them a girl—the one he had been torturing. And he had more girls too. Do you think he is paying them with people?" The thought was so disturbing Clio felt her stomach lurch.

"If he is, then he is going to need more," Riece said.

Tirza's voice pulled Clio's gaze from Riece. "Good thing you are out of Sheehan."

Clio gave Tirza a weak smile. "I'm going back as soon as I can." The conviction in her voice surprised even Clio.

"What can *you* possibly do to stop this man? As the regent, he is too powerful to be stopped by one girl," Riece said.

"What choice do I have? I have to! I can't See these things and not do anything about it. I think the Deities are showing me so that I will go. If Mannix is somehow using the Untouched…I can't leave Sheehan to him. And it's not just one girl. I have Derik to help me."

A shadow crossed Riece's face. "Who?"

"Derik. He is the prince there, but he should be king. Mannix took the throne from him. Derik helped me escape the city. I'm afraid Mannix has imprisoned him. Maybe Mannix is torturing him, too."

A dry laugh escaped Riece's lips. "No. He's not imprisoned. I know where he is."

"How do you know that? Where?" Clio could hear the desperation in her own voice.

"He arrives in Morek tonight. I've been preparing for his arrival for days."

CHAPTER TWENTY-SIX

Clio's heart skipped a beat.

Riece continued, "The Emperor invited him here as a sort of show of friendship with the new king."

"But Mannix is in control." She was still breathless at the thought that Derik might be all right, that he might be coming to her. It sounded in her voice.

Riece's eyes narrowed—clearly aware of Clio's reaction, and he didn't approve.

"I don't think Mannix wants the Emperor to think that. Not yet, anyway."

"Will Mannix be with him? He knows I am here, otherwise he wouldn't have tried to kill you."

"I don't know. All they told us was that the new king, along with his party, will be here for a feast tonight. I don't know who makes up that party. But if what you are telling me is true, then I can't imagine that Mannix would want to leave Sheehan."

She processed that. "If he is here, then I will just have to be careful. I can't pass up the chance to speak to Derik. I have to tell him what Mannix is doing." She didn't say what she really felt—that she had to see him again because she felt a connection to him that she couldn't explain. That the prospect of seeing him again had sent a not unwelcome thrill through Clio's body. She was going to see Derik again, the one person in all the world on whom she could depend, who cared about her for who she really was.

"I could try to talk to him tonight…" Riece suggested.

She shot him a hesitant smile. Somehow this man who felt betrayed by her was still willing to help her. Maybe Derik wasn't the only one who cared about her. But she couldn't fully let her thoughts go there.

"Well, that's that, then." Tirza rose, clearly sensing that Riece's rage had passed. Her eyes darted between Clio and Riece. "Come on. You two really ought to eat something."

She pulled the hanging pelt aside and motioned for them to walk into the room with the fire.

"I have to deal with the bodies first," Riece said.

"Let me help you." The thought of seeing those grimacing, cold faces filled Clio with guilt and disgust.

Riece shook his head. "My men will be coming. It wouldn't be good for them to see you." He left before Clio could argue.

But he was right.

Tirza sat silently before the fire, preparing their meal. Clio knew she would never be able to eat it. Not while she could still feel the memory of her blade cutting flesh.

Instead, she retreated to her own room to clean off the blood. No matter how much she scrubbed, she couldn't seem to keep her hands clean. She wondered if this would be her life now, always cleaning away the day's violence.

Riece returned sooner than Clio would have liked—she still didn't know how to approach him—but Tirza was adamant that they try to eat something. Tirza pulled Clio back into the main room, waved her hand at the meat roasting over the fire, and then ducked behind another hanging pelt into what must have been her room, leaving Riece and Clio uncomfortably alone.

Stiffly, Riece took a seat near the fire. Clio did the same, sure to keep a decent amount of space between them.

They sat for a moment, unsure of what do to. Riece seemed not to hate her anymore, but Clio worried that one wrong word might send him over the edge again. She barely moved a muscle, just waited for him to make the next move.

"I didn't know that you had lost your family. I'm sorry," he said, and he looked it.

She nodded. "Honestly, they stopped being my family a long time ago."

"How's that?"

"I don't need to tell you about how much an Oracle prizes her calling over people." She saw the scar in his neck tighten across his skin. "It was the same with her own daughters."

He remained silent for a long time, and Clio couldn't tell if he was falling back into his former hatred. But finally he spoke. "The

Oracle here did everything to protect her daughter. It was why she took my mother on as a Vessel."

"You said her daughter was too weak to be a Vessel." The thought of someone who didn't share in the Oracle's sacred blood serving as a Vessel felt entirely foreign to Clio.

He nodded. "There was something not right with that girl. I was only a boy when I knew her, but she—well, I've never seen anyone as peculiar. After the Oracle's first daughter was killed, all she was left with was this weak and sickly girl. No amount of training would have made her ready for anything but getting killed, and I don't think the Oracle wanted to risk losing her only blood left. By then she was old and blind and didn't have much power left. So she used my mom instead."

"What happened to the youngest daughter when the Oracle was sacrificed?" Clio asked.

"She wandered off, probably died in the desert. That girl didn't have it in her to survive on her own. I spent a while looking for her. I thought she might have inherited the Sight, or claimed to, but I never found her."

"Riece—I'm so sorry about what happened to your family. I just, I know how hard it must be for you to look at me like this."

"It's not as hard as I want it to be." His eyes found hers between the flickering sparks of the fire.

The moment lasted only a heartbeat, but it was enough to steal the air from Clio's lungs.

He pulled his gaze from hers before she could say anything

more. "Did Mannix kill the king?" he asked.

His question surprised her. "I don't know. He did have the most to gain from his death. But he claims that the Oracle and her Vessels—my sisters—are responsible."

"And what do you think?"

Her eyes fell. "I don't know. Maybe they did. It doesn't really matter. There's nothing I can do about it. I don't want to be like them…but sometimes I'm afraid that it's already too late."

They fell silent again, until finally, Riece reached forward and took the meat out of the flames. He looked around, digging in the soot and sand for something.

"Umm," Clio hesitated.

"Yes?" He looked up from his search, one eyebrow raised.

"The um, blade…" she trailed off, unable to say that she had taken their cleaver in order to kill a man outside.

"Ahh, yes," he nearly chuckled. "I should know by now that if there is a weapon around, you will find it." For a moment, the old Riece was back, the Riece who joked with her in the infirmary, the one who had told her about his past.

He rose and walked over to the basin, where he pulled out another blade. After cutting up and preparing the food, he handed her a portion.

They ate in silence. The food tasted like ash in her mouth. Clio tried to eat as quickly as possible without thinking about what she had done that day.

When she had finished, she rose to wash her hands. As she

walked by Riece, still crouched on the ground, his hand shot out and grabbed her wrist.

His touch was so sudden and so unexpected that all Clio could do was gape at him. His eyes, obscured behind some stray strands of unruly brown hair, burned with a heated intensity.

"What you did for me, you didn't have to. That man would have killed me…and then Tirza."

Slowly, she knelt at his side. His hand stayed locked around her wrist. "I did have to. I owe you everything. I'm sorry that I lied to you. I promise that I won't anymore." Her hair slipped over her shoulder, creating a shimmering white barrier between their faces.

He flinched at the sight. The movement was so slight, but it was enough to break the moment. She slipped her wrist out of his grasp and walked noiselessly over to the water basin.

"You really plan to go back there?" He spoke to her from behind, neither of them turning to face the other.

"I have to. I am so thankful that you are willing to talk to Derik for me, I am. But it's not enough. I have to speak with him about what I've Seen. I don't know where Mannix is keeping the girls, but if I can get in a room with Derik, maybe between us we can figure it out." She dunked her hands in the cool water. "I need to work out a way to go back with him." Her voice was quiet, barely louder than the lapping of the water she disturbed in the basin.

"You can't go back. It's not safe."

She turned to see him standing rigidly behind her. "It's not safe for me anywhere, Riece." She smiled sadly at him.

"I can bring back a message from him." Conflict raged in his expression. It seemed as if he could barely bring himself to look at her face. And yet, she could sense a fierce protectiveness from him. He truly was worried about what would happen to her if she returned home.

"I have to see him."

And there it was. The truth, and he felt the weight of her words as much as she.

"Who is he to you?" For the first time his tone was vulnerable.

"He's my oldest friend in the world. He is the only one I have left."

"That's not true." When he looked up at her, his eyes carried the edges of a promise. "Plus, what has he even done for you? Why hasn't he come for you yet? You could very easily have died up there on that pyramid."

"I don't know. He said he would, but—I don't think he ever suspected that I could have been in such immediate danger."

"Then your friend is a fool. How could he expect anything different when you come into this city as a slave?"

"Well," she said, "you see, I kind of turned myself into a slave. It was the only way I could think of to gain entry into the city." Saying it out loud made her realize just how foolish her plan had been.

He let out a howl of laughter. "By the Deities, Clio, you have got to be the most cocky human being in the world. To think you could actually escape!"

She had to join in in the laughter. "I did, didn't I?"

"Not without some much needed assistance, I might add."

"I do appreciate that, you know."

"Riece," Tirza called from the next room. She appeared on the threshold. "I take it you aren't bringing anyone to the feast with you tonight?" She had a calculating look in her eye.

"Tirza…" He stretched her name out like a groan.

She came in and sat down next to Clio. "If you see Derik, then you two can try to find a way to stop Mannix, right?"

"Eavesdropping is not very becoming, Tirz."

But Tirza just rolled her eyes, and Riece smiled.

"Yes, it would definitely be a start. I don't know how much time we have," Clio said.

Tirza turned to Riece. "So I've thought of a way to repay Clio for saving our lives."

"Whatever could that be?" Riece asked. The suspicious glint in his eyes said he knew exactly what Tirza had planned.

"Really, Tirza, it's not necessary," said Clio. "Riece saved my life too, you know."

Tirza shook her head. "Clio wants to see her old friend, and he's going to be at the feast tonight. Riece, you happen to be invited to the feast, and everyone always expects that you will bring someone…" She bit her lip as a sly smile spread across her face.

Clio felt Riece stiffen next to her.

"Absolutely not, Tirza." His voice was almost a low growl.

"I think you should bring Clio with you. You know, as your companion." Tirza looked knowingly at her brother.

Riece turned to her, eyes narrowed. "Have you completely lost your mind, sister?"

Clio gaped. "Companion?"

"She means have you pose as my lover," Riece clarified.

Clio flushed scarlet.

"No one would suspect a thing!" Tirza argued. "And that way she could get a chance to talk to her friend. And you—"

But Riece cut her off with a look. "Drop it."

"Riece, if you wanted an evening with me, you should have asked me yourself instead of having your sister do it for you." Clio enjoyed teasing him. The look on his face was too precious.

"Riece, you have to get over your embarrassment." Tirza nudged him. "Clio has as good as said that this could be the difference between life and death for a lot of innocent people."

He stood there, gaping at both his sister and Clio. He ran his fingers through his ruffled hair. "To you"—he pointed at Tirza—"That is a horrible plan for so many reasons. First of all, Clio is wanted for murder and escape, remember? Everyone's searching for the Shadow. And on top of that, she is the Deities-forsaken Oracle! Not only does Sheehan want her for that, but I don't think the Emperor has changed his position on their kind. Parading her in front of the Emperor, to say nothing of this Mannix guy, is a sure means of getting her killed."

He turned to Clio. "And to you," he said. "I am perfectly capable of successfully courting women on my own, thank you. And I am still unsure of you, so don't you start with that audacious charm of yours."

Clio turned an even brighter red.

Tirza laughed. "You two really are endlessly entertaining."

An exasperated smile parted Riece's lips. "Well, as long as someone is enjoying this disaster."

"Come on. She isn't even recognizable when she is clean. No one would suspect that she is the Shadow, especially if she is on your arm."

"Let's get this straight. Only I get to decide who is on my arm— or on my anything else, for that matter. And I can't possibly walk into the palace with a girl with hair like that." He pointed to Clio's head. "If the Emperor finds out what we have done for her, it won't matter that I once saved his life."

"Don't be thick. I'll dye her hair. I think red would be sufficiently different from both her Oracle white and her Shadow black. No one will look twice at her."

"Riece, please," Clio begged. "I have to do everything I can to stop Mannix."

His eyes locked on hers, and she could see his will weakening.

"Plus," Tirza added, "how much trouble can you get into with someone who can see the future?"

"Well actually..." Clio began, meaning to tell them about how she couldn't see her own fate, but Riece cut her off.

"A lot." He rose to walk away but then threw up his hands, defeated. "Fine. You get her ready. But if I think she doesn't look different enough, then I am cancelling this whole ill-begotten plan."

Tirza clapped her hands together and ran toward her brother, squeezing him tight in a hug.

Riece softened in her arms. "Whatever makes you happy, little sister."

Clio sat stunned. If someone had asked when she woke up this morning how she thought she would be spending the day, she never would have predicted this. If anything, she thought the best she could hope for would be traveling through the night back to Sheehan.

But now, now she was going to spend the evening with Riece, without lying to him, and if the Deities were with her she would be get to speak with Derik as well.

For some reason, the thought of Derik and Riece in the same room together made Clio a bit nervous, but she pushed the feeling aside. She couldn't worry about sorting out her own feelings when she had a duty to perform. For once she was actually grateful of the distraction of her Visions.

CHAPTER TWENTY-SEVEN

"Well, we are going to have to get to work," Tirza chirped excitedly. She took a long look at Clio. "First thing's first, though. You truly need to wash up. It would be a miracle if you could get through just one day without being covered in every filth imaginable."

Clio looked down at herself and wasn't surprised to see more dirt caking her legs. "Don't I know it," she murmured as she headed back to her room.

Before Clio could even properly wash and redress, Tirza had burst into her room carrying a mountain of colorful wraps and silks. She dropped them on the floor and darted out of the room again, only to return with a couple pails of water and a small, intricately decorated chest.

"Whaa—" Clio started, but Tirza raised a hand to stop her.

"We all agreed the only way you are going tonight is if you look the part."

"But surely all of this"—Clio dug through the fine silks lying on the floor—"is a little much?" She raised her eyes incredulously to Tirza, who only looked amused.

"Deities, you are so much like my brother." Tirza rolled her eyes. "Now, you are going to look nice tonight, and there's nothing you—or Riece, for that matter—can do to stop it." She walked over to Clio and led her to a small, wooden stool in front of the pail of water she had brought in. "Now sit," she commanded.

Before she knew what was happening, Clio found herself dunking her head into a sweet-smelling burgundy concoction.

"It never shows up in my dark hair, but I think it's really going to come through in yours." Tirza had provided a steady flow of high-pitched conversation throughout the whole ordeal. Clio pulled her hair out of the bowl and red droplets showered her feet. Tirza's eyes lit up.

"You do this often? Make girls up for parties?"

"Are you kidding me?" Tirza scoffed. "Riece never lets me have guests over. He's not exactly the trusting type, you know."

Clio fidgeted in her seat. She hadn't helped matters much.

"Bringing you here was big. When he saw that you were going to be all right, he completely changed. It was like seeing a new man. He was always so serious. And so glum. I tell him over and over he should ask for a new post. Shepherding those girls to the slaughter weighs on him awfully hard, but he says that he's the only man for it."

"He's right. Riece makes sure the girls aren't treated badly in the days before their death. I shudder to think about how other men in his position might take advantage of a bunch of scared and weak girls."

"That sounds like Riece, all right. Always sacrificing his well-being for some noble cause. It wears on him, though. I know it does." She smiled at Clio. "But when he brought you back, it was different. He kept going on about how you were going to pull through because you were a fighter. He's used to people dying on him, so I think he only lets himself care about the tough ones."

"I'm not that tough," Clio said. "All this stuff just sort of happened to me. I'm not like Riece." He didn't run away from anything. He suffered everyday at the pyramid, and yet he stayed because he had the chance to help the girls. Clio knew she shouldn't have abandoned her family. If she were truly brave, she wouldn't have run away from home. She would have submitted to her destiny willingly and done everything she could to protect Ali. It had been childish, Clio recognized that. But she was only fifteen. Now she felt so much older.

Tirza laughed. "You know, my brother would say the same about himself." She toweled away the glistening red dye that was threatening to drop from Clio's sopping hair, then clapped her hands and squealed in delight. "All right, now we just have to dress up the rest of you."

The process was long and tiring, taking much more of the day than Clio had thought possible. After what felt like ages, Clio was looking at herself in a tarnished mirror. Her hair was now blood red.

Tirza had spent hours twisting Clio's hair into tight spiraling ringlets that trailed down her neck. Inside each of these spirals, Tirza had knotted in long, delicate strands of what could only be pure gold. They hung, mingling and twirling with the red, giving off an eye-catching sparkle. All of Clio's hair was pulled over so that it draped down her left shoulder, leaving the right side of her neck completely bare.

Clio stared at herself with eyes wide. She felt ridiculous. With all of the changes she had been through in the past couple of days, she no longer had a mental image of her own appearance. Was she the dark-haired girl who just wanted out of her destiny? The snowy white-headed Oracle? The dirt-stained warrior? Or was she this golden red siren?

Tirza had pulled out a midnight blue, silk wrap that clung much too tightly to Clio's muscular curves. It draped down each shoulder and converged at her waist into a straight skirt, leaving much of her sides and back bare. Tirza had to keep pulling Clio's hands down. Her instinct was to cover the exposed skin, especially the sweeping drop in her neckline.

"Truly, Tirza, I think this is a bit much. Or should I say, not enough?" She eyed her bare back.

Tirza was practically glowing with pride behind her.

"Don't be ridiculous, Clio. You are going to be on the arm of the youngest commander in history. You have to look the part." She knelt down and opened the small chest she had brought in. "One last touch," she said more to herself than to Clio as she pulled out two long, dangling earrings that sparkled with every color in the rainbow.

"What *are* those?" Clio came forward to get a better look.

"You've never seen a diamond before? Come on, here," she motioned to Clio to sit in front of her. "They were our mother's." She put them on Clio. The earrings dangled from Clio's ears and brushed along her neck, giving off the effect of falling, glistening droplets of water.

"I really don't think I should wear these."

But Tirza insisted. "I never have anywhere nice enough to wear them. Plus, Riece will like them." The young girl's eyes held a knowing look.

"Tirza, what exactly are you trying to do here?" Clio pulled her eyes away from the enchanting jewels to search Tirza's expression.

She smirked. "Oh, just making you unrecognizable, like Riece requested."

Hesitantly, Clio stepped out of the bedroom. Riece was standing, facing away from her. He was wearing his commander's regalia, his golden cloak hanging powerfully off his shoulders. As he turned, Clio could see that his chest was decorated in swirling blue and black paint that curled into captivating patterns that bespoke delicacy and grace. Placed as they were along the hard and rigidly defined lines of Riece's abdomen and chest, however, the overall impression was one of intimidation, strength and power.

The lines danced all the way up his neck and met in a dramatic peak on his forehead, just below the stray strands of brown hair that always seemed to fall into his eyes.

As her eyes traveled up his body and finally met his face, his eyes did the same. When their eyes met, his were wide with astonishment.

"Deities, Clio, you look…"

"Clean?" she teased.

Her heart warmed when he let out a laugh. "Actually, I was going to go with beautiful on this one, although cleanliness is certainly an accurate attribute as well."

"Think I'm sufficiently disguised?"

"Hmm, I'll need a closer look." His eyes were smoldering as he approached her. Gently, he lifted her arms out away from her so that he could take in her whole frame. "I think Tirza did a fine job. Although she did fail in one respect."

"What?" Her breath caught as he leaned in closer until his breath tickled the bare side of her head.

"She promised that no one would look twice at you."

Shyly, she stepped back from him. Her head was spinning, floating, as if she were light as air. As she pulled herself from his dark eyes, she felt herself grounded again.

"Well, Commander, what is our story tonight?"

"Your accent gives you away as a Sheehan—"

"—I do not have an accent!"

"I assure you that you do."

"What is it like?"

"You swallow your R's more and tend to put some extra space between your consonants. It's actually somewhat charming, but unfortunately, it clearly marks you as Sheehan. I'm thinking that I met you outside the city the last time I was escorting the Emperor."

"And couldn't stay away ever since." She clasped her hands together over her heart in mock sentiment.

He flashed her a grin. "Now, let's not get too carried away."

They had to walk through the winding streets of Morek to get to the palace. The city buzzed with a nighttime energy that Sheehan, with all its lepers and paupers, never had. Everywhere Clio turned, people were gathered together in each other's homes, completely at ease. As they walked, Clio realized they were ascending. Finally they reached a wide road, completely bare except for rows of slave men decked in gold and jewel piercings, each bearing a large torch to light the way up to the palace. The palace itself rose high into the stars, its walls impossibly glittering in the moonlight. Row upon row of steps led up to glowing arches. What was most impressive, however, was the shimmering river that surrounded it all. The reflection of the night's sky in the slow and steady movement of its waters gave the palace the appearance of floating in the sky.

Riece must have heard her breath catch in her lungs, because he turned to her. "Quite a sight, isn't it?"

"I've never seen anything like it." Her voice was hushed in veneration.

"You should see the towers of Cearo. They sparkle ruby red in the night."

Her smile faded. "I would like that very much." Her odds of

surviving long enough to travel all the way to Cearo were slim to none.

"Well, let's make our entrance, shall we?" He clasped her hand in his and led her across a great bridge over the water.

CHAPTER TWENTY-EIGHT

Clio took a deep breath as she crossed the threshold into the palace, but let it all out when her eyes landed on the breathtaking display before her. Everything was gold. Gold of every color and sheen filled the room toe to tip. She was lost in utter amazement as she gazed at the intricately carved patterns on the ceiling: reddish gold mixed with yellow gold in a stunning recreation of the sunlight breaking through the mountain pass.

A gentle pressure on her hand brought her back to focus. That was when she noticed a hush had descended on the entire room. People decked out in glittering jewels and extravagant headpieces were staring at her and Riece. They stood frozen. For one horrible moment, she thought that they somehow knew who she was, what she was.

That was until she realized that most of their gazes were darting between herself and Riece. She turned to look up at Riece and was stunned to see that characteristic smirk slyly creeping across his face.

"Wha—" she started but was interrupted as a jovial fat man

approached and clapped Riece on the back.

"Riece, my boy! Looks like you've stolen the evening. Who is the lovely creature who has finally tempted our most sought-after bachelor?"

Clio's mouth must have been hanging open, because Riece flashed her a satisfied grin before responding to the man.

"Erik, this is Sahi. Sahi, this is Erik, the brother of the Emperor."

Clio was dimly aware that the chatter had restarted in the room around them.

"So glad to meet you!" Erik spoke a little too loudly, and his face was ruddy with drink. He took her hand and laid a very wet kiss on it, refusing to relinquish it.

Clio laughed. "Careful, Riece. I think this one wants to steal me away."

"A foreign girl!" Erik exclaimed as Riece gently took her hand back from his clasp. "Sheehan? You know, just the other day there was a curious incident involving a slave from your city—"

Uncomfortable with the course of the conversation, Riece interjected. "Erik, this is no time to discuss such things."

"Of course, Commander." Erik's gaze fell back on Clio. "You are truly a brave young woman, coming here with this man."

Clio felt every muscle in her body tighten. "What do you mean?" Her eyes flew nervously to Riece, hoping that this all hadn't been some elaborate plan to capture her.

Erik gave a hearty guffaw. "That is just like Riece, to not explain what your presence on his arm would mean to the people of Morek."

"It *shouldn't* mean anything to the people of Morek," Riece growled.

"Yes, well, you can't keep the people from obsessing over the city's greatest and best-looking hero, can you?" He turned to Clio with a sincere smile. "Since this fellow has obviously kept so tight-lipped about himself, let me fill you in. Every girl here has dreamed of winning the warrior Riece for herself ever since he single-handedly saved the Emperor's life. But Riece, villain that he is, has refused them all, at least publicly." He winked at Riece. "So you can't blame us for being surprised when we find this foreign flower of a girl who has finally won him."

She looked to Riece. "Is this true? You're famous?"

He just shrugged and pulled her hand up to his outraised arm, patting it there. "Erik, you have been so kind as to enlighten my guest as to my notoriety, but you must excuse us. We have rounds to make, you know." With that, he swept her across the room.

Out of the corner of her mouth she whispered, "So you're famous because you saved the Emperor?"

"Well, that's only part of it. I'm famous because I saved the Emperor *and* I am ridiculously good looking. And amazingly charming."

"And stunningly obnoxious about it," she said.

"That wasn't a denial."

They made their way through the enormous room. Guests stood over mats on the ground laid out with the finest meats and fruits, more food than Clio had ever seen, but she was the only one looking at any of it. Whenever they passed a group of chattering people, they would suddenly fall silent, eyeing Clio until she was out of sight.

Just then, they approached a great throne gilded in gold and jewels. Clio and Riece made their way slowly down a walkway lined with unmoving warriors dressed in gold-plated armor with the same swirling pattern of paints crisscrossing along their arms and neck. Stunning as it all was, it was the man sitting on the throne who commanded all the attention.

Clio didn't need Riece to tell her that this was the Emperor. She looked around to see if Derik was nearby, but she couldn't spot him.

"Your highness." Riece sank to one knee and bent his head in supplication. The Emperor looked approvingly down at him. Clio could see a father's love in his light brown eyes.

"There's no need for that." The man's voice came out in a rasping whisper. Clio could make out a thick scar encircling the man's neck. In shape it was identical to Riece's, but Clio could tell that the Emperor's scar had done much more damage. The man's tone was so soft but still carried an unnamable strength and power. Riece rose to help the man rise from the throne and descend the steps. He moved with a painful limp. Clio could only guess which injuries came from war and which came from his time as a captive of the Untouched.

"Your highness, this is Sahi, a merchant's daughter from Sheehan."

The man raised his eyebrow at Riece before turning back to her. She felt his eyes piercing her. This was the man responsible for the brutal death of the Oracle of Morek. The man who told his people that the Deities preferred sacrifice to Oracles. The man who would order her execution if he were to find out who she really was. She bowed to him, hoping he wouldn't see through her disguise.

"No guest of Riece's need bow, my dear." She looked up and found his eyes boring into her. "You are absolutely breathtaking, Sahi."

For some reason, Clio found herself happy to have won this man's approval. There was a grandeur to the man, glory born in victories he had clearly won himself. She had no doubts as to how he had managed to amass such an empire in his lifetime. Clio found it hard to remind herself that this majestic man was her enemy.

The Emperor offered Clio his arm. She took it, and he slowly led them deeper into the room. The greatness of the foyer tapered into an elegant open hallway. On either side, archways lined the walls, leaving the room completely exposed to the night. But it was right that way. No amount of gold could be more impressive, more indicative of this city's power than the view offered by these archways. One side looked down on the gleaming and glistening city of Morek; the other faced out over the edge of the mountain.

Breath caught in Clio's throat as she made out the distant flickering of firelight in Sheehan. To look upon it like this was both magnificent and terrifying. There it was, so small, so defenseless— utterly prostrate to the great power lording above it on this mountain. Beyond Sheehan, she could make out more cities, more territories belonging to the Emperor at her side.

The Emperor noted her awe. "What do you think of our city? Is this your first time here?"

Clio bit the inside of her cheek. Lying to the Emperor's face was not something she had expected to do tonight.

"It's the most beautiful place I have ever seen, your highness," she said truthfully.

He smiled warmly at her, his eyes twinkling in the light. "Your beauty glows spectacularly here. I do hope you intend to stay."

"I would like that, sir." Clio was surprised to find that this wasn't a complete lie. She would like to stay in Morek. Riece, as infuriating as he was, was kind, and Tirza reminded Clio of the Ali before all this started—the girl who Clio could stay up all night talking about absolutely nothing and loving every moment of it. To stay here with these people, in this beautiful place, would be the life that she had dreamed of all those nights she spent desperately hoping to escape her grim fate.

With a pang, she remembered that she had not escaped that fate. She could never stay here because she would never be wanted here—not as she truly was, not as the Oracle.

And those lights in the distance, flickering but there, called to her. She liked it here, but she didn't belong here. It was ironic how much she had always yearned for escape, and yet here she was finding that gentle tug of wanting at her heart, pulling her to go back.

She lingered in front of the archway, gazing upon Sheehan, upon what she finally realized was her home.

"Your city." He nodded at what she was already fixated on. "It has true potential. You yourself are a sign of the worth that can be culled from that dust." His words were a jab. He was wrong. Worth needn't be culled from Sheehan; Sheehan already had it in abundance. It was there in the honesty of sunbaked clay, in the simplicity of a city held together not with an army but with a common love of old traditions and older land. Those in Sheehan would never cheer at the butchering of foreign girls as an offering to the Deities. Death was not a thing of revelry for a people who had watched their own numbers slowly dwindle under the blades of others.

He continued, "You see, Sheehan is more centrally located in the Empire than Morek. See how all the other cities circle around it? With some restructuring, it could be reborn as a true sister to Morek."

She knew what that meant—it would be destroyed, but in a subtle way, a way that seemed like improvement. Yes, this improvement would bring with it more gold, but also more warriors, more sacrifices.

"You would like to see that for your city, I'm sure." It wasn't a question. "So then I must ask something of you, my dear."

Riece, walking on Clio's other side, stiffened at the Emperor's words.

"In order to do this, to help your homeland, I need a man there. Someone to make sure that my plans are being enacted, someone I can trust with my very life—because this Empire is my legacy, if not my life itself.

"Such a man is, of course, very rare. So imagine my frustration when I find such a man—and what's more, he is already in my service." He was looking at Riece, who was pointedly looking out the archway.

"Undoubtedly, you, dear Sahi, must have an even better hold on my man's heart than I. And so I must entreat you to beg Riece to go home with you and do this for me. I feel that this request would have much more favorable results coming out of a mouth so delicately sculpted as yours."

"Your highness," Riece tried to interject.

"Now, now, Riece, I am having a word with your guest. You see, Sahi, I don't think overseeing the slave prison is a duty that fully utilizes Riece's potential. I've seen him single-handedly take down ten men. He saved my life." The Emperor's hands glided up to the scar around his neck. "Skill like that must be put to good use—and, well, a prison doesn't allow him the *opportunity* to be who he really is."

A killer, Clio thought. He saw Riece as nothing more than a killer.

"You must have heard about the little stunt one of your city's slaves pulled atop our pyramid?" His eyes were prying, searching for some recognition.

Slowly, she nodded.

"Such a rebellion by a *slave* does not sit well with me. I know it must not sit well with you either, being the civilized lady you are."

Clio couldn't answer. He wasn't giving her the opportunity to speak. Instead, he put the right opinions in her mouth for her. To disagree would be treason.

"We need to correct such notions in Sheehan's populace, before things get out of hand. And Riece could do this. He could bring Sheehan into civility. Now that your king is dead, only a boy sits on the throne. He can't understand everything that is needed in the city. Riece, with the support of his loyal warriors, could affect real change."

Clio hadn't spared one thought for how her stunt would affect Sheehan. Her heart sank with dread. Whatever happened to Sheehan would be due, in part, to her small rebellion.

The Emperor continued. "But Riece, being the stubborn man you must know by now, has the audacity to refuse me." His tone was gentle, but a tinge of frustration lay underneath.

Of course, Riece wouldn't want to take on the job of destroying an entire city. He was smart enough to know the real request behind the Emperor's words. But the horror of it all was that Riece could only refuse for so long. The way Clio saw the muscles in Riece's jaw and neck clench made it clear that he was aware of this.

"Would you do that for me, Sahi?"

"I'll try my best, sir."

He nodded and patted her hand, pleased. "Of course, you will, and I have no doubt that with you as such an incentive, Riece can no longer resist." The threat was there, expertly dressed up as benign, but still apparent for what it was. Riece didn't have a choice in the matter.

"Ah, Riece, Sahi, I want to introduce you to my guest of honor." The Emperor waved his hand to a crowd of people who had entered the room.

Clio turned and saw Derik leading his royal escort.

CHAPTER TWENTY-NINE

The Emperor must have been making formal introductions, but Clio didn't hear any of it. Derik locked eyes with her, and the world around her came to a stop. He looked so tired, so worn down, but the spark of joy and relief in his eyes upon seeing her was unmistakable. No disguise could hide her from him. His whole demeanor changed, and Clio felt as if she were home when she saw that his smile was all for her. The faintest of blushes colored his cheek when his gaze landed her dress and all the skin it left bare.

"Derik, this is our Commander Riece's guest, Sahi. I believe she is from your kingdom."

Derik's eyebrows rose at the word "guest." His eyes narrowed somewhat when they fell upon Riece.

"Now," the Emperor addressed them all, "I believe our entertainment is about to begin."

The Emperor and Derik led the way, with Riece and Clio following several paces behind. Clio strained her ears to catch everything that was passing between the two ahead of her.

"I was sorry to hear about your father. He and I had finally come to an understanding between our kingdoms. I hope that you will continue down the path that he had paved." The Emperor spoke to Derik in a casual, yet authoritative manner.

"I have no intentions of restarting any hostilities with the Empire, your highness."

"That's what I thought. You seem like an intelligent young man. And with Mannix at your side, I feel certain that we will not have any problems. Mannix has done a lot of good for our relationship. I was very pleased to see him acting as regent. I urge you to keep him close."

Of course the Emperor knew Mannix, Clio realized. Mannix had been the one to negotiate the peace between the two cities. He had even been the one to arrange for the offerings. It would be exceedingly difficult to push Mannix from his position of power without some kind of reaction from the Emperor.

Clio wanted so desperately to pull Derik aside, but with the Emperor nearby it was too risky. To have him so close and yet outside her reach was almost more than she could bear.

The steady pulse of a deep drum resounded through the room, calling everyone's attention. A man Clio had never seen before, dressed in a speckled white pelt, stepped in front of the gathered guests.

"To the Emperor of Morek"—his speech was stunted by a heavy, unfamiliar accent—"a gift from the cities lying at the corner of the sea." With that he bowed, and two scantily clad performers took his place. One of the performers, a man, was dressed in black, with a mask adorning his face that looked like a human skull. The other, a girl, wore strips of nearly transparent red fabric. Even her hair was covered in a headdress of fiery red feathers. As she twirled seductively around the man, her dress spun and licked out like flames.

"What is this?" Clio whispered to Riece out of the corner of her mouth.

"The Emperor speaks of conquering the Sea next. This is their attempt to garner his mercy."

"Will it work?"

Riece shrugged, "I doubt it. It takes more than a performance to charm the Emperor."

Clio, however, found the performance mesmerizing. The man was clearly Death himself, a Deity trying to lure a young girl into his kingdom. But the girl would not give in. She twisted and flipped around him, staying ever out of reach. As the drumming came to a crescendo, the girl finally surrendered. Death wrapped her in the folds of his black cape, and when she came out the audience gasped at what they saw.

The girl was no longer wearing red. Instead, white adorned her toe to tip. Red feathers fell from her head, exposing pearly white hair. From where Clio was standing, it was clear that the girl's hair had been powdered, but the effect was the same. This girl was portraying the Oracle.

Death fell beaten at her feet.

"ENOUGH!" roared the Emperor. He tore the spear out of one of his guard's hands.

"The Sea will never be yours, your *highness.*" The announcer stepped forward as he spoke in mock deference. He had barely finished his sentence before the Emperor slit his throat.

Taking advantage of the confusion that spread around her, Clio moved to Derik and pulled him behind her. "We need to talk," she mouthed as she led him back through the room. Riece trailed behind them.

Screaming followed them as they made their way through the arches that overlooked the city.

"What just happened?" Derik asked, trying to get a glimpse of the chaos inside.

"The cities from the Sea just mightily offended the Emperor," Riece answered.

"But how?" Derik looked shaken.

"Truly? *You're* the king of Sheehan?" Riece threw his arms up.

"Riece, come on," Clio said. "Derik became king days ago."

Riece sighed. "They showed an Oracle defeating Death himself. The threat is obvious. Not to mention, the Emperor has a hatred for Oracles in general. To bring them up in his presence is more than disrespectful. Now you two get this conversation over with while I try to restore some order in there." With that, Riece strode back inside.

And suddenly Clio and Derik were alone together, the events of the evening forgotten as their eyes met.

"I knew you would make it." His eyes glowed with triumph.

"Yes, well, it wasn't so easy," Clio said. "I'm actually a fugitive here, for multiple reasons."

He chuckled. "Sounds about right." His face grew somber. "I heard about Ali. I'm so sorry, Clio."

Clio could only nod as she tried to swallow the lump burrowing in her throat.

He looked away. Clio followed his gaze to find Riece watching them out of the corner of his eye while talking to some of Derik's guards.

"Who is this Riece? You came with him?" There was concern in his voice, but with something else too. The faint bitterness of jealousy.

"Yes, I begged him to bring me tonight because I knew you would be here."

"Clio, are you out of your mind? If he finds out what you are—"

She cut him off. "He knows what I am. Riece saved my life. More than once. Derik, tell me what is going on with Mannix."

His face tightened. "I wish I knew, but he has been keeping me out of the city, scheduling me to visit our neighbors so that he can have full reign in Sheehan."

Although the commotion inside covered their conversation, Derik lowered his voice. "Clio, have you been Seeing anything?"

"Yes, that's what I wanted to talk to you about," she said. "I Saw Mannix torturing a girl. I don't know where, but it was some kind of stone room. Since he has been keeping you out of the palace, I think it's fairly safe to say it's somewhere there. And he knows I'm alive, Derik. I Saw him searching for me."

"But what does he want with you?"

"That, I don't know."

"What did he do to the girl you Saw?"

"He cut into her in awful ways. Then he gave her to his men. We think he is using the Untouched."

Clio saw all the color drain from Derik's face.

"Did you recognize the girl?" Clio hadn't noticed Riece's return.

"This is none of *your* business," Derik growled.

Clio shot Derik an admonishing look. "It became his business when he saved my life and put a roof over my head." Derik fell silent. "She was a slave from the pyramid. He was torturing her, trying to get her to tell him something, but she died, or is going to die." She shook her head, trying to sort through the chronology.

"But what information could he possibly want from a slave?" Derik had calmed down some, but Clio could tell he didn't exactly welcome Riece's involvement.

"I don't know," she said. "Maybe he thinks she knows where I am? He definitely wants me for something. He must know I am the Shadow. You have to look through the palace, Derik. You have to find the room, find the slaves."

"I will. I'll leave tomorrow, but Clio, you can't stay here. It's not safe. Let me take you east. We have allies there."

Riece took a step toward him, positioning himself between Clio and Derik. "Your allies cannot be trusted. Remember Mannix is now the one in control of Sheehan."

"You have a better idea? She can't stay in a place that will have her killed if they find out what she is!"

"That's enough, both of you." She laid a hand on Riece, gently pushing him to the side. He resisted at first, but yielded when she implored him with her eyes. She turned to Derik. "Take me any farther away than I am already, and I will be completely useless to you and to Sheehan. I have to stay close."

He opened his mouth to argue, but fell silent at the soft clatter of approaching footsteps.

"We should get back inside. It looks too suspicious for us to be out here alone," Derik whispered.

As Clio turned to enter back through the arches, she caught a flash of red. A man dressed in crimson robes was walking down the hallway toward them.

Mannix.

CHAPTER THIRTY

His red eyes swept through the arches and landed on Clio with all the force a gaze could carry. She expected him to be surprised at her presence, angry maybe, but what she found in his expression was utterly puzzling. His mouth split into a full-toothed smile, pure pleasure igniting his features.

"Now, what could the three of you possibly be discussing out here, all alone?" Mannix leered at her as he spoke.

And they were all alone. Clio had made sure of that. She couldn't see a single guest anywhere.

Riece immediately stepped in front of Clio, shielding her with his body. His hand rested ready on his blade.

Mannix's grin fell. "Riece, commander of Morek's army, the Emperor's prized boy. I didn't get to introduce myself the last time we met. I'm Mannix."

"I figured as much." Riece barely moved his mouth as he spoke.

"I thought I had you killed this morning." Mannix didn't seem too angry about it, just mildly perplexed. "Well, I can't exactly kill you here, nor can I kill you." He turned to Derik. "But…" he turned to the shadows and began to click out a strange pattern with his teeth.

Clio heard rustling all around her. Dark figures took form out of the shadows. A dozen men, all dressed in red robes, surrounded them.

Something—or rather, some*things*—whizzed past Clio's head. In the next instant, both Riece and Derik fell hard to the ground, bolas wrapped tightly around their ankles.

"Clio, run!" Derik shouted.

She did, diving blindly into the darkness. She slid down a steep rocky incline, branches and thorns slowing her descent until she was thrown onto a flat expanse.

Shadows rustled around her as brittle arms grabbed her and began to drag her across the ground, carrying her farther away from the light of the palace. Fingernails dug deep into her arms, urging her non-compliant limbs to bend. Her legs shuffled uselessly along the ground below her, desperately trying to get some kind of hold on the soft dirt, until finally the pressure was too much and no amount of steely determination could keep them from collapsing beneath her. Her knees skimmed and scraped along the ground, but Clio was barely conscious of the pain.

Something heavy collided with her head, and she fell limp.

When she came to, Derik and Riece were nowhere in sight. She was alone.

Well, not all alone. The almost noiseless rustle of robes followed in her wake like a grim funeral procession. Finally, when the sounds of the palace were only a distant hum and the lights of its archways only a dull glow, the force that had been carrying her across all this ground was removed, and without it, Clio dropped heavily to the ground.

Spitting the sand from her mouth and trying to catch the breath that was refusing to fill her lungs, she looked up to find Mannix in all his crimson triumph. She was on all fours at his feet. Her silk dress had been torn up her side, leaving her skin all too exposed and vulnerable to the fire that seemed to emanate from his entire being. With fumbling hands, she tried her best to cover herself up.

He didn't have any weapons on him, but he didn't have any need to—his guards were fully armed. Anyway, Clio knew all too well that it wasn't what a person had that made them dangerous. It was what they didn't have. And Mannix didn't have a soul.

"Clio, my dear, you act as though you are afraid of me." He knelt down to her. "Here, let me help you with that."

Her hands had been shaking too violently to pull the tattered remnants of her skirt back in place. His icy fingers deftly repositioned the silk, deliberately letting them skim along her thigh. All of her hair stood on end under his repulsive touch.

No, he wouldn't have this position of power, her prostrated at his feet. She wouldn't allow it. Biting her cheek to keep from crying out, she raised herself up before him. It was a small victory for her, but he met it with amusement.

"Just can't help yourself, can you? Really, Clio, you should try to be less predictable. An enemy could easily learn to foresee your every move. You see, you just refuse to bend." He was walking around her as if he were inspecting her. "It's how I knew that the little stunt on the pyramid of Morek was to your credit. It had 'Clio' written all over it. Led me straight to you."

She stiffened. What did he want? He could easily have killed her. But instead, he brought her here.

As if he had read her mind, he said, "I see a thousand questions swimming in those big brown eyes of yours, but first I have a question of my own." He leaned in close while pulling her waist toward himself. The gesture was so grotesquely intimate, so wrong in every way. "Answer me honestly, dear. I will know if you lie." She gasped as he pressed a knife into her gut, just hard enough to be very painful and yet not break the skin. "Do you have the Sight?"

She didn't have many choices. The slightest change of pressure, and she would be gutted where she stood. She had no way of knowing what he wanted to hear. Clearly, he wasn't surprised to find her still alive, which meant that he had never intended to eliminate the entire line of Oracles. Why would it matter if she had the Sight? Didn't he want to kill her either way? She stayed silent, weighing her options, trying to think of a way to get out of this.

He sighed. "No need to be so nervous. I'm mostly sure that you do have the Sight. That's part of the plan. I just wondered, since you were underage, whether it might be...delayed in presenting itself." His breath was rank, putrid. It called something back to Clio's mind, and suddenly, the smell was all around her.

Mannix was standing alone in the night, outside of the mouth of a stone structure. The black outlines of mountain peaks rose behind him. He looked around until he found what he needed—a large stone. Picking it up, he knocked it four times against the stone wall, twice fast and twice slow. He tossed it to the side, where it landed with a heavy crunch in a pile of bleached white bones. Clio didn't need to take a step forward to make out that they were human.

Clio shivered even though she couldn't feel the cold night air.

Mannix spoke into the darkness: "Alouwen." The word meant nothing to Clio, but an old man emerged, and with him came that noxious stench of death and decay. The man wore next to nothing, only a thin cloth tied around his groin. Heavy piercings pulled down the folds of skin on his face. In his nose and ears were what looked like delicate finger bones.

The man did not look pleased to see Mannix. His hands began to wave around in a series of quick choppy signals. He was an Untouched.

Mannix must have understood what the man was signaling because he spoke back to him as if bored. "Your people are starving because of the Emperor, not me. I can help you."

The man began to sign again, but Mannix cut him off with his hand. "Send your young warriors back with me, and I promise you will be repaid with more than you have ever known."

He pulled something, a lumpy package, out of his cloak and tossed it at the foot of the man. "There's more of this if you pledge with me."

The man opened the package, and his mouth watered at what he saw. Clio tried to close her eyes, but it was too late. A flash of pale flesh was exposed. All Clio could think of was that dying slave girl. Mannix had promised the Untouched food, and he had brought some to prove it.

Her whole body willed her to leave the Vision behind. She opened her eyes to the real Mannix. He was smiling. He had his answer. Her gaze was fatally drawn to those thin glistening red lips. They didn't even carry a human aspect to them anymore. How could they? How could anyone see Mannix as a human and accept what he did or would do? His lips were the tight snarl of a jackal. A beast. It was the only way her mind could process what her eyes were telling her. Mannix wasn't a human. He couldn't be.

That hand. The hand that moments ago had held human flesh was now encircling her waist, imparting a shadow of its deeds. Human reflex, the same reflex that swats away a hornet or jumps away from a snake in the grass, shoved his hand from her skin.

"What kind of monster are you?" Revulsion colored her voice.

He beamed, but it was all blackness. "Excellent! Oh, how wonderful." He smacked those jackal lips together in satisfaction. "Since you were so kind as to answer my question, I feel it's only gracious to answer one of yours." Spittle bubbled in the corners of his mouth, as if he were salivating in excitement.

Keep him talking, Clio, she told herself. The longer he talked, the more time Riece and Derik would have to find her. She couldn't let herself consider the possibility that they were already dead.

"Why are you hurting those girls? What do you want with me?"

"Tut tut, Clio," he clicked, "that's two questions, and I only agreed to answer one."

"Just kill me then, and be done with it," she spat at him.

"I don't want to kill you. Not yet, anyway. We've got a long road to travel together before then, you and I." Something gleamed in his eyes as he spoke—anticipation.

"I Saw what you did to her. How you tortured her. Is she already dead?"

"I can't be sure of exactly which girl to whom you are referring, but many are dead, yes. You see, I had to test out some *procedures*, and they had information about a girl called 'the Shadow.' I know your kind can't See into your own future—such a glaring oversight, in my opinion—but nonetheless, you might as well treat the sight of that girl's gaping body as a Vision of your own fate. After all, they are only practice for the real thing. Can't have you dying too quickly just because I am rusty." He smiled wickedly down at her. His cloaked guards formed a tight perimeter around them, blocking out the world beyond.

Practice? Whatever he did to that girl, he wanted to do to her. Both the thought and the reality repulsed her to her very core.

Clio knew the funny thing about repulsion, though—no matter how strong, it was never strong enough to stifle curiosity. She burned with it. What was it that he wanted out of her? Clearly, he wasn't only torturing those girls for information about Clio's whereabouts. He wanted to torture Clio, but for what? He had said it himself—he wanted her alive. He wanted to do those things to her, but he wanted to keep her alive.

The point of his blade was still pressed hard into her gut, but she knew he didn't want to kill her. Not here, like this. She had gotten a preview of where his tastes lay.

"Grab her. Let's go." With his free hand, he motioned to his guards to come forward.

He was about to pull the knife away to turn and go, but Clio grabbed the hilt and his hand with it, and forced it back to its threatening position in her abdomen. "No," she said.

For once, she saw fear widen his eyes. "You wouldn't. You don't have it in you to spill your own blood." But his voice was thin, high-pitched. Even he didn't believe what he was saying.

"I assure you I do. But that's not the point, is it? You said it yourself—you want to be able to do those *things* to me without killing me. I am the last Oracle, and for whatever reason, you want to keep me alive."

She could see him fuming. Rage filled his eyes. He had given too much away, made it clear that he needed her.

"Back away now, or it's over for both of us." His hand trembled beneath hers. She could see him weighing his options. A twitch in his forearm alerted her to his effort to pull the knife away, but she just tugged harder on it. It dug into her skin. She had no doubt that it was drawing blood. He looked down at what must have been red blossoming around their hands and with a sigh released the knife.

In an instant, she flipped the blade around in her hand, holding it threateningly to Mannix. "Call off your men."

He smiled. "No, I don't think I will." Turning toward them, he commanded, "Disarm her, but do not kill her."

The circle around her began to tighten as robed figures moved toward her. If she lost the knife, it was over. If any of them knocked her out, it was over.

She spun around in a circle, fending off the approaching men with her single knife. With her back to the distant palace, she planted her feet, ready for the attack. One of the men lunged forward, but before he could reach her, something wrapped around his neck, cutting off his air. As he fell to his knees, trying to untangle the choking bola, Clio made out the shape of an approaching figure behind him.

Before she could discern who it was, she heard a high-pitch whizzing. A spear flew past her, alarmingly close. It embedded itself with a hard thud in the throat of one of Mannix's guards. The scream of another spear split the air, followed by another sickening crunch.

Riece.

At the first sign of attack, Mannix retreated into the night. Clio raced after him, but he was impossibly fast. He found the shadows as if he were one himself. Before she knew it, she was chasing empty air. It was pointless to plunge blindly into this thick darkness while the sounds of battle raged behind her.

She turned back to the action, where Riece was taking on multiple men. Watching him fight was like watching a choreographed dance, and he didn't miss a single step. He spun, twisted, ducked, slid, and lunged—dodging blows and dealing out death to his opponents as if it was the easiest thing in the world. Muscles rippled and stretched across his chest, along his back, down his legs, through his arms, extending and elongating to impossible proportions. Tendons pulled his bones into place, the image of the human body at its most lethal. It was horrible. But it was beautiful.

He had it under control. Clearly. But she would never hear the end of it if she stood by gaping as he rescued her. She didn't need rescuing, anyway. Well, all right—for a moment it had been a little hairy, but now she was fully capable of handling the situation on her own.

Filling her lungs with air, she dove into the fray. Riece was locked in a battle of strengths with a guard whose robe had been slashed from his face. The guard's mouth opened in an otherworldly scream. Clio bit back her surprise when she realized that the reason behind his twisting and wavering cry was that he didn't have a tongue. His mouth stretched wide, opening onto an empty black pit that seemed to stretch right down to his core.

Picking up a spear at her feet she swung it, knocking the man from his feet. He landed hard on the ground. Riece looked up at her, surprised. Clearly, he hadn't noticed her return. His mouth rose in that amused half smile of his. In the brief moment he'd wasted to look at her, another man had pulled himself up from the ground and slammed Riece over the head. Riece stumbled, trying to regain his balance and his composure. The man didn't waste the opportunity. He pulled out a spear and threw it right at Riece's heart.

Without thinking, Clio flung her knife. It flipped end over end in a blink of an eye that seemed to last forever. For one horrifying heartbeat, Clio thought that she had been too late; that the spear was going to pierce its target. But at the final moment, the knife clipped the spear, knocking it off its course and into Riece's shoulder.

Riece looked at his injury. Surprise flickered across his face. Still lightning fast, he pulled the spear out and swiped it perfectly, arcing it to slice the man's throat. The man collapsed to the ground, hopelessly trying to staunch the flow of blood pulsing from his neck. What must have been his attempt at final words bubbled through his throat, but without a tongue, it was only a shapeless moan.

There they stood, among a sea of blood and bodies, but all Clio saw were Riece's brown eyes. A moment passed. They were locked into each other's gazes, hearts racing and blood pumping with exhilaration from battle. Blood colored Clio's cheeks, a flush from either exertion or something else...

Armed to the hilt, with bodies sprinkled around her like dust, she felt vulnerable. And from the look on Riece's face, she knew that he felt it too.

CHAPTER THIRTY-ONE

"Deities…"

Her head snapped to the sound. Both she and Riece turned, prepared for another fight.

"Whoa, it's just me, Clio." The figure stepped into the moonlight. Clio let out the breath she didn't know she was holding. Derik stood in front of her. He was standing in an odd way, putting all of his weight on his left leg, and he held his side as if he was holding back blood.

"When did you learn to do that?" His eyes were wide in amazement. He must have seen the end of their fight. Clio blushed again to think that he had witnessed the confusingly intimate moment that she had shared with Riece.

"It all came with the Sight. I don't know why." Her tone was surprisingly hard. Deities, why was she being so gruff to him? As if she was embarrassed or mad…

He limped painfully over to her. "Are you all right?" He raised his hand to delicately wipe away what must have been some spattered blood on her face. She pulled away from his touch, self-conscious of how she must look in his eyes. This wasn't Clio. This wasn't the girl who had promised never to change. Here she was, blood-spattered and hard. Hard as stone.

No, she didn't want to be this way.

"I'm fine. What about you? You look hurt." She welcomed the concern into her voice. She wanted to feel human again. Vulnerable.

He shrugged. "Nothing that won't heal on its own. We had a little trouble with some of Mannix's men." He looked to Riece. "You could have given me a hand, you know."

Riece bowed his head. "My apologies, but you were not my priority." His eyes found Clio's.

There it was again—that intense gaze that locked every one of Clio's muscles into place. She shook it off before it could set in.

"We should be leaving. Mannix will be back."

Riece nodded his agreement and bent to check the bodies.

"Derik, you have to go back to Sheehan."

"No, I can't leave you behind."

"He is recruiting more Untouched." The words hung heavy in the air. She heard Riece stop his searching and straighten up.

"Wha—? Why?"

"That's what I need to find out. I don't think he knows that I know about it, and we should keep it that way. He's gathering them together and bringing them back to Sheehan for something."

Derik was shaking with rage, or maybe disgust. "How dare he bring those monsters into my city. But why? What does he need them for?"

"I don't know. That's why I have to stay here." Her eyes flashed to Riece for the briefest of moments. "I have to try to stop it. I know where he is going next. Whatever his goal, if he is using the Untouched, then it can't be good."

"Where is he going?" Derik asked. "Let me go with you. You can't possibly face all of them on your own." He grabbed her hand.

"No."

Derik flinched at her rebuke.

She grasped his hand more tightly in hers. "Derik, I need you to try to distract him. Buy me some time. I don't know where exactly it is, but I can find it if you can stall him. Maybe make it seem as if I am hiding out, afraid of his plans for me. And I won't be alone. Riece might be the only person who has faced the Untouched and lived. He can help me—help us—find where I saw Mannix and the Untouched in my Vision. I'll come back once I know more and have a plan. I promise. Sheehan is my home, and I won't let that monster have it."

"Clio, I should be the one going with you, not him." The slightest edge of pain crept into his voice.

"You have to stay in Sheehan. The city needs you now more than ever. If something were to happen to both of us, Sheehan would be left vulnerable."

Swallowing, he nodded. Clio could still see the fight in his eyes, but he would never be able to abandon his kingdom.

Once again, she was going to leave him after seeing him for far too brief a time. "You know, one of these days, we will have to spend more than an evening together."

"Oh, you can count on it." His eyes mirrored the promise in his words. Clio was conscious of Riece standing behind her, and suddenly she felt uncomfortable as Derik brushed his hand along her cheek in the most tender and intimate of gestures.

But it was Derik, and nothing with him could feel uncomfortable for long. They knew each other better than anyone. The gentle curve of his brow, the way it met his nose in defined, sharp angles—she knew those lines better than she knew her own.

His eyes held hers. Before she knew what he was doing, he leaned in, brushing his lips ever so lightly along her cheek. It was so fast, so fleeting and so light that Clio barely believed it had happened. But a trail of fire burned in the kiss's wake, surprising her.

He pulled away, and her body ached in his absence.

"Watch out for yourself," he called as he made his way back up to the palace, leaving her alone in the dark night.

A hurried rustling reminded Clio of Riece's presence. She felt the back of her neck get hot.

"We should get going." Her voice was strangled. *Deities, why am I so embarrassed?* she wondered.

Riece grunted.

"Is that a...a yes? Or..." she stumbled on her words.

"It's a 'keep yourself together for a moment while I search these guys for any clues.'" His tone was like the lash of a whip. He pulled something out of the pocket of one of the men, stowing it away before Clio could get a look.

"All right, we can go now." Instead of going up to the palace, he led the way back to the main road, all the while never looking at her.

He was angry. Very.

"Riece, I..." She tried to catch up to him.

He turned to face her. His chest was heaving. The paint that had been so elegantly swirled on his chest was smudged into a messy tangle of blue, brown and red.

"What?" he snarled.

She flinched. He softened at this, but turned and marched forward, leaving her to trail behind.

"Why are you so angry with me?" she yelled at his back. "What did I do to you—beside save your life?"

He sucked in air, blowing himself up to an even bigger size. "You saved *my* life? What fight were you watching?"

She closed the gap between them. Now she was angry, too. He didn't have any right to be angry with her for what Derik had done. It wasn't as if she had made any promises to Riece. She owed him, but not in that way. Clio tried to shut out the voice in the back of her head that kept reminding her she had felt something between herself and Riece from the very beginning.

"This one." She jabbed her knuckles into the still bleeding wound in his shoulder. He sucked in a painful breath. "Without me to watch your back, this would have been fatal."

He grabbed her hand hard in his, pulling it down and away from his wound. "You distracted me." His voice was suddenly soft, vulnerable. "I've never lost my focus in a fight before." The armor was up again. "Without me, Mannix would have you now."

"I had it under control..." She ripped her hand from his. "But this isn't the point. Riece, don't be jealous." He was too much of a warrior to admit it, but Clio saw it written in the lines of his face.

"I..." he stuttered. "I don't get jealous."

She hadn't noticed, but in the course of their argument, they had made their way back to Riece's home. They crossed through the open archway, and Clio found Tirza eagerly awaiting news of their night. Riece stormed past her, marching toward what must have been his bedroom. A simple curtain separated his room from the living area.

Tirza shrieked at the blood that covered them both. She looked as if she were about to say something to him, but Clio violently shook her head, and Tirza clamped her mouth shut.

Taking a moment to catch her breath, Clio ducked into his bedroom. Exotic pelts lined the walls—animals that had to have been three times the size of Riece when they were alive. Some had shaggy brown and black hair, others sleek and spotted or striped. Also lining the walls were fangs the length of a forearm and tusks the length of Clio's legs.

Instead of the furs that Clio was accustomed to, Clio found Riece sitting on a simple straw mat that must have served as his bed. He had pulled his washbowl to the ground in front of him and was cleaning out his wound.

"I don't remember inviting you in here." He said as he glared up at her.

"Riece, I'm sorry. I do owe you my life. Several times over now." Her hands were clenched tightly into useless fists at her side. He remained silent.

She admired his prized pelts, searching for anything to break the uncomfortable silence between them. "Did you hunt all of these?" After seeing how he fought today, she would believe him capable of taking down any beast.

He shook his head. "Didn't hunt them. Each of them attacked me or my party. I was only doing my job." He refused to look up at her. "Can you please leave now?"

His words hurt, but what pained Clio more was the raw timbre of his voice.

"I don't know what it is you are thinking, but I—"

He cut her off. "I'm thinking that you had me bring you tonight just so you could see your lover again." Finally, he looked up at her.

Clio dropped her eyes as heat filled her cheeks. "He's not my lover."

"Oh no? You make a habit of kissing all the boys you know? Somehow I must have missed my turn..." His half-smile was more of a snarl this time.

"No, Riece...I don't know why Derik did that. He's never...I didn't ask him to." She was stammering again, and the flames in her cheeks were only getting hotter.

He saw how uncomfortable she was. "Deities, I've never seen anyone burn quite as red as you right now." He laughed, finally breaking the coolness between them. "Only a girl unaccustomed to kissing would blush *that* much."

She couldn't help but roll her eyes at him, but inside she was so glad that he didn't seem angry with her. It surprised her how much she wanted his esteem.

"Honestly, I am unaccustomed to men in general." She sat next to him with a sigh.

"Hmm, well, I'd be more than happy to accustom you." There was that grin again. "But you seemed to know what you were doing back in the pyramid."

If it were possible for Clio's cheeks to flame any brighter, they did so. "I don't know what you are talking about."

"Oh, don't play coy with me. It was all rather cruel on your part, unleashing all that charm on a defenseless man."

"You are hardly defenseless." Clio laughed.

"In most areas I'd agree with that." His eyes burned. "So, there's no such understanding between you and Derik?" Was that hope in his voice?

"Of course not. I don't know what that was…"

"That, young, inexperienced, naïve Clio, was a desperate boy's attempt at a kiss." A playful light sparkled in his eyes, and he was really grinning now.

She playfully pushed his head aside. His grin didn't waver.

"Here, give me that. You are completely useless." She grabbed the cloth from his hand and dunked it in the water. Positioning herself so that she was kneeling between his outstretched legs with easy access to his wounded shoulder, she found herself breathtakingly close to him.

His breath was hot on her neck as she leaned forward to get a good look at the damage.

Uncomfortable, she cleared her throat as she started to work at cleaning his wound.

As soon as she pressed the cloth to his shoulder he let out a strangled hiss.

"Gentle!"

"Honestly? I hardly touched you." Clio laughed. "Certainly, a warrior such as yourself can withstand a bit of stinging."

"You've got to learn to be more gentle with your men, Clio."

On her neck, she felt the air displaced by the movement of his lips. Now, she was the distracted one. The heady closeness of his person sent her into a swoon. She slipped, dropping the cloth. To catch her balance, she found both of her hands flat on the hardness of his chest.

His hands shot up to catch her. She knew it was a reflex, but the result was a perfect embrace. Her heart raced, and to her surprise, she could feel Riece's own heartbeat speed up in reply.

It was at that moment—Clio kneeling between Riece's legs, pressed up against his chest with his arms wrapped around her and his head in the crook of her neck—that Tirza walked in.

"Oh my." Clio heard Tirza's startled gasp and the dull thud of her dropping a stack of clean towels.

Clio shot up and out of Riece's arms, stumbling in her haste and nearly collapsing on him again. Riece threw back his head and belted out a booming laugh.

"Dear, dear sister." He was laughing so hard that his eyes were tearing up. "You have the Deities' timing."

Tirza got over her surprise and smiled at her brother in embarrassment.

"It's not what it looks like." Clio was still horrified.

This only made Riece laugh harder, and he collapsed onto his back in a fit of hilarity. "Clio, I don't even think you know what it is this looks like. Don't worry. Tirza won't get the wrong impression of you. I mean, it's not as if you were caught *kissing* a boy."

Stammering, Clio said, "I was seeing to his wounds..."

"Clio, it's fine. I didn't see anything." Tirza was just as red as Clio. Riece was the only one thoroughly amused by the situation.

"I...I, uh, think I will retire for the night. It's nearly dawn, and Riece"—she turned to him, suddenly serious—"I think there is a lot we should go over in the morning."

He waved her away. "Yes, yes. We will deal with saving Sheehan in the morning. Get some rest, Clio. It's been an interesting day for you, no doubt."

Grateful for the escape, Clio nodded and headed out. As she was pulling aside the curtain, Riece called from behind, "Please do let me know who occupies your dreams tonight."

She didn't need to turn around to know that he had that half-smile plastered across his face again. Without replying, she ducked out of the room.

Before she was out of earshot, she heard Riece murmur to Tirza,

"I think it's safe to say she likes me."

It was Tirza's response, though, that heated Clio's blood. "I think it's safe to say that *you* like *her*."

CHAPTER THIRTY-TWO

Clio spent the night in a dreamless sleep. For the first time since before Ali had been taken from her, she woke feeling rested. She stretched out her legs, feeling the strength in them, the power that was hidden under the surface. It didn't feel alien anymore. Instead, it was starting to feel natural, like a part of her. It would take more than a couple assassins to kill Clio and Riece, and Mannix knew that now. There was no way he could attack them in Riece's home with such a force without greatly angering the Emperor. For the moment, she was safe from him.

But Sheehan wasn't.

She rose to dress, choosing a simple white full-length skirt and tunic. She reached for the scarf but realized that her hair was still a bright and fiery red.

Drifting across the room, she caught a glimpse of the vista outside. The sun was barely up, and the ground outside her room was still shrouded in the thick mist, making the whole world seem as if it had floated up into the clouds.

Riece was already seated at the hearth. When she came in, he soundlessly offered her some of the bread he had been eating without even looking up. She ate silently, her eyes on him. His hair was tousled, and the tunic he wore had stretched too wide around his neck, giving her a glimpse of his muscled chest.

He was turning something over and over in his hands, holding it up to the light of the fire. His brow was furrowed, and his lips were held tight, deep in thought.

"What is that?" she asked.

He dropped it, frustrated. She could see a war of memories in the lines of his brow.

"It's early," was all he said. His gaze slid out to the courtyard, where faint rays of sun were just beginning to brush through the trees.

"Riece, we don't have much time. Please, I need to learn as much as I can about the Untouched, and then I'm setting out to stop them." She laid her hand gently on his arm, and for the first time, he didn't make a joke or shrug her off. He only bent down and retrieved the object he had been studying and handed it to her.

It was some kind of woven pattern—a circle with a series of interlocking semi-circles surrounding it, barely bigger than an olive. The pattern reminded Clio of the wild flowers that grew near the river that fed into her mother's temple.

"What is it?" she started, bending the strange material in her fingers. It was coarse, and yet somehow very pliant.

"What do you mean 'setting out?'"

"You don't have to come with me, but I know where Mannix is going next. He is recruiting the Untouched, promising them food beyond belief if they help him. I have to stop him." She squeezed the strange object.

"Careful with that," he cautioned, taking the token gently out of her grip. "This is a token, carried by each man in the Untouched." He pointed to the row of concentric circles. "They keep on adding more and more layers to it. I've seen one as big as a man's hand before."

"What is it for?"

"I suppose it serves a function not unlike our colored cloaks."

"You mean it marks how many lives a man has taken?"

He nodded somberly. "But it's a little more than that. The Untouched believe that harvesting their kills gives them strength."

"And that's why they eat their enemies?" she asked.

"That's part of it." A darkness crossed his face, shading his eyes.

She grabbed the small token back from Riece. Holding it right under her eyes, she saw what she hadn't before. The braids that formed each delicate loop were made out of hair, and Clio had no doubt that it was human.

She shuddered, handing it back to him. "Why did you take this?"

He rose and walked stiffly into his room. When he came out, he was holding a very simple and very small chest. Wordlessly, he handed it to Clio.

Inside were nearly a dozen of these tokens. *Ten*, she realized—the Untouched he had killed. As she looked, he pulled several more from his pocket and added them to the chest's contents. They must have belonged to the men he had killed last night.

"You believe it's true, then? That you will take their strength with these?" She handed the last one back to him as she spoke.

He shrugged. "Not particularly, but it seemed…disrespectful to leave them behind."

She watched his face as he shut the chest and put it aside, keeping a hold on the final token. A dark shadow settled over his eyes.

"I searched each of Mannix's men, and on every body it was the same—they all carried dozens of these."

"But why would they have more than one?" Her voice caught.

"Only from killing each other. But they don't kill each other—or at least they never did before."

"But it's a good thing if they kill each other, isn't it?"

"Not if they are killing the ones who won't side with Mannix." He looked up at her. "You shouldn't go after them."

"We've had this conversation before, Riece."

"You can't help anyone, not if the Untouched are with him." Something was in his eyes that Clio had never seen before. It took her a moment to realize that he was afraid.

"Come on. We didn't have any trouble taking down the ones last night." She tried for a light tone, but the grim look on his face stayed put.

"I don't like this. He is planning something with them. If he is assembling them in any way, any way at all, there is nothing we can do."

"I don't understand. You captured ten of them on your own…Why are you so afraid of them?"

"The Untouched aren't like us. They don't feel loyalty to each other beyond convenience. Their tribes are not made of families. They care about nothing, except for their next victim. It's why they don't have a language. They don't feel the need to communicate even with each other beyond simple gestures."

"So…" She still couldn't make sense of it all. The panic in his voice was real, palpable in the air, and it was beginning to scare her.

"They are born killers. It's what they are made for! And their *only* weakness is their disunity. I was only able to do what I did because they weren't working with each other, because they had never learned to fight as one.

"If Mannix can bring them together, the rest of us will fall."

She was shaking her head. "But don't you see, Riece? We have been given a chance to stop that from happening. He is bringing them together, bringing them into the city, and if that's truly as awful as you say it is, then I have to do something to stop it."

"What can you do?"

"I Saw him. He approached a tribe of Untouched who lived in some kind of stone structure. I don't know exactly where, but it's somewhere near here, in the mountains."

"I know where it is," he said darkly.

"Great! Then you can point me in the right direction, and then—"

"And then what, Clio?" he growled. "What are you going to do?

Reason with the Untouched? Tell them they shouldn't listen to Mannix? Or are you going to kill them all yourself? What? What could you possibly do?"

"I'll think of something," she said. "But first, I have to get there."

"I'm not going to let you march into their den by yourself!"

"Riece, I can't ask you to go with me, I know that. The things you must have suffered…" She stared at the thick scar around his neck. "I can't even imagine. But I can't not go, either." The truth was she didn't know what she could do to stop this. She didn't fully know what she was stopping.

Riece kept turning the token over and over in his hands, thinking.

"Would you please stop that?" she pleaded, taking the object out of his hands. As she held it in her grip, the beginning of an idea began to take shape in her mind. "Wait. You said that each of the Untouched carries one of these?"

"Yes," he answered suspiciously, "each male."

"Do you think it could be used as identification? I mean, I know there are so many different tribes of Untouched. Do you think that carrying one of these could be enough to prove you come from one of them?"

His eyes shot up to hers, catching on. "Are you suggesting we use one to try to pass as Untouched?"

"You said that they don't know each other's tribes," Clio continued. "They won't expect us to know their signs."

"I did pick up the basic ones when I was held prisoner."

"Even better!" She jumped up, relieved to have a plan, or at least part of one. To feel like maybe she could take control. "We can go to them, claim that we were part of a tribe that Mannix came to, and convince them that he betrayed us." It could be enough to get them to turn on Mannix. Maybe word would spread, and no more of them would join Mannix. Maybe they would even kill him.

A warrior dressed in full battle gear swept into the room.

"Sir," he spoke to Riece, "I have a message for you." Riece looked hesitant, clearly he didn't receive many messages. A knot formed in the pit of Clio's stomach.

Riece took the message, then dismissed the man and handed it to Clio without even looking at it. "It's for you."

"How do you know?"

He shrugged. "You think a warrior like me ever learned to read? Go on, open it. It must be from Derik."

She should have known Riece couldn't read. Only nobles and religious figures knew how to read and write. She had been taught at a young age, one of the first steps in serving the Oracle. It was easy to forget that Riece had lived a completely different life. He had accumulated whatever wealth he had as commander, not because he was born into nobility. He most likely never had any formal schooling. She fumbled with the tie around the thin, rolled-up sheet of animal parchment.

Derik's pictographs were rushed and sparse. "He says that Mannix plans to set out on some sort of royal business tomorrow at dawn." She looked up from the note. "That doesn't give us much of a head start. Riece, I have to go now if I'm going to be able to get to the Untouched in time."

"It's a fool of a plan."

"It's all I have." She made to leave.

"Hold on. I'm coming with you." He didn't sound very pleased. "Just give me the afternoon to make arrangements at the palace."

"Thank you." She smiled cautiously at him. "I could use the help."

"It will take the help of the Deities to pull this off."

CHAPTER THIRTY-THREE

It was clear from the way Tirza held herself during the goodbyes that she was not unaccustomed to seeing her brother head off into unknown danger. She kept her chin up, only the slightest twitching of her lip belying her tough exterior.

Riece was gentle with her, pulling her into a tight hug and whispering words into her ear that Clio did not hear.

The sight of the two of them made Clio feel sick for bringing Riece along with her. If anything happened to him, Tirza would be left alone, just as alone as Mannix had left Clio. Just another girl without anyone. A girl who didn't bear the protection of a man's name was left few options in society. It was the same in Sheehan. It was so easy for these girls to fall through the cracks—to end up like Maia with no one but a stranger to mourn her. Tirza couldn't become that. Riece had to make it back.

They set out on foot, carrying enough supplies to last them several days. Riece had informed Clio that the structure she saw in her Vision was in the mountains, a day away. They could only hope that they would find the Untouched before the Untouched found them.

They trudged along the uneven and jagged rocky paths that cut through the mountains of Morek. The land was harsh in many ways, uncompromising to any trees or greenery that tried to put down roots. Clio wondered how humans had been able to live in what nature could not. It was so unforgiving, but sometimes, when the fingers of light broke through the pass or the water trickled down through a spindling ravine, Clio could see why people had refused to give up this place.

"Do you want to kill Mannix?" Riece asked her as he unnecessarily offered her his hand to climb over a fallen tree.

"I don't *want* to kill anyone." His hand brushed along her waist as he guided her.

"But...?" he prompted.

"He's an evil man. And he took my life away from me. If he hadn't done what he did, I wouldn't be talking about killing anyone."

"But you would still have to serve your mother, your sisters, right?" His eyes were on her as they walked side by side.

He was right. She would have become a Vessel either way. A Vessel who killed for the Oracle and her Visions. "I suppose I only moved from one pair of shackles to another."

"I don't think it has to be that way." His words startled her into stopping. He went on a few extra paces and turned when he noticed she was no longer beside him.

"I can't stop myself from having Visions."

"Of course not. I only mean you don't have to be the one to act on your Visions."

She didn't understand where he was trying to go with this. It felt as if he still could not accept who she really was.

"Someone has to," she said.

"No, I know that. I just mean you could gather a force—people like me but from Sheehan, better trained to do what must be done."

That got her thinking. He had a point. No one ever said she had to do all of this alone.

"I guess I never thought about it that way." She started walking again.

"What would you do if you could? Go home and live at the Sheehan palace with your precious prince?" His tone was teasing and playful, but the quick glance he shot down at her carried a hint of something more serious.

"Well, I don't exactly have a home anymore. Why? What would you suggest?"

"The poor boy would probably die of longing if you didn't."

"What do you mean?" She couldn't ignore the bitter tinge in his voice.

"Come on, Clio. The boy is in love with you. Are you blind?"

"Very funny, Riece. But you're being a little dramatic. I've known Derik my whole life—well, most of it, anyway. He's my family now."

"And you think he kissed you, why? Because he wanted your

help with an itch on his lips?"

"I don't know why he kissed me," she stammered. It was the truth. Her relationship with Derik had changed so much, so quickly that she didn't know where either of them stood anymore. "Plus, I can't really think that far ahead. It's not like I can have any sort of life—Oracle or not—until Mannix is stopped."

"But Mannix had a chance to kill you last night, and he didn't."

"He wants me alive." The sight of that dying girl hovered behind her eyes, the one Mannix had called "practice."

"For what?" Clio saw the flash of tension in Riece's jaw.

She shrugged. "Whatever he did to that girl he was torturing, he wants to do to me. I don't know to what end."

He fell silent, only the sounds of their footsteps echoing around their rocky walls. "I don't like it, Clio. He wants something from you, and until you know what that is, you can't risk facing him."

"Of course *I* don't like it either. But it buys me some safety. He doesn't want me dead right away. It scared him when I stole his blade and threatened to stab myself."

"You WHAT?" He grabbed her arm just above the elbow, pulling her to a stop beside him.

"Well, I didn't exactly have many options. I saw that he wanted me alive, and I took advantage of it."

"You are completely out of your mind. You know that, right?" But the hint of a smile lit up his eyes, a warmth that reflected pride. "Tell me truthfully, do you simply have no fear? First, you voluntarily join a group of slaves to enter a city that wants you dead, and then you threaten to kill yourself to avoid being killed."

"You forgot the part where I volunteered to go first on the pyramid."

"Right, that too. If you were a man, you would be a great warrior."

"If I were a man, I wouldn't need to be anything. If I had been a boy, I never would have become the Oracle."

She started walking again. The ground was getting steep below them. Rocks and pebbles dislodged under their feet, rolling down the terrain below them. The sun was concluding its descent, sending fiery spears of red up into the sky.

"But I do have fear." She thought about Mannix's words—about how the girl she had seen in Mannix's chamber might well be a glimpse into her own fate. "I'm afraid of what he will do to me if he gets me. The only thing protecting me is that he believes I am too valuable to be killed right away."

"Well, you are. Clio, you are the only living Oracle below the Great Sea. With the Morek Oracle gone and now your family, you are the only one left."

"And I thought you didn't like Oracles." Clio smiled cautiously at him.

"I don't...or I didn't," his eyes met hers for a moment before he turned back to the terrain. "He made you the last Oracle because he wants something from you."

"An Oracle serves no one but the Deities. I'm no good to him."

"Unless..." A dark look flashed across his face.

Practice. "Unless, he can torture me into giving him whatever it is he wants."

"But we are going to stop him before then." The strength he put into his words almost convinced her, almost made her feel safe as darkness fell.

They kept walking until the night was so thick around them that they couldn't keep from bumping into each other and tripping over the rocky ground beneath them.

"We should be close." Riece's voice came out of the impenetrable darkness around her.

She shook her head, but of course he couldn't see it. "How can you tell? It looks hopeless. There aren't even any trees in all these rocks. I mean really, why would anyone decide that living on top of a mountain was a good idea? Even the trees know better." She couldn't imagine anyone having built something here.

"There's no amount of darkness that could hide this place from me." He fell silent.

"Do you think that they've heard us?"

"If they had, we would be dead. No talking from here on out." His words echoed empty and hollow around them.

With nothing but the moon's feeble light to guide them, they wound their way off the path. After awhile, Riece jumped down, disappearing from view.

Puzzled, Clio approached the sharp dip in the ground. Looking down, she found a small ravine, with a floor of dirt. At one time it must have been a river; now it was dried and gone.

Clio jumped in after him and turned to see where the ravine led.

That was when she saw it. Directly under the waning moon that hung high in the sky was a single-level, stone structure. Clio would recognize one anywhere.

An Oracle's temple.

CHAPTER THIRTY-FOUR

She walked toward the temple, and stood in the very place that Mannix had stood in her Vision. It had been too dark then for her to make it out, but now she knew—the Untouched lived in an Oracle's temple.

"Clio, in the Deities' names, what are you doing?" Riece whispered as he moved to her. "You can't just walk in there. The Untouched could be anywhere!"

"No one is here." She was just outside the great gates. As she laid her hand on the rotted wood of the door, something hummed just beneath her fingertips. Recognition. This place belonged to her. It felt like home.

"How can you be sure?"

A strange compulsion took hold of her, pulling her into the dark depths of the temple.

"Whoa, whoa, whoa." Riece grabbed her arm and pulled her back. "All right, someone truly needs to explain to you general rules of safety. This place belongs to the Untouched!"

"No. It doesn't."

He looked at her, confusion in his eyes. The moonlight lit him from above, giving a soft glow to the brown hair that fell around his face.

"They may have lived here, but it was never theirs. They've gone."

"How can you be sure?"

"I can feel it." They were too late. Mannix already had this tribe of Untouched. "Why didn't you say anything? Your mother—she served the Oracle here, didn't she?"

He nodded. "I never went inside until after my mother was killed, and I came looking for revenge, but I was too late. The Emperor already had her."

"You should have told me. You didn't need to come here. To relive everything." The pain these walls held for him, Clio wished she didn't have to keep dragging him back into those memories.

"And that's exactly why I didn't say anything. It doesn't matter." His face was stone.

"It does matter." She approached him and laid a hand on his arm.

He smiled gently at her. "No, Clio. I am not thinking of the Oracle who was once here, only the one with me here now."

His words warmed her despite the fierce chill that had descended as they rose higher and higher into the mountains.

"We should check inside for some kind of sign of where they might have gone." He began walking into the temple before Clio could protest.

But Clio didn't want to protest. A strange pull tugged on a deep part of her, beckoning her in. She knelt and broke off a piece of the wooden door. "At least light the way first," she called to Riece.

Riece did as she asked. He took a piece of flint from his pocket and sparked it against a stone, lighting the thick beam on fire. He then tossed the flaming wood down into the basin of the temple. They both grabbed more kindling and stepped inside.

It was exactly like her family's temple in Sheehan. Three stepped walls descended downwards in the shape of a triangle. Vines had grown on the unused steps, forming a tangled mat that almost coated the ground below.

The heavy stench of rot hung in the air, the only sign that the Untouched had ever moved within these walls.

The burning log had landed in what would have been the pool of sacrificial waters, but it was as bone dry as the riverbed outside.

Their footsteps echoed off the walls, creating the impression that many people were walking with them, going down.

When they reached the bottom, Riece stopped on the final step, just before the drop into the empty pool, but Clio couldn't stop. She crossed the short pathway that usually parted the waters and moved to the altar. It was a crumbled ruin. Beads were scattered around its base. Bowls and vases were overturned as if someone had been pulled from here in a hurry. Clio wondered why the Untouched had not taken these valuables—pots made out of gold, with intricate carvings along the rims and pearls that sparkled with purity in the flickering light of the fire.

Riece dropped more wood onto the fire. "So you grew up in a temple like this?"

His voice pulled her out of whatever strange compulsion had drawn her down here. "Yes."

"Kind of depressing, isn't it?"

She had to laugh. "I've always thought so."

"Although I suppose yours at home isn't so decayed." He pulled a dead and dried vine up from the ground, crushing it as he spoke.

"Believe me, it's not much of a difference." The feeling she had, of recognition—it was because she belonged here. Or at least, she was supposed to belong here. Something deep in her called, and was called to this place.

But looking at Riece as he peered into the empty pool, Clio knew that something pulled her to him as well—the lines of his shoulders and the curve of his back so at odds with everything around him, the way his skin somehow still managed to look like the sun was shining directly down on him, glistening and glowing in a way no one's ever had in this dark and hollow space. Everything about him was so alive.

But he and this place were so utterly incompatible that Clio wondered how she would ever be able to reconcile the two parts of herself.

"You know men aren't allowed in here," she said. They were standing on opposite banks of the dried up pool.

"I do recall that. I imagine you would never be able to get

whatever it is you do down here done if you had men such as myself distracting you." He started to walk back over to her. "What is it that you do in here, anyway? I know my mother would get her orders here, but what is it *you* are supposed to do?" His words went out into the empty space around them, and for the first time, Clio realized how unnaturally quiet it was. It was never this silent in Sheehan's temple, even when she was alone. The steady trickle of water had always given some kind of life, muted though it was, to the space.

"I don't know exactly," Clio answered. "I know that blessings go on, and private séances, I suppose. I will have to figure it all out on my own. If I ever get the chance, that is." The thought of having to lead this world, a world from which she had tried so hard to get away, felt as if a heavy stone had lodged in her heart.

"Well," Riece kept his tone bright, "with no one to tell you what to do, you can make your own rules. And I say that your first one should be to allow men into the temple. All right, well, maybe not all men. Definitely not Derik, poor love-struck boy..."

"Riece," Clio chided as she leaned over the altar, resting her elbows on its crumbling surface.

"What?" he asked with mock innocence. "But truly, you can decide what you do. I mean, what's going to stop you?"

He had a point. It wasn't as if anyone was left who knew what she was supposed to do. She could abandon the entire temple if she wanted.

"It's not as if you need any of this to have Visions. All of this"— he waved his arm to mean the entire temple—"it just looks like grandeur to me. Like the palace, built to make others see you as someone powerful."

"I don't want that. I don't want any of this."

"Then give it up. Do things your own way."

A grin spread across her face. She would be her own Oracle. She would do things her own way. She dropped down into the empty pool, landing as gracefully and easily as if she were a feather.

Riece quickly jumped in beside her.

"This pool is supposed to hold the sacrificial waters." She remembered Mannix gazing into its unnaturally calm surface.

Mannix's voice echoed in her mind: *They say it carries the power of the Oracle. That she cannot be the servant to the Deities without it.* She could only hope.

"What was it used for?" Riece's voice pulled her from her memories.

"Ritual. My mother would use it to test other's worthiness. Somehow she was able to touch it when it burned almost everyone else. I used to think it was just one of her tricks, but maybe there was something—I don't know, something divine in it." Clio remembered how Maia had been one of the few girls unaffected and smiled.

"I fell in once as a child and came out covered in awful welts." She laughed. "I guess the Deities didn't find me worthy then. But that didn't stop them from burdening me with this." Her smile slipped. "All my life I was so scared." She stared into the crackling flames dancing before her.

"Of what?" He came over. The air between their bodies filled with that same humming energy.

"That I would be like them." She didn't need to explain what she meant. He knew. Of course, he knew. He had spent his whole life hating what she was becoming.

"You could never be like them," he said. A fierce certainty rang in his voice.

"I already am. I've killed. And I'll kill again." Her head fell as she cast her eyes to the floor.

"But not for yourself." He grabbed her face in his hand, lifting it. "Never for your own ambition." His eyes, just a breath away from hers, were blazing. "The hate I have carried for your kind, it's what brought me to where I am today. I've channeled it into my fighting."

She tried to shake her head out of his grasp, but he held her firmly in his calloused hands.

"Let me finish," he said with an almost breathless urgency. "That hate, it's been a bigger part of me than anything else in my life. And when I found out what you were, I would have killed you on the spot. Except"—and his eyes held her with all the raw intensity that rang in his words—"except by then, the hate, it had been burned away. You did that. Being with you...I always thought I was too broken to be happy again, but you showed me that wasn't true.

"I owe you my life a thousand times over, not because you've stopped spears from piercing my heart, but because you've shown me a world where you fight, not out of hate, but because you care, because there is so much worth fighting for."

She wanted to speak, to tell him that he had saved her too. That when all the world had been dark, he had been her light. That without him, she wouldn't have survived in any manner.

She opened her mouth to say everything she felt, but before she could get a single syllable out, he had crushed his mouth against hers. And all the words that had been hanging on the tip of her tongue just melted away. Because nothing else mattered. Nothing else even existed except for the feeling of his lips on hers.

His hands still held her face, locking her to him in an exquisite vise. She parted her lips, leaving herself open to him, enjoying the catch in his breath that this elicited. His lashes brushed against her cheeks, sending quick undulations of pleasure tingling through her skin. Her hands ran over the hard curves of his back, his shoulders, stopping only when her fingers tangled in the messy locks of his hair.

The moment was total bliss, and nothing mattered anymore but this. She wanted to stay locked in his embrace forever, feeling the beat of his heart quicken against her chest.

But she should have known better, because just when the entire world had faded away, a Vision brought it shattering back.

CHAPTER THIRTY-FIVE

Mannix, in his bright red robes, stood like a flame over a huddled form on the ground. A trail of deep red blood led from the crouched figure all the way out of the stone room. Too much blood, Clio thought. Heavy and thick bindings tied the figure's hands to the ground. Another captive.

A man, Clio realized. It wasn't a girl this time.

The sounds of a gentle trickle of water played over the captive's ragged and tired breathing. She wanted to get a better look at him, but her body was still held tightly in Riece's arms. She couldn't budge, couldn't even crane her neck.

"You know I really can't thank you enough." Mannix took a predatory step closer to the man on the ground. Clio could hear the gloating edge to his voice. The light caught the gleam of an obsidian blade. Blood dripped down its black surface, landing with heavy splatters on the floor at Mannix's feet.

"It's noble, really, that you would be willing to die for her," he continued, taking another step closer and bringing the knife forward. "If only she would do the same for you. But unfortunately for us all, they are all the same."

The man tried to get up, rising slowly and painfully onto his knees. Mannix only sighed. Just as the man pulled himself up, Mannix sent a vicious kick into his stomach. He collapsed, and Clio knew he wouldn't be able to get up again. She could hear him spitting blood onto the ground.

"Don't be too hard on yourself, though. There was nothing you could have done to stop her from being mine." And with those words, Mannix slashed down and across. Blood splattered the far wall. The man spluttered and choked as the blood poured down his throat. "I'll tell her you loved her, if that makes any difference."

Mannix left the room before the dying man stopped his agonized wheezing.

Clio didn't need to look at his face to know whose death she was watching. She would know him anywhere. But when Mannix left, it cleared Clio's line of sight, and she was forced to look upon his face as the life bled out of him.

Derik.

When the Vision left her, she found herself staring at a concerned Riece. She hadn't realized it, but she was shaking. Before he could say anything, she untangled herself from his arms, pulling much too forcefully away from him. She could see the hurt flash across his face as he let his arms drop to his side, dimming the eyes that only moments before had been burning with love and want.

"You had a Vision."

She nodded. "We have to go, now." She hugged her arms to her chest, trying to stop the fits of uncontrollable shaking that ran through her body.

"Clio, what did you see?" He reached out to her, as if to take her in his arms again. She wanted to let him, so much, but it was wrong. She pulled away. She didn't know how much time she had, how much time Derik had.

"Don't." She held up a hand to stop him. "It was Derik."

All the tenderness and the vulnerability disappeared from his face. He righted himself back into a guarded stance.

She continued, "He must try to stop Mannix from leaving, or something..."

"You Saw Derik get caught?"

"I Saw Mannix slit his throat." Her words came out as an accusation, as if Riece were the reason Derik was in danger.

As much as Clio hated to admit it, part of her did blame Riece. Because here she was kissing Riece when Derik needed help. Without Riece, she wouldn't have let everything else slip away. If she hadn't let the world fade away in Riece's arms, then somehow Derik wouldn't be in danger.

"You want to just rush into Sheehan, no plan, no idea where they could even be? You'll get us both killed. And for what? A kid who is going to foolishly take on more than he can handle? If we go in there to save him and we get killed, Mannix wins." His tone was hard, and Clio was glad. She deserved it as punishment for forgetting about Derik.

"I have an idea of where they will be." She hadn't realized it until this Vision. She had always assumed that Mannix was in the palace. Whenever she saw him in Sheehan, he was in a stone room. In Sheehan that could only be two places: the palace—and her temple.

It was the trickling water that had given it away. She should have realized it sooner.

"I'm not asking you to come with me," she went on, "but I can't sit by and wait for what I Saw to happen. I should have rushed into Sheehan as soon as I knew that Mannix was hurting people. I should have saved that girl he tortured. But I did nothing, and now he is going to take someone I love away from me."

She saw him bristle at the word "love."

"I'm not letting you go in there by yourself. He's going to be surrounded by Untouched."

"I'm leaving now. I don't need you to protect me. I should be doing this on my own anyway. Go home, Riece. I won't use you for my own problems."

He started gathering their few supplies. "Well, I'm afraid that you don't have any choice in the matter." He started walking up the steps and out of the temple.

"I never do," she said. But he was gone, and she spoke only to the empty temple.

CHAPTER THIRTY-SIX

They ran through the night. Clio wouldn't stop for anything, and it wasn't long before they shed all of their heavy supplies. It was dark, and the ground was jagged and unforgiving until finally they were clear of the mountains. From then on, the moon shone high above them, illuminating the open and rugged road before them.

Riece ran several paces behind Clio, the sound of his heavy breathing a constant reminder of how poorly she had handled everything. She wanted Riece to turn back. She hated endangering one more person, but she knew that arguing with him would just take up Derik's last and limited breaths.

She never should have stayed with Riece. That much was clear. Mannix was going to hurt people with or without her in Sheehan, and she had been selfish, arrogant, and ignorant to assume that staying away could be the right thing.

Derik had needed her. Sheehan had needed her, but she hadn't been ready. She had told herself that she was staying in Morek to learn about the Untouched, but really she stayed because of Riece.

She knew that. And stayed so that she could avoid, if only for a little longer, the prospect of returning to Sheehan and taking up the duties of an Oracle. It was selfish, and it was cowardly.

She sucked in massive breaths of the cold night air that stung her throat, but she didn't have time to worry about any physical pain. Her eyes remained fixed to a distant point, as if she could make out Sheehan on the horizon.

"Clio." Riece's rough voice called to her from behind. She ignored him. Her throat was too raw to speak.

"Clio." He tried again, this time putting on a burst of speed to catch up with her and grab her arm. "Clio, stop! Listen to me. You can't make this run. It's too far. We need to rest."

"No…" she tried to say, but a scratchy whisper was all that came out.

He had slowed her down, but she wouldn't stop. She couldn't. If she did, her whole body would shut down.

"You're bleeding," he huffed besides her, looking down at her feet.

She glanced down and was surprised to find two things. First, he was right. Her feet were a blistered and bleeding mess. She hadn't felt it as layers of skin had been worn off in her flight. Second, she could see the shredded skin on her feet and the faint trail of blood that followed behind, which meant that at some point dawn had come, bringing with it a gentle pink glow. She had been so focused on the horizon that she hadn't noticed the breaking day.

"We're too close," she managed to choke out, coughing on her dry tongue. She willed her body to push through all the pain and charge forward. "We need to head south to my temple."

They ran on, too tired to speak. Clio's feet felt worn down to the bones, and a tiny part of her worried that after this she would never walk normally again.

It doesn't matter, she told herself. All that mattered was reaching Derik before it was too late. If her feet were the price to pay for that, they would be an easy sacrifice.

Finally, they reached the stream that fed the temple pool. She splashed through the icy water, grateful for the stinging relief. They crouched and gulped down mouthful after mouthful of the water, soothing their screaming throats.

"We walk from here," Riece said. It wasn't a question.

She nodded. It wouldn't do any good to barrel into a party of Untouched.

Before long, the all-too-familiar outline of the temple rose out of the ground. In the morning light, she could make out at least a dozen men dressed in Mannix's signature color, standing guard outside the front doors.

"Looks like you were right about where Mannix was hiding."

"I should have known sooner. Some Oracle I am."

"At some point, you are going to have to stop blaming yourself for everything that has happened and start blaming the person actually responsible."

She looked up at him. He must have seen the weary look in her eyes because he sighed and added, "So if Mannix already has Derik, then where in there would they be?"

"What I saw didn't look familiar." There was only one part of the temple that she had never seen before, one part that was for the Oracle's eyes only. "There's a small chamber adjoining the main room of the temple. It was my mother's private chamber. I was never allowed inside. That's where they must be."

"So you sneak in and hope that Derik is alone in there, while I distract Mannix's guests."

She gulped. It was a bad plan. Too many unknowns. Derik might not even be in there. Mannix could be in there torturing him. Or worst of all, Derik could already be dead. Too many possibilities. Not to mention, Riece would be taking on all of those armed guards by himself.

"I'm going to beg you one more time. Please go home, Riece. This isn't your fight."

"You still planning on going in?"

She nodded.

"Then this is the only fight that I've ever needed to be in." His eyes burned with all the words left unsaid.

He grabbed her hand, only for a moment. Clio couldn't allow herself any more comfort than that. She squeezed his rough hand hard in hers. "Be safe," she whispered.

He pulled away from her and headed straight toward the circle of robed men.

For once, she wished the Deities would give her a Vision. She was sending Riece into a fight that she could not foresee.

She held her breath as he went, watching the strong lines of his arms and back, free of his usual golden cloak, as he strode confidently into battle.

The men motioned for Riece to stop, but he feigned confusion and carried on. In the blink of an eye, they all pulled out their weapons. Riece continued on. He marched right up to them, stood for a moment, and then swiped out and grabbed a man's spear, using the other end to ram into another man to the right.

This was it. He was providing the distraction. Now it was her turn. With a final glance at Riece, who was spinning and slashing as if it was the most natural thing in the world, she slipped into the dark and empty temple.

Only it wasn't empty.

For the second time, she had found Mannix inside where men weren't allowed.

He sat atop the altar, the swirling water around him only bringing the violent shade of his robe into sharper focus.

He was studying a long, curved blade, turning it over in his hand as if he were bored and waiting for something.

When he heard her descend the steps, he looked up and smiled.

"Finally," he sighed as he lithely sprung away from the altar. "I worried you'd never come."

CHAPTER THIRTY-SEVEN

She froze. Something was wrong. Where was Derik? Mannix should have been with him. It could only mean that she was too late. "Where is he?"

"I should have known it would take this to get you here." Mannix tucked the blade under his robe and stalked toward her, taking deliberately slow predatory steps in her direction.

She began backing up, toward the thin hallway that led into the Oracle's private chamber. Her bare and raw feet skimmed painfully over the stone floor. "Take what?"

"Your precious prince. You're here because you Saw me killing him, and you wanted to save him. Correct?"

Her eyes darted to the dark hallway that emptied out onto the middle of the far wall's steps. If only she could get to it.

"One would think it would be an impossible feat to lure an Oracle into a trap. After all, you are the one who can See what I am doing, whereas I have no idea where you are. Or at least, I should have no idea, but I know you and your kind pretty well by now."

His eyes shone with triumph, as if her showing up here was the greatest thing in the world. The skin along Clio's exposed arms prickled in warning as she kept backing up toward the dark hallway, hoping that no Untouched lay in wait for her.

"But I have to say—you really did surprise me. I thought you would come when you Saw me torture those girls. I knew the Deities would have to show you my crimes, but you just watched. That wasn't the caring Clio I knew. I worried that maybe you didn't have the Sight yet.

"But then you assured me that you did, in fact, have the Sight, and you were...*somewhat* concerned for the girls. Only not enough to risk your pretty little neck, I guess." He dragged out his words, showing the glint of his teeth as he smirked.

He was wrong. He had it all wrong. She had wanted to save them. She would have done anything to save them if she could. But a nagging voice in her head told her that that wasn't totally true. After all, she had dropped everything for Derik. She should have done the same for that girl. But truthfully, seeing that girl had scared her. She didn't want to be next.

"I'm not the one who tortured them, as what—*practice* for me? You would have used them even if you had me already. Don't want your precious Oracle dying too soon, right? You are a monster, just as barbaric as your Untouched." She flung her words at him as if they were blades that could slice him open and spill his blood across the stone.

"You really are slow, aren't you? Sure, they were practice. Yes, some told me interesting bits of information about you, like an odd connection with a certain commander. But mostly I learned how to push a girl's body to its very edge. Push it to a place where a single word is enough to bring out every hidden secret. And I will put that knowledge to good use." He eyed her viciously. "But they were also bait. Bait *you didn't take.*" He took a step closer. They were only a few paces apart now. He could close the distance in an instant if he wanted.

"Which showed me that you have become more and more heartless, like your dear mother, each day. It's a shame, really. Before all of this, you were such a passionate, caring girl. I remember how ardently you searched for your sister, even stood up to your own mother. That Clio, I'm afraid, is long gone."

Her head was full of an incessant buzzing. He was trying to distract her, to keep her from getting to Derik. She refused to believe that he was already dead. But he was definitely running out of time, and she didn't need to stand here, listening to Mannix's twisted words.

He was several steps below her. Without any of his warriors with him, he was no match for her. Not now. Even though her body screamed out in protest, battered by the all-night journey, she willed it to do the last bit that it could. Without warning, she lunged from her perch.

One moment, Mannix was standing, relaxed, talking to her without a hint of anticipation. She should have landed on him, sending him hard into the jagged ground, slamming his head into the stone. But somehow, she found herself flying across the temple. Her back collided with the corner of the stone altar, sending blinding pain through her spine.

Her entire body revolted, her vision dimmed, and everything in her crumpled to the ground. When she tried to move her legs, tried to rise to face him, she felt a sickening crunch reverberate under her skin. Something was broken—crushed, maybe. Even the smallest movement sent out nauseating waves of pain, making it impossible to so much as crawl away.

She looked up at him, tears blurring her vision, and found that he was holding the long, curved blade at his side. He had moved so fast, unnaturally fast, pulling it out and knocking her across the room with its broad side.

He knelt besides her, jabbing the point of his blade into the skin just above her hip. "Now, now, Clio, will you let me finish? We have some time to kill before my men out there finish with your boy and come down to join us."

She tried to pull away, but the pain was too much. His smooth hands slipped under her chin, turning her face back to his.

"Where was I? Oh, yes. You would not come for a nameless girl, so I had to think of another way to coax you out of hiding—and well, when Derik followed me this morning, spying on me, I figured I might as well give it a try. I'm glad to see that you still have *some* humanity. That your family hadn't robbed you of it all before they died."

"Before you had them butchered, you mean," she spat at him.

He did nothing as the spittle ran down his cheek. When it reached his lips, his tongue flashed out. Clio had to choke down the bile that rose in the back of her throat.

His amused expression faded into a somber one. "But Clio, you too have killed."

"Only to protect others! Only people who left me with no other choice." She found herself screaming. His words—they twisted her thoughts. She knew he was wrong, that she was nothing like the girl he was describing, but the way he spoke in half-truths and over-simplifications made it hard to argue with him.

"Your family was just as murderous as the men you killed."

This stopped her.

"Ah, so you don't doubt this one. No mouthing back at me this time? Of course, you know the truth of your mother as well as I. Although there are secrets about which even you are still in the dark."

She couldn't think about it, and she didn't want to know. Didn't want to know what other crimes had been committed by her own blood.

"The truth is you have killed, just like your family—and even worse, you have done nothing to prevent the deaths your powers have shown you." His hand was still gripping her chin, forcing her to look at him.

"I'm here now. I came to save Derik, to stop you." She was nothing like her family. She was still Clio.

"I thought you would have more compassion. I thought you were still young enough to care about the ones you didn't love, but your mother's talons sank in too deep, too early.

"Nonetheless, I did manage to get you here eventually." He smiled. "Your mother, she would *never* have stormed into danger to fight purely out of love, no matter who it was for. I have to give you that."

"I'm not like her." She didn't know why she felt the need to defend herself, to separate herself from her mother. She had spent her whole life trying to be someone else because she knew she was different. She cared about people. She felt. She loved. "Just because you made it so I would inherit this...curse doesn't mean that I've lost what I am."

"Maybe," he mused. "Then prove it."

A tortured scream carrying all the anguish of death shattered the silence around them.

"The Untouched don't scream," Mannix said, a wicked grin splitting his lips. "Sounds like you brought your boy here to die, used him in a way not unlike how your mother would use her Vessels. It's a shame, really. He was such a gifted warrior. Still, he's not the first to be used by your kind."

His words were like ice freezing her heart, so much so that she felt it struggle to break free and beat. Riece couldn't be dead. She couldn't take another loss. Her mother had been right the night Clio had run away—she should have tried to rein in her emotions more. She shouldn't have let herself fall for someone whom she could never protect. She hadn't wanted him to be here in the first place. She had never asked for any of this, never wanted to be anything but normal. If Riece died, then Clio knew she would have no choice but to become stone. She wouldn't survive otherwise.

"Why are you doing this?" she screamed at Mannix. "What do you want from me?"

"Give yourself up to me." His tone was flat, serious. "This"—he pressed his thumb into her spine, making her cry out—"it's not necessary. Stop your struggling before any more damage is done to you."

She remembered the fear in his eyes when she had threatened to spill her own blood. He still needed her alive for whatever he had planned.

"You know that I'll die fighting you, that I'd sooner take my own life before I let you have what you want." Her voice was ragged, but he must have seen the truth in her eyes.

He lowered his blade.

"Perhaps, but you *will* do as I say, believe me. You may not care about your own life—you've more than proven that. But you killed for Ali and for Riece. And now, you've brought yourself here to die for Derik." He leaned in closer and whispered in her ear. "It doesn't have to be *your* body that I bring to the edges of sanity. All you need do is watch."

Shadows moved across the light shining down on them, followed by the sound of stumbling footsteps. Several Untouched were dragging a bleeding and beaten Riece down into the temple. His arm hung at an unnatural angle. At the end of it, what Clio could make out looked more like raw meat than a hand. His head hung limply forward.

"Prove to me that you aren't heartless, that you aren't like your mother. Sacrifice yourself. Give yourself to me to save him from all this pain."

The Untouched dropped Riece behind Mannix and stood back silent.

She cried out to Riece, tried to use her arms to pull herself toward him, but Mannix held her back.

"Shh, now. Clio, listen to me. I don't have to harm him further. We can save him, you and I. We can save Derik, too. You never wanted this. It's why I picked you. You don't have what it takes to be an Oracle, and that's not a bad thing. It's good. You were good. You care too much to perform this duty, and your mother knew it. But," his voice darkened, "since you have gotten the Sight, you've lost almost everything about yourself.

"All you have to do," he went on, "is tell me everything you See. Every Vision. Tell me that, and no harm needs to come to him."

She was crying. Her tears streamed down her cheeks and onto his thumb that held her face. She couldn't argue with him. Her mother knew that Clio wasn't what an Oracle should be. If Clio didn't care, if she could be like her mother and her sisters, then Mannix wouldn't have this control over her. Everything he said was right. She would give anything to go back to herself before all this. As she remembered her desperate hope that she could possibly leave all of this behind, a Vision was forced behind her eyes.

Mannix stood before a throne in the great palace of Morek. The room was completely empty, save for Mannix and the Emperor. The golden walls that Clio had admired during the feast were scorched black. Burned. The whole palace had been burnt.

The Emperor sat on his throne. Mannix approached, with a wicked grin on his face.

"I have no need for you any longer," Mannix said. "You may leave."

"You'll have to take my body away in pieces before I relinquish my throne."

"That"—Mannix's eyes flared—"can be arranged."

With a snap of Mannix's fingers, men dressed in red robes emerged from every opening. They filed in, filling the space completely.

An army of Untouched.

CHAPTER THIRTY-EIGHT

When she came back, Mannix was staring at her.

"You Saw something. What was it?"

She remained silent. If she told him that he was going to win, nothing would change. He would make her watch as he tortured Riece. She would be forced to tell him everything she Saw, and with that knowledge, he would end up exactly where her Vision had shown him—ruler of the Empire.

No, she couldn't tell him. She had to change his fate.

"Don't do it." Riece's hoarse voice shattered the moment. Her eyes flashed to him. She could see how much of a struggle it was for him to raise his head. Blood dripped down from his lip. His eye was already swollen shut. "Don't tell him. He can't make you do anything."

"Yes, I can." Mannix spoke as he nodded to one of his guards.

A club slammed into Riece's head with a sickening thud.

"Tell me, Clio."

She couldn't watch this. She couldn't watch Riece suffer for her.

The only thing she could think to do, the only way that she could maybe throw Mannix off his course was to lie. "I saw your death." She threw as much conviction into her voice as she could, trying hard not to look at Riece gasping on the ground.

"You lie." Mannix's voice cracked.

"You are going to die, Mannix. I saw it."

Fear dimmed his eyes as he turned to the Untouched. "Bring in the prince." Two left without a word. Her eyes followed them as they entered the dark hallway where Derik must have been kept. They emerged moments later, pushing a man in front of them.

Derik could walk, but his hands were bound in front of him. A long gash split open his cheek, the blood dark and crusted along its edges.

His face fell when his eyes found Clio, taking in the way her legs lay uselessly to the side.

"Don't," she pleaded with Mannix. He wouldn't look at her. With a nod from him, the Untouched moved as one, shoving Derik onto the ground beside Riece. The guards held them both down, immobilizing them, as Mannix swept toward them.

"You can stop all of this, Clio. All you have to do is tell me what you Saw. I've got two men here, and I only need one. Tell me, or one of them dies."

"Don't do it, Clio. He'll kill you," Derik begged, his eyes pleading. Those same gray eyes that had reassured her when everything was falling apart, the eyes that she had grown up dreaming about.

Mannix slowly raised his long blade.

"These two men love you, Clio. Are you going to let them suffer for you? Just tell me!"

Her entire body was shaking. If she gave in to him, Riece and Derik might be all right. But countless others would die at Mannix's will. She had seen Morek scorched black with his fury. She couldn't let it come to that. But if she didn't, she would have to watch as one of the only two people she cared about died in front of her. Because of her. The Oracle would have to make sacrifices. But not this. How could she be expected to do this?

Her eyes slid from Derik's fiercely determined expression over to Riece, and her breath caught in her chest. His face reflected no pain, no fear—nothing but pure, unfiltered love. She couldn't look at them, couldn't bear to watch as their final breaths slid from their chests.

"Pay attention," Mannix yelled, slamming the hilt of his blade into the side of her face. She fell to the floor, her vision doubling from the force of the blow. He dragged the edge of the blade slowly and lightly across Riece's chest, then Derik's.

"Which of you two does the girl love more?" he pondered. "Is it"—he brought the blade up to Derik's neck—"the childhood companion, the prince?"

"Please," she moaned through her tears, "please, no."

"No, not that one?" In a flash he brought the blade over to Riece's neck. "Is it the new lover, the warrior rescuer?"

"It's all right, Clio," was all Riece said.

She bit her tongue, blood filling her mouth. Everything within her was screaming for her to make it stop. She tried to get up, to throw herself at Mannix, but even the slightest movement shot such pain through her that blackness reared in her mind. She had to fight to stay conscious through the grating of her shattered bones.

"Let's see," and he swung the blade out quickly. She screamed. It all happened in a flash. First, the black blur of the blade swooping down on Riece, then the crimson spray of blood shooting out in its wake.

Riece collapsed on all fours, only a choked groan escaping his lips. It took every last drop of resolve in Clio to look at him as he was pulled back up on his knees. The slice had been shallow, only a long, thin red line streaked across his chest. It was not fatal, and the relief brought forth a torrent of sobs.

"TELL ME WHAT YOU SAW!" he bellowed, his blade at the ready.

He would keep hurting them until she said something. She racked her brain for anything, another lie, something believable. "The Untouched," she murmured.

"Yes?" He came over to her. She breathed a sigh of relief as he left Riece and Derik behind him.

"They—they are the ones who kill you. They have no real loyalty to you." It wasn't out of the realm of possibility. With everything that Riece told her, it seemed likely that they could turn on him at any given moment. She met his eyes, sure that she had beaten him at his own game.

But he only laughed. "Clio, Clio, Clio. It's a nice attempt. But it's a lie."

She straightened as much as she could. "No, it's what I Saw."

"It's NOT!" He took a step back and recovered himself.

"You're not one of them. There's no reason for them to feel loyal to you." But she was beginning to feel she was missing something.

Mannix's eyes carried the fatal truth. "No, Clio. That is where you are wrong. You see, I *am* one of them."

CHAPTER THIRTY-NINE

"How can that be?" she stammered. It wasn't possible. He had been living in Sheehan for so long. He could speak. None of it made any sense.

"Until I came to the king in Sheehan, I had spent my entire life among the Untouched. They raised me, and I am one of them."

Still bleeding on the floor, Riece spoke up. "Why did they let you keep your tongue?"

"I know you spent some time among my brothers." Mannix addressed Riece from where he stood. "Can you tell Clio why the Untouched remove their tongues?"

"So that they can become their own warrior. Independent from all the rest." Clio could see that Riece was trying to make sense of it all.

"Correct. And do you know who mutes each child?" Mannix was enjoying this, but Clio couldn't understand why.

"Their mother."

"Correct again. Well, I was raised by the Untouched, but I was not born to them. You are wondering why they let me live, are you not? Let's just say, they recognized that I had a very *interesting* lineage."

"But—" Riece started.

Mannix whipped the blade forward again, perfectly crossing the cut he had just made on Riece's chest. Blood spattered across Mannix's face. "We have other things to discuss now."

He walked over to Derik and jabbed the blade through Derik's shoulder. Without stopping, he raised the weapon and slashed it viciously down Derik's face. It was shallow enough to let him live, but deep enough that Clio knew his face would never be the same again.

Mannix was making it clear—he was not going to stop this time.

"Please!" Clio cried, desperately trying to reach out to him, to pull him back.

Mannix moved behind Riece and pressed the blade into his back, right behind his heart. He growled in frustrated impatience, "I'm done waiting. You lied to me. Now tell me the truth of your Vision or this will kill him, Clio." She could tell he was pressing into Riece's flesh as Riece's face twisted in agony.

"Stop," she screamed, choking on her sobs. "Stop," she said again more calmly. "I Saw you win! I Saw you take the throne in Morek! Now, whatever you want, I'll do it. I'll tell you anything. Just don't hurt them." When she finished speaking, she collapsed onto the ground, her chest heaving, pressing painfully into the stone beneath her.

CHAPTER FORTY

"Thank you." Mannix's eyes rolled back in his head in pleasure, relishing his victory. "Clio, dear." He was back in front of her with some kind of binding in his hands.

She offered her wrists to him, staring into the water below as he tied her hands tightly together. She didn't care anymore. She would do whatever he wanted as long as Derik and Riece were free.

He moved to her legs and knelt as if he were going to tie them together, but stopped. He tossed the unused rope to the men behind him, realizing that it was pointless to bind her broken legs.

"Tie them up." His voice came from right above Clio.

"No!" she yelled. "I'll do whatever you want! I said I would tell you anything. Please," she groaned, "please let them go."

"I'm truly sorry, Clio. But I cannot trust you. I cannot trust that you will continue to cooperate if I let these men go. And I cannot trust that they will not try to rescue you. But I promise that as long as you continue to help me, they will not be harmed."

He was going to hold them as hostages, use them to get her to do whatever he wished. And it would work. He had shown her how effective threatening Riece and Derik was. She would do anything to protect them. People would die because of it.

"Clio, I want you to know that by doing this—by giving yourself to me for these men—you are doing something of which your mother was never capable." Mannix was looking at her as if he really wanted to make her feel better. Almost as if he cared.

"You don't know anything about my mother."

"She killed many. She was even willing to sacrifice her own children."

"She did not. *You* are responsible for my sisters' deaths. Not her."

"It was not to your sisters that I was referring." He spoke very slowly, willing her to understand.

The world seemed to tip around Clio. She stared at him, gaping, trying to figure out what he was talking about.

"Years ago, there was another child. A boy." A chill ran down Clio's spine, but he continued. "Boys, you may not know, cannot inherit the Sight, nor can they be a Vessel. He would have been a dead weight to her. And so, instead of raising him like a mother should, she left him outside to die."

No...Clio thought. What he was saying...it couldn't be true.

"I imagine she never knew that he survived, or maybe she just never cared either way. But the boy did survive. He was picked up by a wandering tribe of Untouched, and he grew up hating the woman who had thrown him away. He grew up and planned to destroy her

319

and take the power that should have been his by birth.

"So, dear sister, I think I know our mother best." His grin was a malicious snarl, showing all of his teeth.

CHAPTER FORTY-ONE

"While I may be unable to inherit the powers of our mother, I will not be left blind. You, sister, you will tell me everything I need to know. You will give me the power that I deserve. Through you, the Deities will speak, and I will listen. You will no longer have to act on what you are Shown. I will take care of everything. In practice, I will be the Oracle, and you can return to being just Clio." Mannix's eyes lit with rapture as he spoke.

As his words rang in her ears, she found herself staring at the trickle of Riece's blood that had rolled to the water's edge. A drop rested precariously on the stone's edge, growing bigger and bigger until the weight was too much, and it tumbled soundlessly into the pool. Bright red spread out in the cool blue of the water, dispersing until it was consumed, dissipated.

Blood and sacrifice. It was all her life had become at this point.

The crimes of the Oracle, of her mother, seemed to never end. So much of Clio wanted to deny Mannix's claim, to say that her mother would never have done such a thing. But Clio knew too much about the Oracle by now. She knew what the Deities could ask of her, what was required to do the sacred tasks. And she knew that her mother was dutiful. Her mother had sacrificed everything for her sacred duty—why not a son? The Untouched would never have kept him alive if he were just ordinary. They had to have known there was something unique in him.

Clio would have felt a spark of sympathy for the man who was once a lost child if she wasn't staring at a trail of Riece's blood. If she didn't have to hear Derik's ragged breathing echoing through the chamber.

If Clio could give them up, her city might make it. Mannix could kill her and he would never have her power at his fingertips. But Clio couldn't sacrifice the ones she loved. She didn't have it in her. Her mother had abandoned her child because of duty. It was easy to see her actions as wrong, easy to lay the blame for all of this on her mother's resolute commitment to duty, but Clio would never know her mother's reasoning. She could never know how hard it must have been for her mother to do this thing. So hard that maybe it was the very action that had petrified her mother.

As Mannix prepared to transport them all out of the temple, Clio stared into the swirling water. She wished she could have just died on top of that pyramid. It would have meant less suffering for everyone she loved. Her passion made it impossible to give up the ones she loved, but it also made it easy to give up herself.

Clio felt strength coursing through her ruined body. Her mother had been wrong. Sacrifice didn't have to come from an absence of feeling. It was the opposite.

She had never understood it before, but looking back, she understood what her sister had told her the night before she was lost:

And if I have to change a little in order to better do this, then that's the sacrifice I am called upon to make.

Ali hadn't been scared to give up part of who she was so that she could become a Vessel and serve an Oracle she truly believed in. Maia too. Even in her last moments, Maia had clung to the assurance that giving up her life would help the people she cared about.

But Clio had been too consumed with remaining herself, with fighting the Oracle in her. And she hated herself for it. Hated the girl who had been too selfish, the girl who had naively clung to what she could no longer be. She had desperately wanted to remain a girl when fate had asked her to become so much more.

Maybe if she had allowed herself to become what was supposed to be, the people she cared about wouldn't be in danger now. She couldn't run from being the Oracle. Running had only hurt more people.

She should have given herself over to it long ago. She should have made the sacrifice as soon she had been called upon.

"You could never be the Oracle." She looked up at Mannix with the iron resolution of someone who had already given up everything reflected in her eyes.

For once he looked surprised, confused at this sudden change in demeanor transpiring before him.

"You don't even know what it means to be the Oracle." She

wouldn't look away from him, wouldn't give herself the pleasure of a quick glance at Derik and Riece. She couldn't be that Clio anymore. They needed the Oracle, not a scared, little girl.

"Really? Enlighten me, Clio." His voice quavered as he glanced at his guards, as if he were trying to discover the source of her sudden display of courage.

"Being the Oracle means being a sacrifice. A sacrifice to the Deities and to man. You don't get a choice anymore. You don't get anything except for what is needed for your people.

"I've stared sacrifice in the eyes. I stood atop the great pyramid of Morek. I've watched as girls gave up everything in the hopes of helping those around them. You, you have done nothing but kill and take for your own pleasure.

"But I can show you." She grabbed his robes tightly in her fists, her two hands still bound together, and pulled him down to her level. He tried to pull away, but nothing could move her. She pulled him closer, so close that she could smell the sweat beading on his brow. She whispered into his ear. "I can give you a taste of what it means to be the Oracle, what it means to be a sacrifice."

With her good leg, she pushed against the stone altar behind her as hard as she could, sending them both off the edge. The pain was blinding, but it didn't matter. In fact, she welcomed it.

They fell, plunging into the sacred pool below, disturbing its still water as they parted the silver surface. As the cool waves lapped over their heads, pushing them farther and farther into its depths, Clio made a promise, a sacrifice to whatever Deities were listening.

She would give herself over as their Vessel in the world of men. She would serve them in everything they Showed her, everything they asked of her, no matter the cost to herself. She would give up her idle visions of a normal life, and she would offer up everything within her power to her sacred duty.

She didn't need to ask for anything in return. It would be up to the Deities to decide if her sacrifice was worthy.

Mannix, twisting in agony, sank like a rock to the bottom. She tried to hold onto his robes, but they were torn from her fingers. Her hand came away with a tiny scrap of material. She couldn't make it out in all the turbulent water roiling around her.

Clio remembered how when she fell into the sacrificial waters as a child, her skin had been painfully blistered. She hadn't been willing to offer anything up that time. She hadn't been the Oracle.

But now the water was soothing, softer than a gentle brush of lips, smoother than a bare caress. She opened her eyes, and the light that broke through the water's surface was splintered into a thousand shards of sparkling and dancing colors.

More colors than Clio had ever known spun and twinkled around her. She turned, trying to see it all, and was alarmed by a red streak fanning out behind her. At first she thought it was blood, that she had been too hurt when she dove in and that she was going to die here in this beautiful prism, but then she caught a glimpse of a stray strand of her hair.

It was back to pure white, almost indistinguishable from the light itself. All of the red dye that had been obscuring who she had to be, that had been keeping her hidden, had been washed away by the purifying water.

She couldn't stay here forever, couldn't remain in this perfect suspension much longer. She had made a promise, and as soon as her body emerged into the air above, she would have to start fulfilling that oath. Pulling with her arms, she began to ascend back into the world. But as she looked up at the pool's surface, admiring the streaks of golden light that cut along the gentle waves, a searing pain cut through her ankle.

She looked down to see Mannix holding her ankle, trying to use her to reach the surface.

The surface moved farther and farther away as Mannix pulled Clio down into the water's depths. She was uncomfortably aware of how tight her lungs felt, as if they would burst in the next moments if she didn't get air.

But Mannix seemed unable to move much, as if he were trapped in the cloud of bubbles that engulfed his entire body, swarming around him like buzzards around a carcass.

He was boiling, his skin blistering and peeling off before her very eyes.

He didn't know how to be a sacrifice, and so the water claimed one of its own.

She kicked, trying to free her foot from his burning vise, preparing herself for the blinding pain that moving her leg would bring, but it never came. Her bones somehow had knotted back together, but Clio couldn't take a moment to marvel at this miracle.

She slammed her foot down on Mannix as hard as she could.

His hand slipped off her, or maybe his skin slipped off his bones. Clio didn't look back to see. Kicking, pulling, and straining with every muscle in her body, she finally breached the surface, gulping in as much air as her lungs could hold.

Blindly, she groped for the stone ledge. When her fingers found its gritty surface, she pulled herself out of the water, ready to fight.

CHAPTER FORTY-TWO

Water streamed down her face, over her eyes, splashing in heavy droplets on the ground below. The temple was dark, so much dimmer than the glittering light within the water, but it didn't matter. She could see every last detail, every shadow that danced across the stone.

Riece and Derik were still restrained, held down firmly on their knees by several Untouched.

Every pair of eyes in the room was locked on her. And on every face, in every expression, on every curve of every mouth, was carved an unadulterated awe.

She knew what they were gazing upon. She could see it in their eyes. Everyone in that temple was looking at the true Oracle.

They had all watched as a beaten and broken girl dove pitifully into a pool of water that she had absolutely no hope of coming out of, and yet somehow she had. Somehow she had not only come out of it without Mannix, but she had come out whole. Healed and more powerful than before. She stood before them without the slightest sign of injury. Not a drop of blood was left anywhere on her body. Water cascaded down the sharp lines of her muscles. Her hair was slicked back, but it still gave off a dazzling white light as if its very strands somehow carried some of the sun's rays.

Riece didn't miss his chance. Taking advantage of his captors' distraction, he threw his head back, smashing the Untouched behind him solidly in the face. Before the man could recover, Riece swung his hands behind him, pulling a dagger from the man's sheath. In the blink of an eye, he rose to face the men around him, his bindings hanging, shredded from his wrists. Blood coated his face, his chest, his hands. Fire burned in his eyes, sharpened by the black edge of the dagger before him.

One of the Untouched made to move toward Riece, but Clio held up her hand.

"Stop," she commanded. It was then that she realized she still had a piece of Mannix's robes in her fist. She lowered her hand, opening it under her eyes, and saw that it wasn't a part of his robes at all.

Nestled in the curves of her palm was something small and brown. It was an intricately woven pattern of a spiraling sun. A token. Somehow in the confusion below, she had managed to pull Mannix's token from his robes.

She tossed it to their feet, letting the Untouched get a good look at what she had taken from Mannix.

At the instant the token touched the ground, the temple began to shake around them. Huge stones from the roof fell with thunderous booms onto the steps, rolling down until they splashed into the pool. The ground beneath their feet began to shake violently, causing the Untouched to stumble to their knees.

Derik rolled out of the way just as a man-sized stone crushed the Untouched holding him down. He swept up the fallen token as he yelled to Clio, "We have to get out now!"

He was answered with a deafening crack that seemed to travel along the entire length of the temple. Looking up, Clio saw the jagged line that split the stone above her. They had only moments before everything would collapse, burying them in the rubble.

The Untouched must have realized the same thing. They clambered over one another, their desperate flinging movements speaking the screams that their mouths left unsaid.

Rocks crashed down on them, but Clio didn't wait to see if any of them made it out of the torrent. "This way!" she called to Riece and Derik. Her footing was sure even though the ground was not. Rubble rained down around them, clattering into the pool and sending waves of water crashing onto the steps.

The very world was falling apart around her, but Clio wasn't scared. This was her temple, and it was called down to the dirt for her to crush her enemies. She didn't flinch as the falling walls crumbled around her.

Deftly, she stepped over shattered rock and broken steps until she reached the black mouth of the Oracle's chamber. The hallway was dark, and Clio had no fire to light her way, but even though Clio had never set foot in this alcove, she felt that hum of familiarity crackle through her veins.

Her body knew what her eyes had never seen. She heard Derik and Riece behind her, treading cautiously in the dark.

They reached a small, circular room. It was mostly bare save for a stone slab holding several urns and a single rolled-up scroll. Roots coated the walls, threading their way down from a dusty opening in the dirt ceiling above.

Clio climbed up onto the slab and felt Derik's gentle hands encircle her waist, lifting her up to the light above.

The sun had fully risen, and when Clio pulled herself up she was facing the back of the temple. As Derik and Riece climbed out of the pit behind her, she watched as the final stones collapsed in a billowing cloud of dirt and sand and dust.

The temple that she had spent her entire life hating lay in ruins at her feet. She knelt down and picked up a shard of stone no bigger than her finger. Had Clio looked upon this rubble only hours earlier, she would have felt more free, more uplifted, more elated than ever before. But now, she had promised her life to this. She had made an oath to the Deities, and that oath would remain with or without a temple.

She flicked the shard of stone onto the ground and turned her back on everything she had left buried in the ruins.

CHAPTER FORTY-THREE

She still hadn't grown used to her room. She had been in Morek a short time, but somehow her body had adjusted to its fresh air, sweeping vistas and colorful walls.

Now that she was back in Sheehan, things were different. No longer did she look out her window and see a glistening and bright city teeming with colors and life. Sheehan was a blur of brown, of the muddy tan in every house's clay. Maybe to some it was boring. Certainly, to anyone who had seen the brilliance of Morek. But in a way, the simplicity of Sheehan made everything else so much more beautiful in comparison. The sky's blue never looked as dramatic as it did hanging over Sheehan. No colors save the earth itself distracted from the beauty above.

Still, Clio couldn't help but feel foreign in her own home. The streets were all familiar, the accents, the food, the dress, even the people—everything was as it had been throughout Clio's whole life. But Clio had come back into all of this as the Oracle. Every look, every word, every gesture carried a new and cold distance. The distance between a commoner and the Oracle of Sheehan. Clio was left feeling just as out of place as she had been when she first set foot in Morek.

Clio didn't want to admit it, but much of her unease had to do with Riece. She hadn't seen him since the temple fell. After they had returned to Sheehan, they found that hordes of the Untouched were camped just outside the city limits, waiting for some kind of signal from Mannix. Riece had had to rush back to Morek. Without the Emperor's help, Sheehan would fall if the Untouched attacked.

She could see them now, distant black dots on the horizon. She sat at her window in the palace, her eyes darting between the threat at their borders and the sparse life in Sheehan's streets. Her city needed her.

"Don't worry, my troops will arrive tomorrow." Riece spoke from just behind her.

Clio jumped at his voice. She hadn't heard him come down the hall. So much for being the Oracle.

"Remember what I said about knocking?" She tried for teasing, but her voice trembled. He was wearing all of his warrior regalia, his gold cloak gleaming behind him. His bandaged hand was the only visible reminder of how close she had come to losing him forever.

He laughed, and for a moment the sight of his warm smile pushed all thoughts of the oath she had made out of her mind. It would be so easy to abandon it all.

But she couldn't.

"I'm sorry, Clio. We didn't find him."

She sighed as she stood. "I know he's out there." They had searched the temple ruins, but found no sign of Mannix in all the rubble.

"How?"

She stared through him as she spoke. "The sacrifice I made, it wasn't blood. I didn't offer up my beating heart, just my life. Only blood can take blood." She understood balance now. She gave up her freedom so that Derik and Riece could have theirs. Sometimes when she was all alone, she wondered if it would have been better to spill her blood in order to kill Mannix.

He must have seen it in her face. "We need you. All of us. It doesn't matter that he's out there as long as we have you."

"I hope that's true." She turned from him, her eyes falling on the horizon. She hoped that if she stared at it long enough, she would be shown what to do.

"I know that I need you." His words hung soft in the air, vulnerable.

Riece didn't waste any more time. He strode over to Clio and swept her up in his arms, covering her face with light, quick kisses that sent her skin into flames, and then cooled it with whispered incantations of her name.

"Riece, stop," she moaned against his lips. "Please, stop." Her voice was breathless, raw, overcome with everything she wanted. But she had to talk to him, to explain. It wouldn't be fair to him. "I need to talk to you."

"Clio, I'm in the middle of something very important right

now." He got the words out, one at a time, as he trailed kisses down her neck, along her collarbone.

It was harder than it should have been to pull away from him. When she did, she could see the dark burn of desire lighting his eyes.

"I'm the Oracle now. Things are different."

"You've always been the Oracle. It hasn't kept me from you yet."

"No." She held her hand up. "What happened in the temple…I made a promise to the Deities."

His arms dropped to his sides. "What kind of promise?"

It would be so easy to back out of the promise she had made. To simply accept what the Deities had done for her and move on with her life. She even reasoned that if Mannix was dead, maybe she could get away with it. Even if he wasn't dead. In her weakest moments she didn't care that Mannix would stop at nothing until he had his revenge on the world. What was the world compared to Riece? A life of Visions and blood compared to just a few breaths, a few heartbeats shared with Riece.

And while his eyes held the promise of everything Clio could have wanted—everything she had dreamed about her whole life—she knew that she couldn't accept it. She had more important promises to live up to, and Riece could not be a part of that. She might be duty bound to the Deities, but he could still live his life. The last time an Oracle had dragged someone else into her mess, Riece's mother had been killed.

"I vowed to fulfill, wholeheartedly, my duties as the Oracle."

When he remained silent, she continued, "That means that I have to stay here, in Sheehan. I have to be here for the city."

He looked as if he was about to protest, but she went on, needing to get everything out. "Whenever I am shown something, I will have to act on it, no matter what that means. I don't know what they will ask me to do, but I won't question it. I know that whatever crimes I commit will somehow be in my people's best interest. And," her voice fell with her eyes, "I can't have a family. My daughters will share in this life. My sons—" She couldn't think straight. "I don't know. But I do know that I can't be what you deserve. I refuse to pull you onto the same path that ruined your mother."

He waited, making sure she had finished. "That it?"

"Were you even listening?" She gaped at him, exasperated.

"Yes, I heard every word you said, but none of those words explained to me why I shouldn't be kissing you right now."

Clio couldn't prevent the thrill that his words sent leaping through her stomach.

"I don't care about any of that. I thought I made this clear to you that night in the old temple. What I feel for you has nothing to do with you being the Oracle or not. You can be the Oracle, or you can turn your back on it. It makes no difference to me. I love Clio, whoever that is, whatever she does or doesn't do."

She wanted to throw her arms around his neck, to revel in everything they felt together. To live the dream that maybe she could be the Oracle and with Riece she could also be Clio. But the all-too-familiar pressure pushed into her head, just behind her eyes, building until another world, another time, burst through.

For a moment, Clio thought something had gone wrong, that she wasn't having a Vision after all. Just as before, she was looking at Riece's face, the same expression of love and unwavering devotion painted across his features.

Only with a second look did Clio make out the differences in their surroundings. The Vision brought with it a black sky. The only light on Riece's face was the flickering glare of a torch.

"What could you possibly be here for?" Mannix's voice came from the darkness. It slid over her skin with the same noxious familiarity.

Riece turned to the sound, but Mannix was folded in shadows. "You know why," Riece said. His face shone with desperate determination.

"For her, of course. Because you love her. I meant, how could you possibly think you could save her? I'll just kill you as well." The voice seemed to drift around them, as if carried on the breeze.

"You kill me, and the Emperor will send his armies to hunt you down," Riece answered.

She didn't understand. Why wasn't he doing anything? Why wasn't he fighting?

Riece's expression didn't change. Not until a shining black spear came through his chest, its point pulsing red in the night's light.

Her name fell from Riece's lips as he dropped to his knees. When Riece crumpled to the ground, Clio could make out a flicker of red robes disappearing into the dark.

The Vision faded away like blood dropped into water, and Clio was left with the real Riece wearing an expression eerily similar to the one in her Vision.

He was going to die for her. She didn't know anything but that. Nothing else was given to her, so that she might stop what she had seen from coming to pass.

It was obvious. If she wanted him to live, she couldn't have him for herself. Riece was too headstrong to hear anything else. If she begged him never to come for her, he would anyway. She knew, because she would do the same if their positions were reversed. She had to stop him now, while the memory of his death hung hauntingly before her.

She took a step away from him, hardening her features into stone as she spoke. "I'm sorry, Riece, but I can't."

"What do you mean you can't? I assure you, you can and quite well." He was still smiling.

Her heart constricted in her chest as she spoke, knowing that she would never see that playful smile of his again. If she did, it would mean the end for the man she loved more than anything.

"No, listen to me. I don't have time for this anymore. I am the Oracle. All other *distractions*"—she said the word as if it disgusted her—"have to be pushed away. Nothing"—she almost choked on the words—"nothing but my duty matters."

"You don't mean that. Come on, Clio. I *know* you. I know you better than anyone. I've seen every side of you, your best and your worst, and I love you despite it all. I know you love me too."

He wouldn't desist. She knew how to make him leave, how to make him leave her forever, but it would mean making him hate her forever too. Maybe that was for the best. Maybe if he hated her with every fiber of his being, maybe only then would he be safe from all this.

"No, you don't get it. I don't *need* you anymore. I've gotten everything I wanted from you. You got me out of that prison, you helped me rescue Derik, you got me back home to him, and now you've brought the Emperor here. There's nothing else I could possibly need from you, so there's no reason for me to pretend that I care about you anymore." Her eyes stung and burned with the pain of tears that she refused to let fall. He had to believe that she was the Oracle he had always hated.

Her heart broke as his face crumbled. But she could see in his eyes that he wasn't going to give up on her.

"Come on, Riece. You've known Oracles before." She hated herself as she said it, but it was the only way. "What you and I had—it was only useful to me at the time. But now that Derik sits on the throne, it's over. *He's* the only one I've ever wanted. I just needed you to get me back to him."

"Derik? I don't believe—" he started.

"Of course, Derik! He is a king. He can offer me so much more than you ever could. It's always been him. Riece, for once in my life, I am being honest with you. Please just go."

"Look me in the eye and tell me you love him and not me, and I will. I swear it." His eyes were pleading with her.

It took everything within her to not give in. She fixed her gaze on him with a cold stare as she spoke. "I love him. I never loved you. I used you. That's what Oracles do."

She could see the battle being waged in his heart. It tore across his face, leaving pain and betrayal in its path.

Without another word, he turned and left. *He will be safe now*, she thought, desperately trying to remain strong. *I'll never see him again, but he will be safe.* It was right. Just another sacrifice she had to make.

She couldn't watch as he left her room, left her life forever. She turned away before he could see the tears that she could no longer fight back.

Suddenly, his footsteps stopped. *No*, she thought, *please keep going. I don't have it in me for anything more.*

But when he spoke, it wasn't to her. "She's all yours now. I'm done." And with that, he was gone.

Clio's heart stilled. Derik had been outside. He'd heard everything.

"Clio." Derik's voice was soft. He limped into the room on a crutch. No one could say whether he would ever walk normally again. "What you said, is it true?"

She could hear the hope in his voice, and it splintered her heart yet again. She couldn't turn to him. Couldn't look into his gray shaded eyes, couldn't look upon his black curling hair, or the jagged scar that now ran down his cheek. Her heart ached for him, like for a home she'd left behind.

"Clio?" he took a step closer.

Finally she turned, tears still spilling down her cheeks.

He saw the tears in her eyes, understood what they meant. His face fell. "You *do* love him." Jealousy flashed across his face. "Then why did you lie?"

"I'm the Oracle. I can't love anyone." She wanted to say that it would only get him killed. That her mother had always been right.

She couldn't hold it back anymore. Huge sobs broke through her body.

He should have been angry, but he came to her and held her just like the night when she ran away to him.

She couldn't look into those eyes. She couldn't gaze into gray when what she really wanted was brown.

"It was the only way I could keep him away," she said between sobs.

He pulled away from her. "There's no keeping a man in love away. Trust me." His mouth set in a straight line, trying to hold back what he was feeling. "He'll be back. What are you going to do then?"

"I'll manage." He was right. Riece was the most determined person she knew.

"When he comes, I can pretend with you. I know it won't be real. I know that you think you can't love anyone. But if it's the closest I can get to you, then I'll take it."

She didn't know what to say. What he was offering her wasn't right. He shouldn't have to suffer like this.

"Derik, you can't love me. I'm different now. The girl you love, she's gone forever. You will see it soon enough."

He shook his head. "Clio, she's not gone. She's only grown up some." He brushed a tear from her cheek with his thumb before he turned to go.

As soon as his footsteps faded down the hallway, Clio walked shakily back to her window where her city lay sprawled out before her.

She thought she would break down completely, but as she looked out over the city that she would stop at nothing to protect, all she felt was relief. She had proved that she could do anything to keep the ones she loved safe. Most of all, she had proved that despite everything that had happened, everything that had been taken away from her, Clio would not be beaten into deadened stone. She felt, sometimes more than she could handle. She felt so much that she was able to give up her own happiness so that others could be safe.

Maybe there was worse to come. Maybe more sacrifice, devastating pain and unendurable remorse were just on the horizon. But Clio knew that she wouldn't leave behind the girl who had rebelled so desperately against the coldness of her mother's ways. That no matter what, she would always remain Clio.

Looking down out of that window, she felt that she was once again atop that great pyramid.

Only this time Clio was truly the Oracle, and she had made her sacrifice.

To be continued in Books II and III
of The Last Oracle Series...
FORSWORN and *DIVINED*

Want a chance to enter exclusive The Last Oracle giveaways? Want to hear predictions from the Oracle about other young adult books Emily's writing? Sign up for her newsletter on her website:

www.emilywibberley.com

The Oracle promises not to barrage your inbox with spammy Visions of the future from the Deities, and you can unsubscribe at any time.

ABOUT THE AUTHOR

Emily Wibberley grew up in the South Bay where she spent her formative years battling zombies on her Xbox, watching *Buffy the Vampire Slayer*, and voraciously reading Jane Austen and books like *The Hunger Games*, where her love for feisty young heroines was born.

After graduating from Princeton University Magna Cum Laude in 2014, she began writing. Her debut novel, *Sacrificed*, was named a finalist in the Young Adult category of the 2015 International Book Awards, in the Young Adult category of the 2015 Beverly Hills Book Awards, and in the Young Author category of the 2015 Next Generation Indie Book Awards. Since its release, *Sacrificed* has spent over a year as a Kindle Top Ten Teen and Young Adult Bestseller.

When she isn't reading the latest YA book, Emily enjoys watching kick-butt action movies with her two rescue German Shepherds, Hudson and Bishop, named after characters from James Cameron's *Aliens*.